HOW TO SET THE WORLD ON WORLD ON fire

HOW TO SET THE WORLD ON fire

T.K. RIGGINS

Franchise Publishing
Vancouver, British Columbia

Published in 2017 in accordance with Franchise Publishing.

Library and Archives Canada Cataloguing in Publication

Riggins, T. K., 1981-, author
How to set the world on fire / T.K. Riggins.

Issued in print and electronic formats.
ISBN 978-0-9959002-0-2 (softcover). -- ISBN 978-0-9959002-1-9 (PDF)

I. Title.

PS8635.I533H69 2017   jC813'.6   C2017-901545-1
                    C2017-901546-X

Printed in Canada

For Kelly,
You are my ride or die.

Table of Contents

Prologue

K ase didn't know what kind of creature it was, but its dark fur begged to be touched. The hairs seemed to glimmer as the creature's sides rose and fell to the calm rhythm of its breathing. One moment they were as black as the darkest night, and the next they were bright like morning sunlight. He had never seen anything like it while growing up on the farm. It was strange. It was chaotic. It was magical. He reached his hand out.

"Don't touch it!" yelled his uncle, who had finally caught up. Eowin ran well for a chubby old wizard, but Kase was born a warrior, and was lightning fast in comparison.

Kase yanked his hand back.

The beast woke up and abruptly made its way to its feet, stretching its wings to their full span: nearly twice as wide as the creature was long. Its paws were broad, with claws that cut through the bark and mulch as cleanly as a sword. Its legs alone were longer than Kase was tall. Soft, black fur covered its massive body from the base of its tail to the tips of its fluffy wings, flowing into a ruff that surrounded its head like a mane. It had a mean glare that was further amplified by the baring of a set of sharp, ferocious teeth.

The creature towered above them, casting a long shadow. It leaned back and opened its jaws wide, as if to let out a crippling roar, but its madness quickly faded. Its head lolled at its own movement, and its piercing blue eyes fluttered. It slumped back to the ground in a tailspin of awkwardness.

"What is it?" Kase asked curiously.

Eowin stayed quiet as he examined the animal from a safe distance. He took a few steps to his left, and then took a few more to his right. He stroked his greying beard. "I thought these were creatures of myth," he finally mumbled.

"What is it?" Kase repeated eagerly. He could feel his heart pound faster. It had been a long time since anything exciting had happened.

"Stay calm," Eowin replied. He made his way towards the head of the winged animal and put his hand below its nose. Its breathing was slow and difficult. A warm glow shone from his hand, and he touched it to the creature's forehead. His power seemed to soothe it.

"It's a langara," Eowin said in a soft, monotone voice. "A giant beast of legend. With the body of a lion and the wings of a dragon, they're said to be the guardians of the enchanted Forest of Moiras. They are dangerous creatures: natural born killers. That's why no one has actually seen one: because chances are, if they have, they're already dead."

"If it's the guardian of the Forest of Moiras, why is it here?" Kase asked, making sure to keep his voice low so as to not startle the legendary beast.

"That's a great question," replied Eowin. "I'm not entirely sure if I want to find out." He began to walk around the langara, keeping his hands, still glowing with their soothing magic, against it. He made his way across its outstretched paws and giant, powerful legs, stopping at the belly of the beast.

He turned towards Kase with a stern look. "Kase," he said calmly, "I need you to go inside and get Anna, my staff, and a bottle of ginger bear elixir."

"Yes, sir," Kase replied, like a trained soldier accepting an order from his commander. He still had questions, but the look on his uncle's face was serious, and he knew they had to act quickly.

He ran across the field and back to the farmhouse as fast as his legs could carry him. He went straight into the common room. There was a large, stone fireplace in the centre of the main wall, while the others were lined with bookshelves and homespun tapestries. Beside the fireplace was his uncle's old rocking chair, the staff leaning against it.

Kase nearly tripped on the area rug as he rushed through the room. He grabbed the first item he had been sent for, and headed into the kitchen to find the second.

He dropped the staff on the table and flung open one of the two large cabinets beside the hearth, where a tarnished, black cauldron hung over the coals. The cabinet was full of brewing ingredients, and he rummaged through it, looking for a pear-shaped bottle. There was frog's heart, spirit juice, troll's toenails, roibus fruit jelly, greensbane, and spider's breath. He stood on his tiptoes to peek at the top shelf, and moved his long hair away from his face so he could get a better look.

He heard footsteps from behind him.

"Kase, how many times have I told you not to put things on the table," his aunt scolded. "It's for food and potion preparation, not for dirty tools and staffs."

Kase spun towards her, but was in such a rush that he didn't have time to apologize. "Where's the ginger bear elixir?" he shouted in panic.

Anna gave him a quizzical look. Her soft eyes made him feel a little guilty about his behaviour. "What's going on?" she replied calmly.

Kase took a step back from the cabinet and quickly explained what was happening outside the house in short breaths.

In response, his aunt went to the small cupboard on the other side of the cauldron and unerringly grabbed out the oblong bottle, filled to the top with an amber liquid. "Whatever Eowin needs this for, it must be serious. Grab the staff. Let's go," she said sternly.

They left the house and made their way across the field. When they arrived, they found Eowin resting his entire body against the belly of the langara. As it breathed in, its belly moved outward, taking the wizard along with it. As it exhaled, the belly, and wizard, moved back in.

When he noticed them, Eowin left his position and walked over. He took the bottle of ginger bear elixir from his wife.

"What are you going to use that for?" she asked as she stared at the langara.

"Oh Anna, this is just for me." Eowin removed the cap from the bottle, took a swig, and shook his head side to side. "Woo—that really wakes a man up!" he said with a chuckle.

"It's way too early in the morning for that." Anna rolled her eyes. "Give me that back." She grabbed the bottle, and then took a swig herself. She walked up to the foot of the beast, but Eowin grabbed her hand, and led her to its belly instead. He placed her hands gently on the animal where he had initially put his. A soft glow appeared as she touched it.

"Oh my," Anna murmured.

"I know, right?" replied Eowin.

"But it's not quite ..." she said.

"I know," he replied.

"So why is it ..." she asked.

"I don't know that," he replied.

"The—"

"Is anyone going to tell me what's going on?" Kase asked, impatient with his aunt and uncle's secret conversation.

"This is a mother langara," Eowin explained. "She is with child. It appears that the baby's body is twisted, so it's unable to be born naturally. Because it can't be born, it will die in the womb, and will probably kill the mother as well."

Kase glanced at the mother worriedly.

"I think the langara has flown all this way out of panic. She is in shock, and a great deal of pain, because of the complications." Eowin walked over to Kase and grabbed his staff. "Lucky for them though, they found us."

Eowin made his way back to his wife. "I need you to expand the womb while I try and turn the baby around," he instructed.

Anna acknowledged and closed her eyes in concentration. A brighter glow emanated from her hands, which she lifted slightly off the dark fur.

Eowin took a step back, lifted his staff, and drove the base of it into the ground. He reached out with one hand and placed it beside Anna's. He closed his eyes and started moving his palm, which glowed vibrantly. It went up, and it went down. It went in a clockwise circle, and then a counter-clockwise circle. He pushed his arm in, and pulled it back out. After a few intense moments, his calm expression turned into one of frustration.

"What are you trying to do?" asked Anna.

"I almost have it; I just have to turn it a little bit left," replied Eowin.

"Do you really want to go left?" she asked.

"Yeah, that's what I said. That's where I'm going," he replied sharply.

"But are you sure?" she asked.

Eowin frowned in irritation. "I know what I'm—no, wait … you're right. I need to go to the other left." He adjusted his position.

"There it is," Anna said with a smirk. Both wizards half-opened their eyes, looked at each other, and giggled. Their calm expressions returned thereafter.

Kase couldn't help but roll his eyes.

"All right, Kase. We need your help now," said Eowin.

Kase was ready to jump into action. "Of course! What do you need?" he asked.

"I need you to go to the rear of the beast," Eowin instructed.

Kase made his way past the giant legs and paws, and steadied himself at the tail end. He was out of view of his aunt and uncle. "Now what?" he shouted over the hind legs.

"We're going to try and deliver this baby, but the mother has no strength," Eowin shouted back. "We need you to extend your arms, reach inside her, and try and pull the baby out. Your aunt and I are going to try and push from this end."

"Hold on, you want me to what?" Kase tried to wrap his head around his uncle's request.

"Just reach inside the animal, grab the baby, and pull it out while your aunt and I push from this end," Eowin repeated. "It's not that complicated."

Kase stared at the rear end of the langara, turned away, and then back again. There was an odour coming from it; the shifting of the baby on the inside was causing gases to escape the womb. The raunchy stench hit him right in the face as he tried to contemplate his next move. For a magical animal, it sure had some hygiene problems.

"Are you ready?" shouted Eowin. "We're starting to push."

Kase steadied himself as best he could. He reached his arms out, braced his legs, and moved towards the animal. Just as his hand was about to enter the mother, he froze. He noticed some white, slimy fur coming slowly out of her body. Before he knew it, an entire paw the size of his own hand appeared before him, followed by a second. It was like the baby was trying to swan dive out of its mother's womb.

"Are you pulling?" shouted Eowin. Kase quickly grabbed onto the paws, leaned back, and pulled with all his might. His grip slipped, and he went crashing to the ground.

He pushed himself back up and noticed that his hands were covered in dirt, sticking because of the birthing slime. He grabbed the paws again, but this time his grip was better. He leaned back, and, with a little more success, helped the baby come out of the womb. With one pull, he was able to see the baby's forelegs. With another, the wings emerged. On his next pull, the baby shot out of the womb like lightning. Kase and the baby langara landed together on the ground in a heap of slime and dust.

More than a little grossed out, Kase tried to sit up and shift away, but he couldn't move with the cub on top of him. It was motionless, and didn't appear to be breathing at all. Its face was resting on his shoulder, eyes closed and its neck limp.

Although he was covered in afterbirth, Kase's focus was on the health of the baby langara. "Come on, little one, wake up," Kase said to the cub in a wishful tone. He shrugged his shoulder in order to rock the baby's head, hoping beyond hope that he could somehow save it. "Come on, little one," he said again, but he felt powerless. He closed his eyes and clenched his fists, wishing there was more he could do.

His aunt and uncle joined him behind the mother langara.

"Oh no," said Anna. Both wizards rushed to help. Just as his aunt was about to touch the langara and try to use her power, it sneezed all over Kase's face. He felt the cold, slimy mucus and afterbirth combination cover his eyelids, surround his mouth, and go up his nose. He turned his head and tried not to vomit.

"It's alive!" exclaimed Eowin. The baby langara nestled its head into Kase's neck with its eyes closed, and then began licking his face. "Aww, would you look at that; she thinks you're her mother."

Kase started to giggle as the baby langara's rough tongue tickled his cheeks. The cub was purring softly to show its affection. She stopped licking and opened a vibrant set of green eyes. Kase was mesmerized by the power that seemed to radiate from the young, giant beast.

The cub shifted itself off his body, and tried to take her first few steps. At first, she could barely stand: her legs were shaking like a plucked lute string as she tried to balance herself.

As soon as she took a few strong strides, she stopped and shook herself clean, flinging the afterbirth in every direction. Kase, Eowin, and Anna turned away and tried to shield themselves from the viscous liquid. The cub started to lope in circles, excited with the newfound power in her legs.

"I'm a little surprised at how fast the young one recovered from the birth," said Eowin. "I actually thought she was dead, but look at her now! She's not only alive; she's healthy, and surprisingly mobile for being born just moments ago. It really is a magical creature to have recovered so well."

Kase stood up and tried to clean himself off as best he could. He wasn't as impressed as his uncle was. As he brushed his legs, the cub tackled him in a pounce, and they both went to the ground. The baby langara furiously licked his face again as he laughed and tried to break free.

The cub moved back away, sat down on the ground, twitched her tail, and waited for him to get up.

"I think your new friend wants to play," said Anna. "Maybe you should take her for a run through the field."

Kase got up again, brushed himself off—this time keeping a close eye on the langara cub—and then took off as fast as he could. He looked over his shoulder and saw her follow playfully. It didn't take long for her to catch up and tackle him again.

As he stood up, the langara looked at him and almost appeared to smile. Her eyes dazzled wickedly. She took off running, as if it was her turn to be chased.

Kase ran after her, but she was a lot faster than he was. She looked over her shoulder, and seemed to slow down. He caught up, stretched his arms out, and pushed her as hard as he could. She rolled across the grass like a white, furry tumbleweed.

Their game continued as they ran across the field. He would chase her, she would chase him. At one point, he heard her make a sharp, pulsating purr. He liked it, and somehow it made him think of laughter. He knew that she was enjoying herself.

Then, he felt her fear.

She stopped abruptly in their chase game and looked back. Her tail straightened, her head moved up, and her eyes stared at the sky. Kase stopped running, and heard something hit the ground behind him. It sounded like thunder.

Slowly, he turned to meet the gaze of the mother langara. Her blue eyes were angry, her wings spread wide. Her fangs were dripping with saliva. She let out a roar so powerful that he felt the wind of her breath rush through his hair.

Kase was frozen in place, but he didn't feel scared. He felt warm, calm, and confident.

Before he had a chance to react, the young langara cub ran between him and her mother, and let out a roar in return. The baby's roar was like a kitten's purr compared to the mother's angry bellow.

The mother looked at her baby and calmed, her fur smoothing. She looked back at Kase, and though her gaze was piercing, her teeth were no longer bared. For some reason, he felt that the langaras were communicating somehow. The mother's gaze softened even more while watching the baby pace back and forth.

The langara cub turned to Kase, and gave him another soft lick on the cheek, as if to say goodbye. The cub then went over to her mother and stood beside the enormous left paw of the beast.

The mother moved forward, dropped her head towards Kase and moved it to within a whisker-length of his face. He wanted to reach out and touch her. He felt peaceful, safe, and comfortable as he stared at the deadly creature. He believed that she was not going to harm him, even though she was still making a low, mean growl under her breath.

The langara mother ducked her head, scooped her baby up gently in her mouth, and fluttered her wings. She slowly rose into the sky, heading back to where she came from.

"Goodbye," Kase said in a low voice. He stared at them until they disappeared.

"Kase!" yelled the old wizards as they ran across the field. He didn't look in their direction.

"Kase!" they yelled louder. When they finally reached him, both of them wrapped their arms around him in relief as they caught their breath.

"I could feel it." Kase kept his eyes on the sky. "We were connected. How is that possible?" He had never experienced anything like this before; he didn't know how to deal with the emotional chaos.

"I don't really know how to answer that, Kase," replied Anna. "Maybe the magic of the langara caused you to feel that way, or maybe it was something that generated inside of you. As wizards, it's easy for us to make connections with the animals around us, but I don't know how to explain it in your case."

"Maybe you're a wizard after all," added Eowin with a proud smirk.

"Don't tease him," scolded Anna. "He's all ready to go to The Academy to become the warrior he has always dreamed. Don't fill his head with nonsense."

"I wish she didn't have to go." Kase continued to ignore his aunt and uncle. His eyes never left the sky.

"She doesn't belong here," Anna said as she put her arm around him. "Sometimes the connections we make are important, and require a lot of strength. Sometimes letting them go is even more important, and is even harder to do. The langaras are on their own path. They're magical creatures, and we have to let them be what they're meant to be. We have to let them go."

Kase knew she was right, even if he wished otherwise. He wanted to keep hold of his special connection, without worrying his aunt and uncle. He hoped he would see the langara again. He hoped he would feel its power again.

He hoped it wasn't gone forever.

CHAPTER 1

Sparks

Kase's heart started to race. He felt alive.

The horse sprinted down the narrow path, dragging the cart through the forest of crooked trees at a breakneck speed. Even though branches dangled over the edge, and the road softly wound its way through the forest, the horse seemed to be staying on course.

Instead of grabbing the reins that were flailing about on the bench beside him, Kase leaned away and sat on his hands. He glanced towards his uncle and gave him a confident grin. "I could do this all day," he said cockily. "You should just give up!"

The old wizard laughed, and stroked his greying beard. "Well, Kase, I hope we don't get hurt today, because there's no way I'm grabbing those reins," Eowin replied. He leaned forward a little more and gave the horse another slap on the rear.

It seemed to speed up, and the cart rocked back and forth even more uncontrollably. It veered left, and swerved right. Kase tried to fight the nervousness that was creeping in, but he could feel goosebumps on his arms as the thrill of the ride started to get to him.

"Watch out for that tree!" Eowin said as he laughed and pointed. "Watch out for that one!" He laughed again and swung his arm in the opposite direction. The horse started to move more erratically; the road was getting bumpier, and the path was getting narrower. Kase tried to focus ahead instead of acknowledging his uncle. They were headed for a T-junction.

"Wooooo, do you think the horse is going to make the turn?" asked Eowin slyly, as if reading Kase's mind. "Better grab the reins!" he added.

They needed to make a right turn in order to continue on their way, but the horse was heading into the junction too fast, and was going to hit the brush head on.

Kase turned to his uncle and met his gaze. Eowin's brow looked calm, but his eyes shone with an evil twinkle. His hands still remained at his sides. Kase knew that the crazy old man was not going to budge.

He moved his attention back towards the approaching junction and quickly grabbed the reins. He pulled them sharply, and the horse and cart skidded to a stop.

As the dust settled, Kase hunched over in defeat and looked away from his uncle. He had lost again. He knew that the old man would not be able to hide his beaming, cocky, victorious smirk.

"Chicken," Eowin muttered jokingly as he happily took the reins from Kase. "I'm going to miss this," Eowin admitted as he righted the horse and cart, and continued their journey in a less thrilling fashion.

Eowin guided the horse through the rest of the forest that surrounded their farm, across the grasslands meadow, and to a hillside where the portal gateway was located.

At this particular gateway, there were five large, smooth, black boulders that surrounded a row of three triangular, grey stone doorways. The doorways were about twenty feet high, and twenty feet wide at the base, each made of two leaning pillars that met at the centre. Two stone panels, flat and upright, fit snugly between them. The grey doorways served as a connection between other portals in the rest of the realm, while the boulders acted as a shield from any outside magic. Only the power of the gateway portals was evident within the circle, for the safety of travellers as they were transported from one area to another.

Eowin led them to the first door on the left. Kase dismounted, grabbed his sac and his aunt's care package, and said goodbye to his uncle. Eowin wasn't much of one for words. Kase walked over to the door's keystone, which was used to pinpoint the desired destination of travel. It also had a slot for payment. He set the keystone for The Academy, and put in his two gold Aileron coins.

A bright, white light shone through the crack down the centre of the doorway, between the two door panels. As each second passed, the light pulsated, a sign of the portal calibrating itself for transport. Each pulse gave off a soft hum and a slight radiance of heat.

After the seventh pulse, the panels slowly slid apart with the grating sound of stone grinding on stone. The panels seemed to disintegrate into the edge of the archway, and disappeared from view as a glimmer of the other side was revealed. Kase could see the hustle and bustle of The Academy through the magical opening.

"I'm proud of you, Kase," said Eowin from atop the cart. Kase turned back to see his uncle's loving smile. "Your parents would have been proud of you, too." Eowin wiped his eye.

Kase swung his sac over his shoulder, said goodbye to his uncle again, and then walked through the portal with a confident stride.

The Academy portal gateway had ten doors that opened up into a park surrounded by tall, beige, brick walls. The park was alive, and sunshine bounced off the green grass, beautiful trees, and bright flowerbeds. There were some students lounging in the shade, others running and playing games, and new students twirling around in bewilderment as they tried to look at everything all at once. Kase didn't even hear the portal door close, because he was trying to take it all in. He suddenly felt dizzy.

"Kase!" shouted a familiar voice. He looked around, and saw his older sister running towards him. She had a big grin on her face, and buried it into his chest as she wrapped her arms around him.

"It's nice to see you too, Cali." Kase tried to return the hug. He had his sac in one hand and the basket in the other, so it was hard for him to embrace her.

"Look how big you are now!" Cali exclaimed as she shook her head in disbelief. The top of her head nearly reached Kase's broad shoulders. "Your hair is so long and wavy, but you still can't grow any on your face!" she said mockingly.

Kase laughed. "Auntie Anna sent this gift basket for you." He was more nervous than excited at the moment.

"Are there scuffles inside? Cookies?" Cali was excited as she grabbed the basket and looked inside. She searched wildly for her favourite treats. She pulled out a jar and raised it in the air like a trophy. "Scuffles!" she exclaimed. She opened it, took out one of the cinnamon pastries, and shoved it in her mouth. "So good," she mumbled. She ate another one, put the lid back on the jar without offering one to Kase, and returned it to the basket.

After she was done chewing, she started with some small talk. "So how are Uncle Eowin and Auntie Anna?"

"They're good, I guess," Kase said as he continued to look around at all the buildings, the windows, and the people.

"Still not much of a talker, are you?" Cali said, as she playfully punched him in the stomach. Kase didn't even flinch, but Cali shook her hand. "Wow, you've grown. Come on, I'll show you around."

Cali picked up the basket and started pointing things out as they walked. "The scholar castle is straight ahead," she explained, pointing to the tall, flat-topped structure ahead of them. The crenellations appeared more decorative than defensive. "We'll go there first so I can drop off this basket. Over there is the main castle, where the administration, ceremonies, and cafeteria can be found." She gestured flippantly to what was easily the largest building Kase had ever seen, just as tall as the other three, but far more sprawling.

4

"Next to it is the wizard castle, but you don't have to worry about that one. Back there is the warrior castle, where you'll spend most of your time. You can tell which one is which by the flags and banners attached to each one. The symbol of the scholar school is a midnight owl; the wizard school, a unicorn; the warrior school is a three-headed dragon; and the main castle is a peach tree."

Cali led Kase up some stairs and into the scholar castle. Kase could hear their footsteps echo off the stone floor in the eerily quiet halls. There were a lot of students around, but most of them seemed to be mesmerised by the tiny mirrors that they were holding. Some students were even whispering into them.

"What are those things?" Kase asked, as he pointed to one of the students.

"Those things are dwarves," Cali whispered in an embarrassed tone. "And don't call them 'those things'. That's rude!"

"No, I know what a dwarf is," Kase replied. "I meant, what is he holding?"

"Oh." Cali laughed, and they stopped walking. "Sorry, that's a sage mirror. It's something that was created last year at the wizard castle. It's so cool and innovative! I have one," she added as she reached into her pocket. She pulled out a small mirror and gave it to Kase to look at. "Just don't drop it. They break easily."

Kase held it carefully and studied it. It was a rectangle the size of his hand. The edges were tapered on all four sides, but there was no frame around it. He turned it around, flipped it over a couple times. His reflection was muddled by his own fingerprints. "It looks like a regular mirror," he said, unsatisfied.

"You have to talk to it," Cali said with a laugh. She took the mirror back, rubbed the face of it with her sleeve to clear the smudges off, and moved it in front of her face. "Like this. Mirror, mirror, show me information on the midnight owl," she said. Then she gave it back to him. This time, he didn't see his own reflection, but instead saw a twirling grey cloud where his reflection should have been. Suddenly, the cloud disappeared and he saw a picture of a midnight owl with a written description underneath.

"That's incredible!" Kase said in delight.

"It's basically like having a book in your hand," Cali replied with a smile. "Draw your finger across the face of the mirror, like you're turning pages in a book."

Kase did as instructed, and the image of the midnight owl was replaced with more descriptive words. He kept swiping his finger, and looked at different pages and images on the mirror's face. He couldn't believe his eyes.

"That's a report I did," Cali said, pointing at the mirror's face with a joyous expression. "I'm one of the many students at the scholar school that have been hired for imaging and documenting all the books in the scholar library. It's a good way for me to earn some extra Aileron. Basically, the information from the library is being copied into the magical archive of the mirror, so that anyone with a sage mirror can access the information. Instead of only being able to carry a few books with you at a time, you can carry hundreds all around in your hand!"

"That's amazing!" Kase said. "People here must be reading every day with all these at their fingertips."

"People are getting smarter by using them," Cali said as she took the sage mirror back. "Check this out though." She moved closer to Kase and held the mirror in front of them. He could see their reflection looking back at them. "Mirror, mirror, capture image. Smile, Kase!"

Kase was confused, but then he saw a flash of light. An image of his confused look and Cali's gleaming smile was captured in the sage mirror. "You look like such a dork," she said as she laughed and elbowed him in the ribs.

"I'm pretty sure you're the nerd in the family," Kase shot back.

The smile on her face turned into a sneer. "I missed you, baby brother." With a laugh, she looked at the mirror again. "Mirror, mirror, label that image as 'Kase's dork face'. Store that image in my personal collection." The image disappeared, and it became a mirror once again.

"I've heard that this year, they're developing sage mirrors that will be able to capture moving images! Can you imagine?" Cali's excitement was contagious, and Kase suddenly felt the need to own one, even though he didn't know what he would really do with it. "Come on, dork face, let's keep going."

Cali led him through the halls of the scholar castle and pointed out some of the lecture rooms where she attended training classes. Along the way, she stopped to talk to some of her friends and introduced him. Everyone at The Academy seemed pleasant and upbeat.

They eventually made it to Cali's dorm room, where she ate a couple more scuffles before ditching the basket.

"Let's go to your dorm now," she said. "I'll—"

Cali was interrupted by the sound of bells chiming in the distance. "Oh no, is it that time already? Come on, we have to go to your first day orientation assembly!"

They rushed back through the halls of the scholar castle and over to the main castle. There was a large crowd gathered at the entrance steps, but it was moving slowly as people made their way in. Kase was feeling overwhelmed by how many people there were at The Academy, and felt like a cow being guided into a large barn with the rest of the herd.

He felt his sister tug at his sleeve. "Come this way," she said. She pulled him away from the middle of the crowd, and led him over to the left side of the entrance steps. There were a few older people standing there, dressed in colourful robes, helping guide everyone along. Cali made her way over to two gentlemen. One of them looked like he was a professor at the school; the other was young enough to be a student, and was preoccupied with his sage mirror.

As they approached, the student looked up at them, and then quickly put his sage mirror in his pocket. He stretched his arms out wide. "Hey girl," he said as Cali embraced him. "Who's your friend?"

"This is my brother, Kase. I told you he was starting today." Cali disengaged and gestured over to him. "Kase, I want you to meet my boyfriend, Niveous, and his father, Professor Winters."

The professor extended his hand. "Nice to meet you," he said as he shook Kase's hand vigorously. He turned to Cali and put his arm around her. "Cali, I was riveted by your report on the midnight owl. It was very well-written." He pulled her aside, leaving Kase and Niveous a few steps away on the stairwell.

"Nice to meet you, Niveous," Kase said as he extended his hand. Niveous had the body of a skeleton in comparison, and Kase was a little worried he'd hurt him if he touched him.

Niveous raised his eyebrows and nodded his head in awkward silence. He did not extend his arm in return; he simply turned his back and pulled his sage mirror out from his pocket.

Kase looked over Niveous's shoulder curiously, and saw that he was swiping through various images captured in the mirror. Kase thought he should try to be friendly with his sister's boyfriend, and start a conversation. He saw an image of Niveous holding the hand of a girl he didn't recognize.

"Who's that?" Kase asked. "Is that your sister?"

Niveous startled in surprise, and quickly turned his head to sneer at Kase. "Mind your own business." He tried to push Kase away.

Kase took a quick step back and turned slightly, causing Niveous to miss him completely. Niveous stumbled forward. He lost his balance, and tumbled down a few steps to the bottom. He landed with an awkward thud, but his sage mirror crashed and shattered to pieces.

Everyone around them stopped moving and stared, including Cali and Professor Winters. Niveous was looking at the shards of glass around him, as if someone he cared about had just died.

"My sage mirror!" cried Niveous in desperate shock.

"Son, what happened?" Professor Winters exclaimed as he rushed down the stairs.

"He pushed me," Niveous said, fighting tears from his eyes. "Now my mirror is broken!"

"Kase, what did you do?" said Cali furiously.

"I ... I didn't do anything. He just ..." Kase stumbled for an explanation for the bizarre accident that just occurred.

"He tried taking my sage mirror, but I wouldn't just let him *have* it," Niveous interrupted Kase. "I slipped when he tried yanking it away, and fell down the stairs. I think my arm was hurt in the fall too," he added as he clutched his elbow.

Professor Winters glared first at Cali, then at Kase. "Mister Garrick, I think you will find that that sort of behaviour is considered unacceptable here at The Academy. And over what, a sage mirror? You will report to the Administration Disciplinary Room at once, and we will deal with you after the opening assembly!"

Kase was shocked and dumbfounded. He didn't even know what had just happened, but he didn't think that he should be the one to blame; certainly not in the manner that Niveous claimed. "But, I ..." He looked around at the crowd, and at the professor still glaring at him, and felt the humility sink in. Had he made a misstep? He dropped his head in shame. "I don't even know where that is," he said, trying not to make the situation any worse.

"I'll take you," Cali said angrily. She grabbed his arm and quickly led him over to a separate entrance of the main castle. He was happy to get away from the judging eyes of the crowd, but he couldn't help but look back as they walked. Niveous was being helped up by his father, and shot a quick glare in his and Cali's direction.

He turned back to his sister, and tried to shake his arm away from her death grip. He wanted to explain what happened. He thought he would at least have her on his side. "Cali, I didn't even touch him. And I didn't want his mirror. I was just asking him what it was about. He was looking at a captured image of himself holding—"

"Don't Kase," Cali said angrily. "Just don't even talk to me right now. I'm so embarrassed. How could you? Never mind. Just don't talk."

"Cali ..." Kase started.

"Just don't," she retorted. They walked in silence. She led him into the main castle, and down a dark, empty hallway. The walls loomed closely in on him. He thought the thick scent of stone and stagnant air was worse than any animal smells at home on the farm.

When they finally arrived, Cali stopped, crossed her arms, and nudged her chin towards the door. He looked at her with sad eyes, grabbed the knob, and walked in without saying goodbye.

The disciplinary room was square and plain. There was a large wooden desk at the front, with four rows of tables and chairs lined down the room. In the middle of the first row sat a small girl with perfectly combed blonde hair. She was sitting with a stiff and straight posture, reading a small, red book. She looked up with curious, blue eyes, but quickly looked back to her book without acknowledging him at all.

At the end of the third row was another girl, but she was hunched over the table. Her hooded head was resting on her arms, and her eyes were closed. The fingers on her right hand were wrapped around a black object, while her thumb was repeatedly flicking its top edge. It made a small flame for only half a second, and then disappeared until she ignited it again. This girl didn't seem to care that he had entered the room, either.

He closed the door behind him, walked to the end of the fourth row, tossed his sac onto the floor, and slumped down into his chair. He put his elbows onto the table and held his face with his hands, hoping he could somehow escape the dark thoughts and feelings that were creeping in.

"What are you in for?" said the hooded girl, still flicking her fire starter.

Kase didn't move. He didn't want to talk to anyone. He just wanted to crawl into a hole and be alone. The hooded girl stopped flicking her fire starter, sat up, and turned around in her chair to face him.

"Hey, what are you here for?" she repeated in a soft tone. She put her elbows on the table like Kase had.

He lifted his head up to look at her, but didn't realize how close she was, and jerked his body back to get some space. The momentum sent the back of his chair into a tipping motion. The chair and Kase fell straight back, and he landed on the floor with a thud.

He didn't move, just looked back at the top of the table and saw the girl's fingertips curl around the edge of it. Slowly, the top of her black hood and the long, brown hair escaping it came into view, followed by her eyebrows. The girl stopped moving when her eyes were barely peeking over the edge and met Kase's gaze for the first time.

"You're fun," she said, giggling slightly.

Kase stared at her eyes. They were green and glowing with life. They sparkled with delight after watching him fall, but were still softly empathetic. They were steady and calm, but burned with an adventurous passion. They were pure chaos, and were drawing him in.

At that moment, he forgot where he was, what he was doing, and how he got there. The rest of the world didn't seem to matter in the wake of those magical eyes. For the first time since his arrival, he felt alive.

CHAPTER 2

A Hot Moment

"Who are you?" The hooded girl's soft voice comfortably broke through his reverie. She tilted her head, and Kase thought he could see the beginnings of a smile.

Before Kase could answer, he heard the door of the room fly open. The hooded girl spun around and sat up straight at the table. Kase didn't move. A spider ran across the floor next to him. Beyond the spider, the small shoes of a professor were pacing at the front of the room.

"Girls," said the professor. He cleared his throat. He was breathing quickly. "I don't have time to supervise your detainment. As punishment for your crimes, you will stay here during the assembly and do some extra homework."

The professor's voice grew softer. "Talen, I want you to write a ten page essay on why you should not trespass in restricted areas of the castle. Lenia ..."

The professor stopped talking, and sighed instead. "Yes, Talen," he said regretfully.

"Thank you, Professor Dowie," replied the girl from the front row. "Do you want me to write about the school policy, or divulge into the laws of the realm in regards to trespassing? If I just have to write about the school policy, then my report will be about ..." Talen paused for a second. "Twelve pages long. But if I have to write about the laws of the realm, then my report will be ..." she paused again. "Thirty-four and a half pages long."

"Just write about the school policy," replied Professor Dowie with a frustrated sigh. "If you finish before I come back, then keep going on the laws of the realm." Kase saw Talen's hand reach down into her sac and take out a quill.

"Lenia, I want you to get out a notebook and write the following sentence down one hundred times." Professor Dowie raised his voice to drive the message home. "I will not light anything on fire!"

"Lines?" Lenia quipped. "You want me to write lines? Isn't that a little juvenile?"

"Two hundred," said Professor Dowie with a stern voice.

Lenia sighed and shook her head.

"Don't roll your eyes at me, young lady," the Professor said angrily. "Three hundred!"

Lenia pulled her hood down to cover her face and went silent. The professor seemed satisfied with that response, and walked back towards the door. "I will return after the assembly. I expect you both to still be here," he added, and rushed out of the room.

As soon as the door closed, Lenia turned again to look at the overlooked inmate. Kase was still on the floor, but he was rubbing his face in angst. He pushed his hair back, and their eyes met for a second time.

"You're not going to light me on fire, are you?" he asked.

Lenia giggled. "That depends." Her green eyes darted to the right in a playful sort of way. "How come you're in here?"

"I don't really know, to be honest," Kase replied as he stood up. He picked up his chair, put it back in its spot, and sat down. Lenia grabbed her chair and turned it around so that she could sit down and face him. She put one elbow on the table and cupped her chin in her hand. Her green eyes glowed with anticipation.

"I guess I was in the wrong place at the wrong time," Kase looked down and twirled his thumbs. As he explained his story, he felt like he was in serious trouble. But when he finished, Lenia just laughed. He was confused, but her laugh relieved him.

"I can't believe you got sent here on your first day!" Lenia said in awe. "That's got to be some sort of record, even for a warrior. You haven't even been to your dorm yet!" She shook her head in disbelief. "I got sent here for the first time in my third month here, and I thought that was good!"

"I don't really think it's a good thing that I'm here," Kase replied with a shocked look.

Lenia laughed again. "I was being a little sarcastic," she said with a wink. "I've been known to be sarcastic from time to time. Seriously though, it doesn't sound like you really did anything wrong, and I'm sure this Niveous will get caught up in his lies eventually."

"Sorry," Kase replied nervously. His dimples accompanied his confused grin. "I just …"

Lenia reached across the table and tapped him softly on the shoulder. "Relax," she said. "I have just the thing to take your mind off the mess you got yourself into today. It will be fun!" She turned around in her seat and reached into her sac. She pulled out a quill and a notebook and put it on the table in front of Kase. "See, you can help me with my assignment," she said casually.

Kase's smile disappeared. "That doesn't sound like fun," he said.

"Trust me," she said, and their eyes met again. She opened the notebook up to the first page and held the quill, pointing the tail end in Kase's direction with a playful grin. He accepted it with a cautious hand.

"Now write 'I will not light anything on fire' on the first line of the page," she said, pointing to the notebook. Kase held the quill firmly, concentrating on the letters. He wrote the line as Lenia instructed, and then leaned back in his chair once he was finished.

"I'm not writing that three hundred times," he said as she reviewed his entry.

"You have really nice writing for a warrior," said Lenia, ignoring Kase's comment. "Actually, I didn't think a lot of warriors even knew how to write, or read, for that matter." She reached over and took the quill back, and turned the book towards her. "Now watch this," she said as she stood up.

Lenia moved the quill to the second line of the notebook and held it steady. She moved her free hand over the top of the quill and slowly started to wave it around. She closed her eyes. "Oh magic quill, do not be still; copy this line, three hundred times."

She opened her eyes and let go of the quill, but it didn't fall. It was hanging in the air, as if her hand were still holding it. Kase watched as it began to move on its own, copying the line that he had written just moments ago. Once the quill finished on the second line, it moved to the third and started again. Kase's face lit up with excitement and wonder.

"Cool, huh," Lenia said proudly.

"That's brilliant!" Kase said with a smile. "Do you just leave it now while it does your assignment for you?"

"That's it. Just let it do its thing, and soon the work will be done," Lenia replied happily.

"That's cheating," Talen finally spoke up. She had turned in her seat, and must have watched the whole thing unfold.

Lenia looked over her shoulder, and as soon as their eyes met, Talen quickly turned around and huddled over her book. "What are you going to do about it?" snickered Lenia as she glared at Talen. "Are you going to tell on me? I dare you." She turned back towards Kase and sat down in disgust.

"Come on now," Kase tried to keep the peace. "We're all in this together, aren't we? We're all 'troublemakers' here, but that doesn't mean we have to cause trouble for each other." He pointed to the quill, writing away in Lenia's notebook. "Isn't there a way we can use the same magic on Talen's assignment, so that she doesn't have to worry about hers either?"

"It doesn't really work like that," said Talen from the front of the room. Her back was still turned to Kase and Lenia. She appeared to be working on her own assignment, but her focus was obviously on them instead.

"She's right, it doesn't really work like that," chimed in Lenia. She was a little calmer, but there was still tension in the room.

"What do you mean?" Kase asked curiously.

"The magic involved in making the quill write out lines doesn't really come from the words of the spell, it comes from me," Lenia responded. She pulled out her fire starter and held it tight. "The power that comes from a wizard is not the same as the power that comes from the muscles of a warrior, or the visualization and thoughts of the scholars."

She flicked the fire starter on and stared at the flame. "The power that comes from a wizard comes from the very core of their being: their emotions, their soul, and their connection to everything in the world. The key is not only being able to access that power, but to control it: to focus it on whatever the wizard desires."

She took a deep breath, and looked back at the notebook. The flame went out as she gestured to the quill. "Some wizards use wands or staffs as tools to focus the power that comes from within. In the same way, the words I used in the spell are a focus. They don't really mean anything; they're just a tool." Her eyes brightened. "Hopefully, once I get stronger as a wizard, I won't have to use words, or a wand, or a staff, or even my hands in order to channel it."

"So, the quill ..." Kase moved closer to examine it.

"Think of it as an extension of my being." Lenia leaned forward, too. "What keeps that quill writing is me: my power, my soul, my heart, and everything I believe in. Think of it like a part of me is actually writing the lines, even though I'm just sitting here."

"So you don't have enough energy left over to use your power on a second one?" Kase's brow furrowed as he tried to understand Lenia's words.

She scoffed, and then shook her head, an amused look on her face. "It's not about the amount of power; it's about the focus of the power. The problem with helping out Talen comes from the nature of her assignment. It requires a knowledge base and facts to report."

She leaned back, and put her fire starter back in her pocket. "A knowledge that I don't have within my being. The magic for my assignment is easy, because the quill is just copying something that already exists, and the power within me relates to the first line that you wrote down. Talen's assignment doesn't exist yet, and it needs to be created from the knowledge in her own mind, and organizing those thoughts into a proper report."

Kase's face relaxed as he understood Lenia's words this time. "I'm going to go talk to her," he whispered.

"What are you going to say?" Lenia whispered back.

"Trust me," Kase smiled and gave Lenia a wink. He got a skeptical look in return, but he could tell that she was at least intrigued by his positivity. He didn't know what he was going to do, but he felt confident nonetheless.

He got up from his chair and walked over to the first row. Talen had her head buried in her notebook, and was busy scribbling down all of her thoughts into her report. He made his way in front of her, and knelt down. He crossed his arms on the table and laid his head on top of them, so that he was at the same level as her. Talen stopped writing, but seemed too shy to look up.

"Hi, I'm Kase," he said in a friendly voice. A few seconds went by as he waited for a response, but she said nothing.

He tried again. "I heard the professor call you Talen. That's a nice name." She still didn't move, and a couple more seconds went by. "Is it all right if I call you Tal instead?" he asked. The awkwardness felt like it was starting to drive a wedge between them, and the silence of the room was getting heavy. He glanced over at Lenia for some help, but all he got in response was a confused grin and a shoulder shrug. He felt like she was enjoying herself, but it was at his expense.

He turned his attention back to Talen. "Alright Tal, I have a secret. Do you want to hear it?" he asked. A few more seconds passed. "I practiced for weeks just so that I could do a pretty good duck call." Still nothing.

Kase puffed up his right cheek and tightened the muscles around his upper lip. He forced the air through the small gap between his lip and his gums, and a duck sound escaped from his mouth.

Talen turned her head away from Kase's. Her lips curled up in a smile.

Kase jumped up in victory and laughed. "I did it!" he exclaimed. "I got through to you, Tal!"

"My name isn't Tal," she said as she looked down. "It's Talen. Talen Sparwood."

"Aw, come on, Tal," replied Kase. "We're friends now, aren't we? I can call you Tal for short."

Talen finally looked up at Kase. "You …" she started, then paused. "You want to be friends … with me?"

"Yeah, why not?" Kase asked. He looked at Lenia, who shook her head in disbelief.

"You're a warrior. I'm a scholar. We don't have anything in common," replied Talen factually. "Warriors are friends with warriors. Scholars are usually friends with other scholars. Except for me, I guess." She looked down in shame. "I don't have any friends," she added.

"Well, I don't have any friends here yet, either," Kase admitted. He put his hand over his heart. "I would be honoured if you would be my friend. Who cares if I'm a warrior and you're a scholar. We're all in here together, and that has to count for something, right?"

Talen looked back up at Kase and couldn't hide her smile any longer.

"Would you like to come with me back to my seat and talk with us?" Kase asked as he gestured over to Lenia.

Talen gathered her notebook, quill, and her sac and walked to the back of the room. Kase followed behind with a cocky strut and a stupid grin. They both sat down in the fourth row, and Talen looked at the magic quill, which was still writing lines for Lenia.

"That is actually a pretty good trick," Talen admitted. "It looks like you're already thirty-three percent done."

"Threes!" Kase said in support.

Lenia didn't respond. She seemed awestruck at the turn of events.

"What are you in for anyway? The professor said he caught you trespassing somewhere?"

Talen excitedly got out her notebook and opened it up to a page that looked like a large map. The drawing was labelled 'F2: Peach Tree'.

"This is a diagram of the second floor of the main castle," said Talen. "I've been doing some research on the floor plans of all the castles. I've looked at all the maps that are on record in the scholar library, but I've noticed that there are some areas in each one that don't match the actual floor plans of each castle. For example, there is a staircase on the map here"—Talen pointed to a section that was labelled 'Staircase 3'—"but when I went looking around, I couldn't find a staircase at all."

Talen flipped to another page that was labelled 'B1: Unicorn'. She pointed to a section with a long hallway, but her finger stopped halfway down. "This is a map of the basement of the wizard castle. I was walking down the hallway here, but ran into a wall that doesn't appear on the map."

Lenia frowned in puzzlement. It was all new to Kase, and he followed along with Talen's explanation with interest.

Talen flipped to a third page, labelled 'F1: Midnight Owl'. "This is the first floor of the scholar castle. I found a door at the end of the hallway here." Talen pointed to a line on the map that showed the end of a hallway, but a door wasn't there. "It was locked when I tried to open it. There was no one around, so I decided to pick the lock. I thought I was successful, but as soon as I tried to open the door, Professor Dowie came around the corner and caught me. As such, I am now in detention."

Kase was glad that she had shared her criminal past, and was intrigued by her story. "It sounds like you're becoming a professional sleuth," he said with a smile.

Talen smiled sheepishly back. "When I started this research," she said, a little less rigidly, "I thought it would be good practice for mapping out my surroundings. Once I'm done my four years of scholar training, I want to travel the realm and help discover new things about the world. But now that I've started this search, I think it's quite peculiar that there are hidden things even within these castle walls. It's kind of exhilarating to try and figure out this puzzle, even if it has gotten me into a little trouble."

She looked over again at Lenia's assignment. "Forty-two percent done," she said. It seemed like her attention was always on many things at once.

"Only one left," Kase said as he looked at the wizard. "Why are you here, Lenia?"

She puffed up her chest proudly, sat straight, and cleared her throat. "Have you ever lit a dandelion on fire?" she asked Kase and Talen. Her green eyes lit up.

They both shook their heads. Lenia's excitement was contagious. Kase couldn't wait to hear more.

"There comes a time in a dandelion's life when the yellow flower petals turn to seeds, and they look like a little white cloud hovering above the ground."

Lenia reached into her pocket again. "If you take a fire starter like this one and light the edge of the white dandelion, the whole thing lights up like a tiny fireball!" Lenia sparked a flame, and then waved her other hand across it. The flame grew larger, and then disappeared. Both Kase and Talen were impressed with the show.

"Lighting one dandelion can be beautiful, but imagine lighting a whole garden full of white dandelions!" Lenia looked over at Talen's book. It was still open to the page that showed the first floor of the scholar castle. Lenia pointed at an area beyond the walls of the castle. "This morning, I found a large patch of white-topped dandelions here, and I just couldn't help myself. It was like nature was giving me an early birthday present! I took my fire starter, lit the very edge of the patch, and watched as the entire thing burst into one beautiful, magnificent, raging firestorm." Lenia sat down. She seemed exhausted from re-living her own experience.

"Unfortunately, Professor Dowie saw the fire and caught me, but it was worth it." She smiled.

"So we have a burglar and a pyromaniac," Kase said after listening to the stories of his fellow criminals.

"And an idiot," said Lenia as she winked at Kase.

Kase laughed. "You're being sarcastic again, aren't you?" he said.

"No," Lenia replied. She tried to keep a straight face, but then Talen chuckled, and they all broke out into laughter together.

"Let's play a game," Lenia said as she reached into her sac. She grabbed a small jar filled with raisins and a purple, ceramic bowl. The inside of the bowl was charred and rough. "Have you two ever heard of Flapdragon?"

Kase and Talen looked at each other, and then shook their heads in unison.

Lenia was oozing with excitement. "I'm going to put a handful of raisins in this bowl, and then light it on fire. The name of the game is to quickly grab a raisin out of the blaze and eat it."

Lenia took the jar of raisins, and placed a few of them in the centre of the bowl. Kase and Talen looked on as Lenia sparked her fire starter. "Fire light, fire bright; stay ablaze, til time is right." The outside rim of the bowl was instantly lined with a small fire; the flame flickered just beyond the top edge.

"I'll go first," Lenia said as she looked slyly at her audience. Kase was a little nervous, but eager to play. He studied Lenia's technique as her hand darted in quickly and snatched a raisin out of the centre of the bowl, like a falcon snapping its prey from above. She showed the raisin to Kase and Talen, and then popped it in her mouth proudly. "See, it's that easy. Who's next?"

"Kase will go," Talen said as she looked at the bowl of raisins. She couldn't take her eyes off the creeping flame.

Kase gave Talen a quizzical look, and then moved his hand over to the bowl without hesitation. He concentrated as hard as he could, and tried to mimic Lenia's technique.

Unfortunately, his movement was not nearly as elegant as Lenia's, and when he swiped his hand down, he hit the edge of the bowl. It wobbled from the impact. He brought his hand up, and proved that his clumsiness wasn't indicative of failure. He proudly showed off his raisin.

"That was easy," Kase said. He popped the raisin in his mouth and grinned. Lenia and Talen both laughed, since his form was clearly graceless.

"You're starting to get this whole sarcasm thing, aren't you," said Lenia.

He smiled and looked away shyly. He *was* enjoying himself.

"Talen, you're up," Lenia said as she turned her attention to the third player.

Talen looked a little nervous still. "That's okay, I'll just watch, thank you," she replied politely, but skeptically. "If that's fine with everyone?"

"That's fine, Talen," Lenia said with a smile. She turned her attention to Kase, and squinted a little, as if studying him. "Let's take this up a notch." She put her hands under the rim of the bowl and closed her eyes. The fire in the bowl rose higher, stopping when it had tripled in size. Kase had to move his seat back a little bit; the heat was more intense.

Lenia stood up and took a step back. She moved her right arm high and behind her head in order to get some extra momentum for her attack. She drove her arm down into the bowl. She brought it back out, shook her hand for effect, and then revealed her raisin. "That was close," she said as she popped it into her mouth.

Kase could tell that she was trying to sound cocky so that he would attempt the much more challenging level of Flapdragon. Fortunately for her, he was ready for the challenge.

Kase stood and steadied himself. He tried to move a little closer to the bowl, but the heat was a little uncomfortable. Nevertheless, he reached his arm behind his head like Lenia did, and then drove his hand at the bowl.

His hand was swift, but it struck the edge of the bowl instead of the centre. There was a loud bang as the edge dipped down and hit the tabletop with great force. The bowl then skipped back up, tumbled around, and danced down the length of the table. It crashed into the magic quill. Raisins flew everywhere, and both Lenia and Talen ducked for cover. It landed at the end of the table face-down. The fire was out.

Lenia and Talen both looked back up and started to laugh. Kase tried to remain confident, even though his effort had ended in failure. "That means I win, right?" he said confidently, but he couldn't help but laugh at his own mistake.

"Almost," joked Lenia, as she started to gather the scattered raisins. Kase and Talen joined in, and they all worked together to help clean up his mess.

Talen picked up the quill and returned it to Lenia. "Looks like it's still in good shape, and you're already done seventy-nine percent of your assignment," she said reassuringly.

"Thanks, Talen," Lenia replied as she set the quill on top of her book. "I'll just have to re-do that spell to finish it off."

When they were done cleaning up the mess, Kase turned to Lenia. "What's it like to control fire like that?" he asked curiously.

"I feel both nervous and exhilarated," Lenia responded with a wicked smile. "It's nexhilarating." She sat back down in her chair. She set the bowl back in front of her, and started the fire again. "Fire is my favourite element to play with, because it's warm, and bright, and alive; but then, it can also be dangerous, chaotic, and unpredictable. When I feel it with everything I have, it's the closest thing to being free that I've ever experienced."

Lenia looked at the fire with hypnotic eyes, making the flames dance up and down effortlessly in the bowl. "I'll try and show you. Just put your hands under the bowl like I did."

Kase put his arms on the table, and cradled the bowl in his hands. He didn't feel nervous, exhilarated or nexhilarated, but he did feel calm and happy.

At the safe end of the table, Talen sat down and watched the experiment.

"Now close your eyes," Lenia said soothingly. "Try and clear your mind of everything around you." Kase followed Lenia's direction precisely. His face relaxed, and he tried to keep his mind open. Unfortunately, he couldn't stop thinking about the beautiful wizard in front of him.

"Good," said Lenia as she continued. "Now, when I do this, I try and feel the fire from within. Don't think about it; just feel it. Feel the warmth of the fingertips of the fire. Feel the strength in the arms of the fire. Feel the deepness within the heart of the fire." Lenia took her hands and put them over Kase's. Her touch was soft. Kase felt his heart start to beat faster.

The fire jumped up with an ambitious roar. The tips of the flame almost reached the roof. Kase and Lenia could feel the heat rush out at them in the instant blaze, and they both leaned back and withdrew their hands from the bottom of the bowl. As quickly as the fire shot up, it went back down, and extinguished into nothingness.

"What happened?" asked a surprised Talen.

Lenia just stared at the bowl in disbelief and awe. "That's impossible," she muttered.

Kase moved his hand over his heart, and could feel it trying to escape his chest. He felt excited, alive, and dangerous, all at the same time. He didn't want to let go of that feeling

Lenia tilted her head, looked at him, at her own hands, and then back at the bowl. It was as if she tried to study what had happened from a better angle. "What was that?" Lenia asked in a slow, soft voice.

Before any of them could respond, the door of the room flew open again. This time, a burly man entered. Lenia was still fixated on her bowl, but Kase and Talen turned their attention to the man, who had to duck in order to enter the room.

"Kase Garrick," the man said, in a low, powerful voice. "Come with me."

Kase nodded at the monstrous man, and then looked back at Lenia, smiled, and shrugged his shoulders. He stood up from his chair and grabbed his sac. As he passed by Talen, he gave her a pat on the shoulder. "See ya, Tal."

"Goodbye, Kase Garrick," Talen responded.

Kase stopped and looked back at Lenia one last time. "Goodbye, Lenia…"

"Rie," Lenia responded quickly. She smiled, a playful expression that crinkled up her cheeks. "My name is Lenia Rie."

CHAPTER 3

A Flight of Dragons

The arrow tore through the air with effortless celerity. The deadly projectile was in pursuit of perfection, and would not accept anything less than total victory. It reached its destination with full force, and plunged its head deep into the heart of its prey. For a moment, all was silent.

"Ladies and gentlemen," said Professor Tusk as he lifted his bow in triumph and turned to his students. "That is what you call a bulls-eye. I assure you that, one day, all of you will be able to replicate this perfect shot. Until that day comes, you must practice. You must hone your skill so that when you are ready, whether that is as a High Guardian, city watch, or just a protector of your home village, hitting a bulls-eye will be as natural and as automatic as breathing."

The professor reached behind his head and grabbed another arrow from his quiver. In one fast, fluid motion, he drew, turned, and fired. The arrow tore through the air in the same trajectory as the first, and pierced the same wooden target. The arrow stood, quivering, its point touching that of its brother. Another bulls-eye.

The professor put his bow down on the table in front of him. He removed the quiver from his back, and placed it next to the bow. "As you can see, there are twenty-five stations set up with all of the instruments we have been talking about in our ranged weapons class. There are throwing knives, axes, spears, and bows. Get together into groups of four, and pick a station to practice the techniques we went over. Help each other out, but safety is of utmost importance."

Professor Tusk raised his voice to stress his point further. "Do not, I repeat, do not ever use a weapon while your fellow warriors are near a target! Anyone who ignores the safety of others will be punished accordingly! Do I make myself clear?"

The class universally replied with the chant of the warriors in a low, grumbling tone. "Dragoon!"

Kase felt someone gently poke his rib cage. He looked back, and saw John gesture with a quick chin-lift to join him for the group work. Kase acknowledged in the same way, and as the other class members were scrambling and calling to each other in excitement, Kase and John walked calmly towards one of the empty stations. Along the way, John silently gestured to the two other members of their foursome, Rocky and A.J.

A.J. went to the far end of the table and grabbed the bow. She looked it over and studied its construction to see if it was up to her standards.

Rocky quickly ran up beside her and grabbed a spear that was on the table beside the bow. "You look good holding that bow," Rocky said as he moved closer to her.

A.J.'s expression did not change. She was fixated on her weapon. "Do you think you can throw that axe better than I can use this bow?" She ran her hand over the bowstring, barely touching it in an almost seductive gesture.

Rocky looked at his spear in confusion. "I'm … not holding an axe?"

A.J. put the bow back down on the table and turned to Rocky. "I wasn't talking to you, I was talking to John. He's obviously the only one I'm concerned about beating in this session." She looked at John over Rocky's shoulder.

Rocky turned around in disbelief. His cool and sly demeanour unravelled in the process. "Wait. What? You didn't just … I can't believe … you can't be …" he stuttered in a panic.

Everyone laughed.

"At a loss for words?" A.J. said, as Rocky mumbled and scrambled to keep his quick tongue from stopping.

Rocky brought his palms up, as if to slow his own thinking. "Okay," he started, "first of all, I'm the best long range weapons warrior west of Kimroad."

A.J. and Kase laughed harder, and this time John couldn't help but smile.

"Second, the only one I'm really worried about is Kase."

A.J. stopped laughing and opened her mouth wide. "Is that so?" She turned to Kase. "It's on then," she said with a wink.

"Hey," Rocky said as he tried to regain A.J.'s attention. "I'm ..."

"Attention!" yelled Professor Tusk from the other end of the practice field. The students went quiet, and stood straight in acknowledgment. "Make sure that each group member gets to use each weapon. This is a training exercise for *all* long range weapons, so I expect everyone to familiarize themselves with each one today. Don't just focus on one weapon; you will need to know how to successfully use each one in this class, and beyond. Also, don't hesitate to help each other with form and technique. Helping each other will make you stronger as a whole, as well as an individual. Understood?"

"Dragoon!" the class responded in unison.

The group turned back to the table. "Would you like to go first, Kase?" A.J. gestured towards the table.

"I'll go first," Rocky said confidently, and playfully pushed A.J. out of the way. "Then after I'm done, you'll be calling me Bulls-eye for the rest of the class."

A.J. started laughing again. "Alright, Bulls-eye. Show us how it's done," she said sarcastically.

"Watch and learn," Rocky replied as he grabbed one of the spears from the table. There were four sets of each weapon, so each team member had multiple chances before they had to re-gather their ammo from the target.

Rocky followed the instructions laid out by Professor Tusk in their earlier classes. He lifted the spear to his shoulder with a loose grip, and held it at its balance point. He faced the target, bent his knees, and turned slightly sideways to get in his ready position. He focused on the bulls-eye, stepped forward, and launched it.

The spear flew through the air with poise and precision. Its nose was heading straight for the centre of the target, but started to flutter and dip. Rocky held his breath while he watched the spear lose its speed. It landed well in front of the target.

"Looks like you fell a little short of the bulls-eye," said A.J. as she reached over and touched Rocky's slumping shoulder. "I guess we'll just call you Shorty." Kase, A.J., and even John started to laugh.

"That is not funny," said Rocky as he looked at A.J. and shook his head. He grabbed another spear right away, and tried to redeem himself.

"Wait," said Kase, still laughing. In a steadier voice, he tried to give his teammate some advice. "I noticed your release point was a little low. Try releasing it a little higher, so that it carries a little more, Shorty."

Rocky looked at Kase and gave him an unenthusiastic glare, but acknowledged with a nod. He turned back towards the target, steadied himself again, and made another throw. This time, the spear had a lot more speed as it flew towards the target, but it curved left and missed again. Rocky's shoulders seemed to slump forward a little more in defeat.

"It looked like your grip was a little tight." A.J. tried to give encouragement this time.

Rocky looked at her and nodded as he tried to take in the advice. He steadied himself again and turned towards the target.

"Also, your legs look a little stiff, and your chest was angled forward and down, Shorty."

Rocky seemed unimpressed with A.J's last comment, but took her advice nonetheless. He steadied himself again, and concentrated. "High release, loose grip, bend the knees, chest up," he said softly to himself. He repeated it over and over as he stared at the target. He took one step and threw the third spear, ending his throw with a soft grunt. Although this spear was on line, he must have put too much into it: it flew well over the target.

Rocky seemed frustrated, and grabbed the last spear forcefully. He didn't look at his friends, or wait for any more advice. He readied himself for a quick throw.

Before he could heave the last spear, John reached out and touched his shoulder. "Breathe," said John in a deep and calming voice. Rocky took a deep breath and seemed a little more relaxed. "You've got this, Rocky," added John as he released his hand from Rocky's back.

Rocky suddenly stood tall and focused on the target again. He threw his last spear. The spearhead cut through the wood, piercing the top of the target. Although the spear had hit the largest of the five rings, Rocky couldn't help but show his excitement.

"You did it!" cried Kase.

Rocky let a smile cross his lips as he turned to A.J. "It's not exactly a bulls-eye," he said to her, "but that was a good shot, right?"

"It was a great shot, Rocky," she said, and gave him a jab to the shoulder. "Just keep trying. You'll hit that bulls-eye soon enough."

"Are you going to show us how it's done, then?" replied Rocky with a sly grin.

"Watch and learn," replied A.J. She slung the quiver of arrows across her shoulders and walked to the target line, holding the bow loosely in her left hand. She raised the bow towards the target and drew an arrow back with the elegance and grace of a seasoned marksman. With her form confident and relaxed, she released and sent the arrow on its way. The whole group watched on as the arrow flew effortlessly through the air, and lodged itself in the second smallest ring on the target.

"Great shot!" said Kase in encouragement.

"Not exactly a bulls-eye," Rocky chipped in softly.

"What was that?" A.J. turned to Rocky and grinned.

"Nothing," Rocky said as he looked towards the target, and couldn't help but smile.

"That's what I thought," replied A.J., who was still grinning. She grabbed another arrow, reloaded her bow, and shot again. This time, her shot was a little closer, but still on the second ring. She grabbed her third arrow, and ended up with the same result. She took a breath before loading the last one, and then drew it back and fired. Unlike the others, this arrow found the centre of the target.

"Finally!" said A.J. in triumph. She looked at Rocky for a response, but he didn't turn from the target in order to give her the satisfaction.

"Great shot, A.J.," said Kase, as he tried to keep things going. "John, do you want to go next?"

John nodded at Kase, axe still in hand. A.J. and Rocky's bickering didn't affect him as he threw each axe at the target. Although his form was nearly perfect, his aim was a little off. All the axes hit the target, but they landed in the three to five ring range.

Kase was up next, and grabbed the first of four weighted throwing knives. He judged the distance and decided to pinch the blade instead of the handle. Keeping his wrist straight, he threw it in one quick motion, and watched as it slowly spun through the air. The knife landed, point-first, beside the arrow in the centre.

"Bulls-eye!" exclaimed Rocky. Instead of congratulating Kase, he turned to A.J. "Looks like someone else can hit a bulls-eye too!" he said, mockingly.

"Nice shot Kase," A.J. said, ignoring Rocky's immature comment.

"Thanks," Kase replied as he picked up another knife. Holding it like the first, he threw it at the target. It landed in the bull-eye too. This time, all of the group members were as quiet as John.

Kase threw the third and fourth knives in the same way, and both ended up hitting the bulls-eye, just as the first two did.

"That's amazing Kase!" said Rocky. His eyes were locked on the target.

"How did you do that?" asked A.J. as she stared at the target too.

Kase shrugged casually. "I used to practice at home, before I came to The Academy," he said. "I had targets set up all over the farm, and I tried to work as much as I could. It's pretty easy once you get the hang of it, but when we start doing moving target training next year, it will be a little more challenging."

"I understand," said A.J. "I mean, I practiced too. Still, you must have spent hours and hours crafting your skill. You're crazy!" A.J. finally looked at Kase and smiled. "If you see something wrong with my technique, please let me know!"

"Me too!" chimed in Rocky.

John swung his arm and tapped Kase's shoulder. He nodded his head at Kase and pointed to himself.

Kase was beaming with pride; he was glad that his group looked up to him. "Absolutely!" he replied with excitement.

The four members walked to the target and gathered their weapons. Along the way, Rocky kept talking about the tosses that Kase made, and was very enthusiastic about improving his knife-throwing with Kase's help. He didn't stop talking, not even to sweet talk A.J.

Once they gathered the weapons, they went back to the table and arranged them how they originally were. The three members took a step back and got ready to watch Kase with the next weapon.

Kase grabbed a throwing axe. He steadied himself, looked at

the target, and threw it: bulls-eye. He took the second throwing axe, relaxed, and threw it: bulls-eye. He threw the third axe: bulls-eye. Before throwing the fourth, he flipped it in his hand, showing how steady he was with the weapon.

"I bet Kase could hit the bulls-eye with his eyes closed!" exclaimed Rocky. Kase looked back at him and grinned. Instead of focusing on the target ahead, Kase closed his eyes and threw the axe with confidence. He stood tall and waited for the reaction from his friends.

"Ooh …" A.J said as she winced. Kase turned to see the result. The axe was lodged on the edge of the outermost ring. "Looks like you're human after all," A.J. quipped.

Kase laughed. "To be honest, I didn't really practice blind shots," he admitted.

"Maybe next time," A.J. jabbed him in the shoulder and moved towards the table. She grabbed the throwing kives and got ready for her next session. Kase backed up and stood with Rocky and John.

"Still impressive," Rocky whispered.

Kase had won over the respect of the other group members, and for the rest of the class, he helped his friends with their techniques. All of them improved, which made them elated in the process. Rocky even got a bulls-eye with one of the throwing knives, which made all of the group members happy, until they realized that he would not stop talking about it.

"Did you see that throw?" Rocky kept asking. He was proud of his accomplishment, and very thankful that Kase had improved his throwing technique in such a short amount of time. "I think Kase is even better than the professor. He should teach the class next time!"

Unfortunately for Kase, the professor happened to be walking by at the time. "Is that so?" said Professor Tusk upon overhearing Rocky's remark.

"No, I didn't mean …" Rocky said nervously. He scrambled for the right words.

"Why don't you show me your skills, Kase," interrupted the professor. "I want you to use each weapon once, so I can see your technique."

"Yes, sir," Kase said with confidence. The other group members cleared away from the table so that Kase had enough room. Just as he had done before, Kase grabbed the throwing knife. He steadied himself and threw the knife at the target: bulls-eye. He looked back at Professor Tusk to see what he thought, and received an encouraging nod.

"Very good," said Professor Tusk. "Keep going." He rotated his hand in a move along gesture.

Kase hit the bulls-eye using the axe, spear, and bow and arrow. As he was setting the bow down, he heard a slow clapping from the professor's direction.

"Excellent, Kase," Professor Tusk replied. "Your technique is exquisite. You're very skilled with the long range weapons, and I'm excited to see what else you can do in this class."

"Thank you, Professor Tusk," replied Kase. "It was an honour to demonstrate for you." He smiled. "It was actually pretty fun, too."

"It was exciting," Professor Tusk admitted with a nod of approval. He left the group and continued on helping the other students with their attempts.

When the professor was out of earshot, A.J. punched Kase in the arm. "Are you kidding me?" she exclaimed, her face beaming. "Professor Tusk never gives out compliments! You have to teach me everything you know!"

"Me too!" exclaimed Rocky.

"And me!" said John. Everyone turned and stared at this uncharacteristic outburst. Kase was thrilled that Professor Tusk had complimented him, but he was even more delighted to be the reason John spoke.

"Absolutely," he replied with a proud smile.

Kase, A.J., John, and Rocky continued with their long range weapons practice for the rest of the period. When their class was dismissed, they had a break for lunch, and all went their separate ways. After a quick stop at his dorm room, Kase headed out of the warrior castle and to the administration castle to eat.

While he was walking through the common area, feeling elated with his day, he noticed Niveous and his friends standing around a tree on the far side of the park. They were laughing together, and pointing at someone in their group.

Kase suddenly felt his mood start to deflate. He was about to turn away, until he recognized the girl that they were laughing at. It was Talen. Niveous was holding something above his head and out of her reach. She was outnumbered. He wanted to change that.

"Give that back, Niveous," Talen said sternly. She had her arm extended with her palm facing up. Her tiny stature didn't even reach his bony shoulders.

"Hey, Sharaine, look at this image of Talen," Niveous said to one of his female friends in the group. "She's not the prettiest girl, is she?" He dangled the sage mirror out in front of her; Sharaine looked at the image and laughed. Talen tried to reach for it, but he pulled it up and out of her reach.

"Too slow, Talen," Niveous said as he held the mirror above his head. "Looks like this is mine now."

Niveous hadn't noticed Kase sneak up behind him. He wrapped his fingers around Niveous's tiny wrist like a vice. Niveous's body instantly went limp, but Kase remained strong. The mirror fell from Niveous's grip, but instead of letting it fall to the ground and shatter, Kase reached out and caught it. Niveous's friends were shocked. Talen was expressionless.

"Hi, Tal," said Kase. "Is this yours?"

"Hi, Kase," Talen responded. Kase knew she was happy to see him, even if she didn't show any emotion. "That is my sage mirror. May I have it back, please?"

"No problem, Tal." Kase handed it to her.

"Please let go of me," said Niveous in a hurt whisper. His arm and upper body were trembling.

"Oh, Niveous? Is that you?" Kase asked sarcastically. "I didn't recognize you there."

"This hurts so much," replied Niveous.

"Let him go!" cried Sharaine in a high-pitched, terrified shriek.

"I'll let go of you, but you and your friends have to make a promise to me," said Kase in a calm and direct voice. "I want you to promise that you won't bother Talen anymore. Tal is a friend of mine, and if she tells me that you're causing her trouble, I will make sure that the next time we meet, your wrist won't be the only thing that hurts."

Kase let go of Niveous, who fell to the ground and grabbed his wrist with his other hand. His friends gathered around him in concern, but Niveous was able to get up on his own. He looked back at Kase with a glare. "You're going to regret this." He walked away with his friends, defeated, and did not look back.

After watching Niveous and his posse walk away, Kase turned to Talen and shrugged. "Problem solved," he said casually as he brushed his hands together.

"I can handle my own problems, thank you very much," Talen said as she sat down. There was a thin blanket beneath her, now rumpled with everyone's passing. "Bullies often pick on someone that they feel they have power over: someone who is different, someone who bothers them, or someone they know they can get a big reaction from. From what I've read, when dealing with bullies, the best thing you can do is ignore their advances, stand up for yourself, and walk away the bigger person. The worst thing you can do is sink to their level and hurt them back. Bullying is not the answer to bullying."

Kase took a step back. He was confused. "I'm sorry, Tal," he replied solemnly. "I saw that you were in trouble, and I know that

Niveous isn't a nice person, so I came over to lend a hand. I didn't mean to say that you needed my help; it's just that, where I come from, friends help each other out."

Talen stared up at him, but didn't respond. It was awkward silence.

"I guess I'll be going then," Kase said. "Bye, Tal. It was good to see you again."

He turned to walk away. After a few steps, Talen made a high-pitched, short shriek. He stopped, raised an eyebrow, and turned back. She made the same noise again, and then stopped; her face was expressionless.

"That's the sound a mother rainbow sloth makes," she said. "She lets out a high-pitched squeak when calling for her baby. The baby makes more of a lower 'ah' sound to communicate back, like this." Talen imitated the baby sloth sound, and Kase couldn't help but smile.

"I know it's no duck sound, but it's something that I know." She looked down at the large, mostly empty blanket, and back up at Kase. "Would you like some of my lunch?"

"I'd love some," Kase said as he sat down next to her.

Talen and Kase had a picnic together in the common area park, and talked about the cuteness of rainbow sloths, their habitat, and random facts that Talen knew about this favourite animal of hers. They also talked about where they grew up, their families, and life at The Academy. Kase was learning that Talen's experience as a scholar was quite different than his at the warrior castle had been thus far.

But as their friendship was blossoming, a dark shadow slowly crept across the field. The two of them were too involved in conversation to notice the group that was approaching them, until the shadow fell onto the sunny edge of the blanket that they were sitting on.

"Mister Garrick," said Professor Winters in an unimpressed tone.

Kase and Talen looked up at the group that had assembled around them, which included the professor, Niveous, and the rest of the bullies. The professor pointed at Niveous's injured wrist. "Are you responsible for this act of violence?" he asked.

"Yes, Professor Winters, but—" Kase started to plead, but was cut off instantly.

"You apparently have not learned. Two violent outbursts in so little time is a serious matter. Come with me: we are going to see the Grand Master of The Academy immediately."

The professor reached under his robe and pulled out a set of restraints. "To prevent further outbursts, please extend your arms so I can put these on. I will be escorting you to his office personally."

Kase got up from the blanket. "Is that really necessary?" he asked. "I'll come with you, but I don't think I—"

"Extend your arms!" Professor Winters commanded. Kase acknowledged and let the professor restrain him. He looked back at Talen, but didn't have a chance to say goodbye. He walked away in silence.

CHAPTER 4

The G.O.A.T.

K ase felt trapped. He was shackled to a chair outside one of the main offices. He had only been at The Academy for three weeks, but this was already the second time he was in trouble. He felt different this time, because his actions helped out Talen, and he wasn't going to feel ashamed. He was ready to accept the consequences.

He did know that things were more serious this time, though. He could hear Professor Winters arguing with the Grand Master from behind the closed door.

"This isn't the first time he's hurt my son," the professor shouted. "Who knows if he has done this to others? Is student safety less important than the future of one renegade?"

He tried to ignore the argument by staring at the painting on the wall across from him. It was faded, and had an old emblem of The Academy on it. There were three circles in succession. The first one had a sword in the middle of it, while the other two had a flame and a quill, respectively. Underneath the emblem was a phrase that read 'Strength in Unity.'

He tried to remain calm and keep a clear mind, so he kept reading the phrase over and over. Strength in unity. He assumed it meant unity between the warriors, scholars, and wizards, as depicted in the symbols. Strength in unity. His mind wandered, and he thought of the scholars and wizards he knew. Strength in unity.

He was so focused on the phrase he didn't even notice Lenia walking down the hall. She stopped in front of him and obstructed his view. "Wrong place, wrong time?" she asked him, as she gestured towards the shackles.

Kase met her playful gaze. Her green eyes glowed in the gloomy halls. Her hood was down, and her long, brown hair was braided across her left shoulder. There was something glimmering within it.

"Unfortunately, I think I deserve to be here this time," he replied as he laughed. He yanked his arm up and made the shackles dance and rattle against the chair. He quickly changed the subject. "Where did you get the unicorn hair for your braid?" he asked.

"You can see it? Have you met Luna before?" she responded with a shocked look.

"Who's Luna?" Kase replied with a shrug.

"Luna is the unicorn that my class went to see," Lenia replied as she studied him. "She spends time at the stables. I was the only one that was able to take a hair from her mane, but the rest of the class didn't even see her. Did you have a class there, too?"

"Not really," Kase replied, not understanding why no one saw Luna. She was hard to miss. "As punishment for my first detention, I have to tend the stables for the entire semester. It's not that difficult; I just have to clean them, and then feed the horses before my morning classes." He paused. "Well, I guess after my afternoon classes, too. I look after the six horses, and the two unicorns that sometimes stay there. I think ..."

"What do you mean, 'two unicorns'?" Lenia interrupted. Her eyes glowed with excitement.

"Well, there's the white one, which I guess is named Luna," he replied with a smile. "Then there's the black one. He's a little different; he has wings, so sometimes he takes off for a few days. The white one seems to stick around, even though she can leave anytime. I like to think she stays because she enjoys the Kase Unicorn Spa more." He laughed at his own joke, but Lenia didn't chuckle. Her mouth was wide open, but she didn't say anything.

He turned his head in embarrassment, and hoped he hadn't said something stupid. He continued talking to fill the silence. "No one else really comes to the stables in the morning, so sometimes I spend a little time brushing the unicorns' hair and running around with them a little bit. They seem to enjoy it. I really think …"

"I, more than anything, want to see the black unicorn with wings," Lenia said bluntly.

Kase was delighted that she was interested in his morning routine. "Well, like I said, there's no one else around early in the morning, so you're welcome to come and join me whenever you want."

"Can I come next Thursday?" Lenia asked eagerly. She reached up and twirled her braid, wrapping her fingers around the end of the unicorn hair she had weaved into it.

"Absolutely," he said with a smile, "I'm looking forward to—"

The door to the main office swung open, and Professor Winters came storming out. "He should be expelled from The Academy," he called behind him before continuing briskly down the hall.

The Grand Master emerged from behind the open door with a key to remove the shackles. Kase shook his hands after he was free, while the Grand Master looked up at Lenia. "Hello, Miss Rie; how are you today?"

"I'm fine, Grand Master Carter," Lenia said with a smile.

"I like what you've done with your hair," he replied in a soft voice. "Come on, Kase, let's get to it."

Kase stood up. "Thursday?" He smiled at her one last time.

"Thursday," she replied, and she smiled right back. She turned away and continued on down the hall.

Grand Master Carter led Kase into the office, and gestured for him to sit down.

The brown leather chair was in front of a desk piled high with different books and papers, contracts and documents, notes and letters.

Bookshelves lined the office walls, and held even more books and papers. Kase wondered if the Grand Master knew everything that was on those shelves, and how he could keep track of it all.

Grand Master Carter sat down behind the desk, took out a notebook, and grabbed his quill. "Okay, Kase," he said calmly. "In your own words, tell me what happened."

Kase took a deep breath, and unveiled the events from earlier that afternoon. He did not bend the truth, or shy away from the trouble he was in. When he was finished, he leaned back in his chair, and awaited punishment.

The Grand Master had written down some notes, but didn't seem angry or disappointed. He looked concerned. "What are you doing here, Kase?" he asked gently. "Why are you at The Academy?"

Kase was a little surprised at the question, but he gave his answer without having to think about it. "I want to become a great warrior," he said.

It didn't seem to be what the Grand Master was looking for; he put his quill down, leaned back in his chair, and crossed his arms. "Sure, there are a lot of students here that want to be the best warriors they can be," he replied. "But I'm interested in you. Why do *you* want to become a great warrior?"

"I guess I want to be like my grandfather," replied Kase. "He was a great warrior, so I want to be like him, or even better."

The Grand Master moved his hand to his chin and tapped it a few times. "Your grandfather," he repeated slowly. "I knew him. I knew Roman Garrick. He was arguably the greatest warrior in history, and you want to be better than him? That's admirable and ambitious. But let me ask you: why was he so great?"

Kase was starting to get a little annoyed by the indirect questions. "He was a great warrior because he won a lot of battles," he replied impatiently. Grand Master Carter looked at him in silence, as if he'd expected a perfect answer, but didn't get it.

After an awkward moment, Kase decided to keep answering until the Grand Master was satisfied. "He was a great warrior because no one was a match to his unbelievable strength." Still nothing. "He could fight many enemies at the same time." Nothing again. "He was feared by his enemies, and beloved by his comrades?" he asked instead of stating.

The Grand Master gently shook his head and waved his hand, gesturing for Kase to stop answering. "It's true, your grandfather was a very powerful man," he replied calmly. "His mêlée prowess was unmatched, and his bravery and relentlessness in battle was contagious to those that fought with him. Those are all good answers, Kase, and they are all good qualities that a great warrior can have, but those aren't the only qualities a warrior must possess."

Kase sat back in his chair, frowning.

"One of the qualities I admired most about your grandfather was that he knew balance. He knew when to fight, and when not to fight. He knew that there are many situations in life where it would seem that the simplest answer would be to use one's strength to quickly solve a problem; but that doesn't necessarily solve the bigger issue. Even for the most powerful warrior, strength in fighting can give you a victory in a battle, but it doesn't necessarily win the war."

Grand Master Carter leaned forward in his seat. "Let's take your situation with Niveous as an example. Now, I'm not saying that he didn't deserve to be punished for teasing your friend Talen. Bullying is a serious issue at The Academy, and should not be tolerated by anyone. However, did hurting his wrist really solve the issue?"

Kase was about to answer, but the Grand Master continued without waiting for a response. "Did fighting someone who was clearly outmatched by your strength really persuade him not to repeat his offence? It would seem that the stronger person won the battle, but the war was lost, because here you are, sitting at my desk."

Kase sulked into his chair a little deeper. He knew that the Grand Master was right. It was the same sort of lecture that his uncle Eowin would have given him. For the first time, he started to feel guilt churn his stomach. He thought about what Talen had said to him. "Bullying is not the answer to bullying," he muttered.

Grand Master Carter tilted his head, and continued. "Again, I'm not saying that your motivations were wrong, Kase. You used your strength to handle a bad situation, and you ended up winning a battle. Unfortunately for you, the decision to use your strength in the first place was an impulsive one, driven by emotion rather than proper analysis of the situation. And so, the other party ended up winning the war."

The Grand Master took a breath, and then leaned forward. "Do you know what happened to your grandfather?"

"What do you mean?" Kase felt his heart drop a little at the sudden change in topic. "Like, how he died?"

"Well, yes," the Grand Master replied. "Do you know the story of his final battle?"

"Kind of." Kase hesitated. He wasn't really comfortable talking about it, but he pushed through anyway. "I know he died during the Battle of the Pink Lakes, at the hands of Mardious Hood." Kase cleared his throat, and his voice became softer. "Mardious Hood killed both of my grandparents, actually."

"That is true," Grand Master Carter responded carefully. "It still saddens me to this day to think of the number of people who died defending the realm against that madman. However, I think that we can always learn from history, and if you are okay with hearing the story, I think we can learn something today."

Kase nodded his head slowly. He watched the Grand Master get up from his seat, go over to one of the shelves, and select a book. It looked old and dusty. He sat back down, confidently flipped through the pages, and then stopped to read a section. Kase was nervous, but also a little excited to hear the story from someone other than his family.

"I made some notes of my own in regards to the Battle of the Pink Lakes," Grand Master Carter said. "I was just a young scholar at the time, but I was working for the Triple Crown when the battle began."

At this, Kase sat up on the edge of his chair. "You were there?"

Grand Master Carter nodded slowly. "At the time, Mardious Hood's reputation for terror had quickly spread through the land. He had many names: The Death Dealer, The Firewalker, The Saviour of the Badlands, the Unkillable. The common people knew him to be an evil wizard, who had bathed in violence uncountable times, but always escaped death."

Grand Master Carter tapped the book in front of him. "What many did not know was that this man, this wizard, had a noble vision: that the people of The Badlands should be entitled to the same wealth and riches of the rest of the realm."

His face grew sad as he stared down at the pages. "Unfortunately, his path for equality was paved with carnage and death. In order to get the attention of The Triple Crown, he and his rebels—the Brotherhood, they called themselves—murdered hundreds of people, and put dozens of Guardians to the sword."

Grand Master Carter finally looked up at Kase. "As both the size of their small army and the body count grew, so did The Triple Crown's concern for Mardious's methods. Roman Garrick was the High Warrior at the time, along with the High Wizard Jolene and the High Scholar Robert. They agreed that the threat was real, and that the realm had to be protected."

"And thus the Battle of the Pink Lakes," Kase said with a sigh.

Grand Master Carter nodded slowly. "The Pink Lakes was where it all ended, or so some people claim."

The Grand Master stared off into nothing for a moment, but then shook his head and continued. "Everything came to a head on Confederation Day, in the midst of the capital's annual celebration festival."

Kase nodded. His Uncle Eowin and Aunt Anna had taken him and Cali to the Confederation Day celebration a few times when they were younger. It marked the date of the official formation of the Triple Crown, formally uniting warriors, wizards, and scholars.

"Even that year, thousands gathered at the castle of the Triple Crown; with so many people in one location, it was a prime target for The Brotherhood. Because of the looming threats within the realm, the Triple Crown decided that higher security would be needed at the celebration, and at each of the portal gates, in order to deter The Brotherhood."

"But it wasn't good enough to stop Mardious Hood," Kase said, looking down at his hands.

"Not as intended, no," continued the Grand Master. "Unfortunately, The Brotherhood succeeded in striking one of the smallest gates, located at The Pink Lakes. Some people think that Mardious chose this gate because it was rural, and rarely used. However, I was one of the scholars assigned to report on the gates, and monitor their use. I can confidently say that the Brotherhood did not intend to pass through and attack the celebration; you see, The Pink Lakes was the gate that your grandmother, Helena Garrick, was stationed."

Kase nodded slowly. "She was a great warrior too." He closed his eyes. "She was outnumbered, and fought them off as best she could, but she died with her warrior brethren defending the gate."

"Not exactly," The Grand Master replied.

Kase opened his eyes and gave the Grand Master a confused look.

"Mardious Hood kept Helena alive in order to draw your grandfather into a trap. He succeeded."

46

Kase leaned forward. He had never heard this part of the story before.

"Upon hearing of his wife's trouble," the Grand Master continued, "Roman rushed to the portal gate and entered the breach. He led the charge with a full contingent of Guardians behind him. However, when The High Warrior was beyond the black stones of the gate, Mardious Hood erected a shield of fire, preventing any other warriors from following."

The Grand Master stared off at the bookshelves that lined the walls, looking past them to the events of that day. "We frantically called upon more wizards to come through the portal and reverse the fire shield spell, but in the meantime Roman stood alone against the small army of The Brotherhood. There was nothing more we could do. Beyond the fire we could see Mardious Hood, standing on a rise well behind the front lines, where he held Helena Garrick hostage. They'd had to subdue her and bind her in chains to keep her at his feet.

"I can still remember hearing their chant: 'Oliyeah, Oliyeah, Oliyeah', over the crackle of the flames. The chant was a symbol, an ode that represented the Brotherhood's unity and uprising. For a moment, all stood still. I do not know if Mardious tried to make a deal with your grandfather, to trade for his prisoner, or if he was merely gloating."

Grand Master Carter turned back to Kase and purposefully met his eyes, a gentle expression on his face. "Whatever anyone says about that day, you should know that your grandmother died well. She never gave in. She, and your grandfather, lived by the oath of the warrior: to sacrifice themselves for the greater good; to never hesitate, never negotiate, and never surrender to the hands of evil. In the end, yes, Mardious is the one who murdered her. A single sword stroke to the neck; a quick death."

Grand Master Carter stopped, as if to gauge Kase's reaction, but Kase remained calm. The new details were a little unsettling, but he was eager to hear more. He wondered what other secrets the Grand Master had in his notebook.

The Grand Master continued. "Seeing his wife die at the hands of the evil wizard seemed to break whatever honour was instilled in the High Warrior. In his rage, he became as murderous as the villains in front of him. His nickname was 'The Bull', and he lived up to it that day. Instead of waiting for the rest of his comrades, he charged at the crowd separating him from Mardious. One man, with one sword and one shield, against hundreds would normally be certain death, but The Bull was not just one man. He was too strong, too fast, and too skilled to be taken down easily."

Grand Master Carter rubbed a hand over his eyes. "Finally, we got a few skilled wizards through the portal, and the fire shield surrounding the gate was removed. The other guardians could, at last, join in. From there, the battle quickly became one-sided. Some of the Brotherhood fought valiantly, but stupidly, and were quickly outmatched and arrested. Others scattered and fled. Through the portal, I never saw the standoff between Mardious and The Bull. But I heard of it."

Kase knew what was coming next, and yet he was still riveted. It was the most detailed account he had ever been told of that day.

"By this time, the High Warrior was soaked in the blood of war; his rage was controlling him. And though his strength, speed, and skill heavily outmatched the evil wizard, Mardious had a trick up his sleeve. Delirium dust. In his rage, and his grief, Roman fell right into the trap. The dust blown at him was overpowering, and the High Warrior fell to his knees. Hypnotized by the dust and oblivious to his surroundings, he was at the mercy of his opponent. Mardious Hood obliged. He buried his sword in Roman Garrick's chest."

Grand Master Carter looked down at the book on his desk in silence, then closed it suddenly. He looked back up at Kase and took a deep breath. "I'm not saying that your situation is as dire as one of the greatest battles of all time," he said. "But I do believe that we can learn something from history, and apply it to your situation. Your grandfather was a great leader, and was put in a position of great power because he made the right decisions; he had balance. His demise came from making decisions that were emotionally driven and unbalanced; because of it, he not only lost the battle, he lost the war."

"But I thought Mardious Hood died right after that?" Kase said, confused.

"You're right." The Grand Master nodded. "He died in his cell awaiting trial."

"And didn't the Brotherhood stop the bloodshed when Mardious died?" Kase said.

"You certainly know your history," the Grand Master said with a smile. "What I'm saying is, there may have been a better way to handle the situation. Roman Garrick knew balance, but he made a passionate decision based on the love of his wife that was imbalanced, and that decision cost him his life.

"Similarly, by protecting your friend Talen based on your own personal emotions, you put yourself in an unstable situation. If you truly are here at The Academy in order to become a great warrior like your grandfather, then there is a lot more that you need to learn in order to understand the self-possession that your grandfather knew. I honestly believe that there is potential in you, Kase, and that you will not only become like your grandfather, but that you will go beyond the level you want to achieve."

Kase couldn't help but grin.

Grand Master Carter held up a forestalling hand. "That being said, you have a long way to go before you fight a war like your grandfather did. The Battle of The Pink Lakes famously defined Roman Garrick as legendary. It is proof that he was indeed a great warrior, but he was great for other things besides standing up to Mardious Hood: he captured other criminals throughout his career, ruled as High Warrior, and instilled professionalism and confidence that are still apparent in the actions of warriors today. He treated every situation with the same amount of greatness, no matter how large or small it was."

Grand Master Carter leaned back. "I remember having a conversation like this with your father," he added.

Kase fidgeted in his chair. Just hearing about his father made him want to escape the room, but he tried to remain calm.

The Grand Master continued without noticing his discomfort. "Like you, your father dreamed of becoming a great warrior like Roman Garrick, but he was born to be a scholar. He did not have the physical attributes needed for becoming a warrior, but instead had a greater gift of intelligence. Unfortunately for him, he interpreted it as a burden instead of a gift. Even though your father was registered as a scholar, he tried to prove the system wrong. He tried to prove himself worthy of being a warrior by starting fights with other students, training on the warrior grounds after regular class hours, and studying combat skills. However, he was simply trying to be something that he wasn't.

"He ended up in the same position as you: sitting in a chair across from me. Instead of punishing him with detention, suspension, or expulsion, I decided to challenge him to change his attitude and reach his full potential. I told him that if he wanted to be like Roman Garrick, then he should take pride in what he does, and do everything in his own power to be great. He didn't have to be a warrior to understand the warrior. He didn't have to become a wizard in order to appreciate wizards. He needed to accept himself as a scholar; then The Academy could support him, by challenging him academically. He was an incredible student, and learned how to be great in his own right instead of trying to live in the shadow of 'The Bull'. He even made it to the finals of The Quest Series!"

"What's the Quest Series?" Kase asked. He had never heard of it from his sister, and his father certainly hadn't mentioned anything about it.

"Well, it's not something that many students worry about in their first year, but all students are welcome to participate." Grand Master Carter seemed to glow with pride, and he leaned forward excitedly. "The Quest Series is a multi-faculty, annual event here at The Academy. It's a competition that tests intelligence, strength, and emotions through a series of puzzling challenges. In teams of four, students work together to complete a different test every week for five weeks. Sometimes teams have to gather something from a different part of the realm, or race against each other towards a goal, or build something new. The eight teams that rank the highest after those first five challenges compete in a final tournament, with the victor being crowned the champion."

Based on the Grand Master's expression, Kase felt like he should be excited, but it didn't sound that interesting. "Do the winners get anything special?" he asked.

"The winners receive golden medals, but that's more a formality than anything," Carter replied. "More importantly, it's a measure of greatness. Although the Quest Series is not mandatory for all students, the team that succeeds usually consists of students that go on to do great things after their tenure at The Academy. It's not the only thing that matters, but it's definitely a good measure of character and skill."

Kase considered the Grand Master's words. He wanted to be the best at everything, and the Quest Series sounded like something to help him do just that. Or at least, prove that he could do just that. "I'll do it," he said with a smile.

The Grand Master laughed. "I admire your enthusiasm, Kase," he said. "I think you would be a powerful competitor in the Quest Series one day, and it would certainly be something that would be challenging for you. More importantly, preparing for it would be a great way for you to focus your energy, and not get into trouble with Niveous and his friends anymore. However, in the meantime I want you to be the best at everything you do, not just training for the Quest Series. I want you to study hard, treat your fellow students with respect, and obey all the rules here at The Academy. I don't want you to *try* and become the greatest warrior. I want you to *be* the greatest warrior right now."

Kase could feel the excitement start to creep in. He was ready for the challenge. "Thank you, Grand Master. I will definitely be the greatest right now."

"I know, Kase," replied Grand Master Carter with a smile. He grabbed a book from the left corner of his desk, opened it, and set it down in front of him. His finger scanned one of the pages in the book rather quickly. "Yes, it looks like I have Fridays open," he said to himself. He looked up. "As punishment for your behaviour, Kase, you will come to my office every Friday at the lunch period. We'll talk about your development and your classes, and I will expect a weekly report on how you are improving at each."

Kase deflated somewhat. "During lunch?"

"Every Friday. I am going to take a personal interest in your development, Kase Garrick, and hold you accountable for your actions during the week. Think of it as an opportunity to monitor how great you actually are. I think it will satisfy Professor Winters, but I must warn you: if you get into trouble with Niveous again, I will have no choice but to expel you."

Kase remembered Professor Winter's initial anger. He knew that he was lucky, and he wasn't going to do anything to ruin his new opportunity. He thanked the Grand Master again for his generosity, and left the office. He was so excited that he ran to his next class as fast as his legs could carry him. He felt free.

CHAPTER 5

Unicorns

The gate swayed in the morning breeze, causing the rusty hinges to creak. Kase couldn't help but glance at it every time it echoed through the stable. He heard it while filling the water buckets, but no one had entered. It rattled while he was cleaning out one of the stalls, but there was no one there.

Although the fluttering of the gate caught his attention enough for him to stop working for countless moments throughout the morning, he still completed his chores long before his first classes. It gave him time to provide the unicorns with some extra attention.

The unicorns didn't really have a stable of their own. They were wild, free from any control. Some days they would be running around the stable yard, playing games with each other. Other days, they disappeared.

There or not, he would always stash some extra hay where the unicorns laid, along the outer west wall of the stable. He supplied them with food, and placed some water buckets near their area. If they were going to spend a day at Kase's Unicorn Spa, they were going to be treated like the royalty they were.

He didn't see the black unicorn anywhere, but he found the white unicorn, Luna, standing in her usual spot. He grabbed a brush and approached her. He liked to talk to the unicorns as he tended to them, and felt that they could understand him. Secretly, he was waiting for the day when they would talk back.

"Your mane is looking extra beautiful today," he said as he brushed Luna's hair. In response, she lifted her head and shook it back and forth, as if to show off the long, silvery strands. She moved closer so he could brush a little deeper.

"I have a surprise for you," he told Luna. "We're hopefully going to have a visitor this morning. Her name is Lenia, and I know you've met her before. She's ..." he paused, thinking about her mischievous quill spell, her passion for fire, and her vibrant green eyes. "She's the most magical girl I've ever met."

Luna jerked her head up and gave him a disbelieving look.

"I'm sorry." Kase laughed. "I didn't mean to offend you! You're magical too!"

Luna snorted in skeptical satisfaction, and then gingerly returned her head to his soft hand. He continued to brush her mane, but his mind was focused on Lenia. He checked the entrance of the stable again. No one had entered.

"I hope she shows up soon," he admitted. Maybe she had forgotten? Or was too busy? She probably had something better to do than come to the warrior stable first thing in the morning.

The gate creaked. He looked at the entrance. This time, his guest had arrived.

She looked over and saw him and Luna right away, and smiled. "Luna!" She stopped in front of the unicorn to softly stroke her glimmering snout.

Kase continued to stand at her side and brush her. "It looks like you're getting twice the pampering today, Luna," Kase said, and he reached up and scratched her behind the ear. Luna whinnied in delight and bobbed her head up and down.

Lenia laughed. "I think she understood you. Do you usually talk to animals?"

"I don't *think* she understood me," Kase replied with a wicked

54

smile. "I know she did. I've noticed that both unicorns pay attention to me, so we've had a lot of good conversations together."

Lenia laughed again. "What do you talk about?" she asked. "Do you talk about the weather? Catch up on all the gossip around The Academy? Do they know all of your deepest and darkest secrets?"

Kase turned his head away. "So, what were you doing at the administration building the other day?" he asked. He was too embarrassed to meet her eyes.

Lenia laughed even harder this time. "So it's true! You do tell them all of your deepest and darkest secrets!" she said jokingly. "You're going to tell me all of his secrets, aren't you Luna?" she said as she rubbed Luna's snout again. Luna whinnied and moved her head up and down.

"Oh, come on, Luna!" Kase said playfully. "I can't believe you're teaming up with Lenia on this one. I thought you were the nice one!" Luna snorted, and shook her head from side to side this time. Kase couldn't tell who was enjoying playing games with him more.

"Where is the other unicorn?" Lenia looked around the stable yard.

"I haven't seen him all morning, unfortunately," Kase replied. He was a little disappointed that he was unable to make Lenia's wish come true.

"What's his name?" Lenia asked. "Maybe if we call him, he'll hear us and come by?"

"I don't know his name," Kase said. "He hasn't exactly told me yet." Kase laughed at his own joke, and waited for Lenia's reaction.

He could see a smile in her eyes, even if the rest of her face didn't agree. "Talking too much about your own hopes and dreams to ask him his name? You know, it's not always about you, warrior-boy." Lenia poked Kase in the ribs.

"Warrior-boy?" Kase said with a grin. "That's kind of a lame nickname, don't you think?"

Lenia tried to replicate Kase's grin. "How about trouble-making, flapdragon-losing, unicorn-whispering stable boy?" she replied.

Kase tried to stay serious. "That one's a little short, don't you think?"

They both laughed. "You sure seem to be a pretty good judge of nicknames for someone who can't seem to name a black unicorn," she retorted.

"Okay," replied Kase, "I'll make a deal with you then. I'll figure out a name for the black unicorn, and you figure out a better nickname for me."

"Deal," said Lenia. "Now, how are you going to come up with a name for the black unicorn?"

Kase laughed. "I have no idea," he admitted. "He's actually quite different from Luna, so I don't know what name would suit him."

"What do you mean?" Lenia looked up at him in wonder. Kase knew she was seriously interested in his relationship with the unicorns, and wasn't joking around anymore.

"Well, even ignoring the colour of their coats, I would say that Luna is completely different from the black unicorn. I suppose you could say it's their personalities." Kase stopped brushing Luna's mane, and rested his hand on her back. "A couple days ago, I was running a little late with the chores. Because I was in a rush, I was sprinting across the yard with a water bucket in each hand. I'm usually pretty light on my feet, but my toe caught the edge of a divot, and I ended up falling pretty hard. I scraped my knee and shin, but I didn't spill any of the water."

"Good thing you saved the water," Lenia said mockingly. "You're a hero."

Kase laughed. "Don't tease. There was quite a bit of blood. Before I could assess the injury, though, Luna was standing directly over me. She touched my leg with her snout." Kase gestured down at his right leg. "Her touch healed my leg instantly, and I was able to get up and continue on with my chores as if nothing had happened."

Lenia blinked, once at Kase, and then at Luna. "I didn't know unicorns could do that," she admitted. She looked back at Kase and smiled. "Tell me more."

Kase nodded, and couldn't help but smile, too. "She's caring and compassionate. She's slow to take and quick to give. I thanked her, but I don't think she did it for the praise, or the glory." Kase moved his hand along Luna's head. He was grateful that he had a friend in Luna, and appreciated the time they spent together.

"And the black one?" Lenia asked softly.

Kase stopped stroking Luna, and dropped his hand to his side. "Well, like I said before, the black one is different. He's unique in the sense that he's more of a maverick: a lone soul. He can be extremely intimidating, and hard to get close to.

"When I first saw him, I was actually tending to Luna. He was across the yard watching the both of us with a stare that was warm, but … dark, you know? His stillness made me uncomfortable, but it didn't stop me from walking up to him. Just as I was about to touch his coat, I heard a sound from the stable. I looked away for half a second, but when I turned back, he was gone."

Lenia raised an eyebrow. "Where'd he go?"

Kase shrugged. "I don't know. I thought he'd disappeared into thin air, but he's just that fast. I'll sometimes see him at one end of the yard, and then a second later he will be right beside me. It took a few days, but he eventually let me pet him on the snout, and stroke him behind the ear like I do with Luna. He doesn't do it to try and bond with me, and he doesn't exude the same compassion that Luna does; he's still a little distant."

"Tough love," Lenia said, and she shook her head in disbelief. "Your description of the unicorns is nothing like what I've learned about any magical beasts. It's so …" Lenia looked down at the ground.

Kase felt his heart drop. He wondered if he'd said something wrong.

"It's so ... refreshing." She looked up and smiled brightly. "In my class, my professor focused on what we have to do to see the unicorns, rather than describing them. He explained how the unicorn hides in plain sight. Its camouflage is a reflection: a mirror of the intentions of those wanting to see it. If someone is willing to do harm to the unicorn, or is living in fear, or anger, or hate, then it stays invisible. If someone is wearing a mask, or otherwise hiding their own true form, then it remains unseen. The unicorn only reveals itself to those who are worthy of looking at themselves with nobility and confidence, and not pretending to be something they're not. When you reveal your true nature, the unicorn reveals its."

"That sounds pretty intense," Kase admitted, rubbing the back of his neck.

"The way you're describing them, it really feels like you know them well; I wouldn't be surprised if they knew you well, too," Lenia said with a smile. "I hope I get a chance to get to know both unicorns like you do. I want to share my secrets with gentle Luna. I want to see for myself how much of a rebel the black unicorn really is!"

"I'm sure you'll get a chance to meet him." Kase sighed. "I hope he warms up to you more than he does me! Luna likes to run around, and lets me lie on her back when it's sunny and warm. I thought I could do the same with him, but every time I go to do so, he just moves out of the way as I jump up. I get the feeling that he enjoys seeing me fall on my face, and is messing with me a little bit."

He noticed Lenia chuckle. "It's not that funny, I mean, just between you and me, he's a bit of a jerk."

He suddenly felt the presence of something behind him. He noticed Luna look up and over his shoulder. He didn't have to turn around. He knew what it was.

"Oh no," he whispered to Lenia, "I think he heard me."

Lenia looked around excitedly. "I don't think so; I don't see him anywhere."

Kase slowly turned around and saw the black unicorn staring right at him, just a few steps away. It let out a disgusted snort, and the power from the wind blowing out of his nose created a dust cloud around Kase's feet.

Kase spun around, ducked under Luna's head, and hid on the other side of her. He looked at Lenia, and pointed to where he'd been standing. "He's over there," he whispered.

"I still don't see him," she said with a confused look.

Kase peeked around Luna, and discovered that the black unicorn was nowhere to be seen. "He's not there anymore," he said in relief. "I guess he's gone."

At that instant, Kase felt something move up his spine. Something long and slender was sliding itself in between his shirt and his back.

"Oh no," he said again.

His body was flung up in the air, dangling from the black unicorn's horn. The unicorn lightly bounced him up and down, and moved him around in circles. He couldn't help but laugh uncontrollably at the playfully rough ride that he was getting.

Lenia looked on in astonishment. Her hand covered her gaping mouth.

"Put me down," Kase yelled as he laughed. "I'm sorry I called you a jerk!" The horn was actually tickling him a little bit. With a sudden lurch, Kase's body flew to the ground. He landed flat on his face and belly.

He rolled over and looked at Lenia, who was in tears from laughing so hard.

He felt the hoof of the great unicorn rest on his chest, pinning him to the ground. Its snout moved closer to his nose. Deep, dark eyes met his and pierced through him.

"I'm sorry, I'm sorry," Kase repeated. He was still beaming. "You're not a jerk. You're a kind and loving magical being." Kase moved his arm to pet the unicorn's snout, and in response it licked his hand as a gesture of forgiveness.

Lenia rushed over to Kase and knelt down beside him. "Are you okay?" she asked as she giggled.

"I'll be fine," he replied. "Are you still unable to see him? He's standing on top of me."

Lenia looked, but shook her head. Her smile slowly faded away.

"My hand is right on his nose, maybe you can feel it too?" he asked hopefully.

Lenia lifted her arm, but then hesitated. She held her palm up for what seemed like an eternity, but then placed it on the back of his hand. She pushed gently, but it was held strong by the unicorn. "I know he's there," she admitted. "I just can't see him yet."

Kase noticed how soft Lenia's touch was. He glanced up at her face. The way the morning sunlight was shining across her eyes made him forget about the hard ground he was resting on, the dust in his hair, and the black hoof on his chest.

His blissful moment was interrupted by his own voice. "His name is Turanus." Somehow, the black unicorn's name had been implanted in his mind, but he didn't care how it got there.

"Turanus," Lenia repeated. Her smile crept back onto her face.

"Do you see him now?" Kase asked her excitedly.

"No," Lenia said. She looked down at him. "At least you gave him a name, though."

Kase laughed. "That fulfills my part of the deal," he said. "So, what's my nickname?"

"I have to get to class," Lenia replied with a wink. She moved her hand back down to her side, and stood up to leave.

"Wait," Kase said. He couldn't get up; Turanus still had him pinned. He struggled a little bit, but knew that he wasn't going anywhere. "I'm sorry you weren't able to see Turanus yet."

"Don't worry, Kase," Lenia replied with a smile. "I'm sure we'll meet someday. Thank you for letting me join you this morning. I had a wonderful time."

She said goodbye to Luna and started to make her way back towards the entrance of the stable. She stopped to look back, smiled again, and made the hinges creak as she disappeared.

Kase took a deep breath, and then turned back to Turanus. "Couldn't help a guy out, could you?" he said. All he got in reply was a disgusted snort and a face full of dust.

CHAPTER 6

Cloud Game

K ase raced to the administration castle, his heart pounding with excitement. It was Friday afternoon. He had just finished a combat training class on shield tactics, where he had outlasted every warrior he faced, even against multiple opponents. A.J. had volunteered to show him some hand-to-hand training techniques, and this week he had managed to beat Rocky while they were sparring. His peers were asking him for more sword-and-shield training tips after class, which made him feel like he was part of the warrior family. He couldn't wait to tell the Grand Master of his latest accomplishments.

Grand Master Carter welcomed him into his office, and they both sat down to begin their conversation. Kase tried to remain calm, but his blood was still pumping wildly.

"So, Kase," Carter began, "how were your classes this week?"

Kase couldn't contain his enthusiasm any longer. He began talking so fast, he could barely keep up with all the details floating through his mind. He recounted his battle with Rocky, who, although a lot smaller, was nearly impossible to hold down in unarmed combat. He explained how his strategy changed when he was matched up with John, who was still the best in their class at hand-to-hand. Kase had lasted longer this week than he had last. He ended with the shield tactics class, and how Professor Tusk had taken him aside to show him some advanced sword-and-shield moves. He admitted how elated he was that he had earned the respect of his fellow warriors, enough so that they were willing to ask him for advice. His smile was so big, he could feel his dimples showing.

"That is wonderful, Kase!" Grand Master Carter replied. "Your relationship development with your peers is important. Your warrior brethren are like a family. They can be supportive in your accomplishments, and they can help you when you are struggling. It is admirable that you have gained the trust and respect of those in your class, and it appears that your relationship with them is growing stronger."

He fiddled with the weekly assignment that Kase had handed him at the beginning of lunch. "Speaking of relationships, how is your sister? I haven't noticed any mention of her in your reports."

Kase was a little startled by the quick turn of events. "Oh. Uh ... Cali and I haven't really talked since the first day of school, so ... I guess I don't really know how she's doing."

"Why haven't you spoken with her?" asked Grand Master Carter.

Kase shared the story of his first interaction with Niveous, including how frustrated Cali had been with him, and how ashamed he was for disappointing her.

The Grand Master listened intently. "Thank you, Kase. It is good to get your side of the story," he said. "I heard a different one from Professor Winters. As to where you stand with Cali, I don't think the situation is as bad as you think. I know I said that you and your fellow warriors are like family, and as such, you will go through some ups and downs together."

Grand Master Carter leaned forward in his seat. "However, you and Cali *are* family; the ups and downs may be more severe than those with your classmates, but with a little bit of effort, I think you can even them out. You wouldn't want her to give up so easily on you, would you?"

A little sheepish, Kase shook his head.

"Then you shouldn't give up on her." Grand Master Carter pulled a small sheaf of papers from one of the piles on his desk. "She has been on my absentee report the last few days for missing classes. Her professors haven't been able to follow up with her, but maybe you would have better luck? It might also give you two a chance to reconcile."

"Yes, Grand Master," Kase replied begrudgingly. He was worried—skipping classes wasn't like Cali at all—but he was a little reluctant to confront her and his past mistakes. He knew the Grand Master was right, though.

On his way out of the office, Grand Master Carter thanked him and sent him on his way.

He still had a lot of time before his next class, so he rushed over to the scholar castle. He remembered where Cali's dorm was, so he headed there first. Unfortunately, he didn't find her. He walked back through the halls, hoping that he would somehow run into her, but he didn't. He had no idea where he was going, and was nearly lost in the hallways, but eventually managed to find his way outside to the common area.

As he was slowly making his way back to the warrior castle, he scanned the park for anyone or anything he recognized that might help him. He saw a girl lying on the grass by herself, looking up at the partly-clouded sky, and knew it was his sister. He rushed over and tried to think about what he would say when he reached her.

"Hi sis!" he said in a simple, upbeat tone. He stopped at her side.

She didn't acknowledge him, or even move. She continued staring at the sky, as if lost in the complexity of it all. He could see that her eyes were red and her cheeks were rosy, as if she had been crying.

"Are you okay?"

"Do you remember when we were kids, and we'd try to figure out what the clouds looked like?" she asked. She remained motionless.

"Sure," Kase replied cautiously.

Cali pointed up towards the sky. "What about that one?" she asked.

Kase lay down on the ground next to her. He didn't really know why she was there, or how she was feeling towards him, but he was happy that she was talking to him, at least.

He looked at the general area where she was pointing, and saw a large cloud that was almost fading into nonexistence. "That one reminds me of your hairstyle," he said, hoping it would make her laugh. It didn't.

"I think it looks like a giant, dead, lonely tree with no leaves," said Cali. She started to sniffle. "Its branches are all crooked, but nobody cares."

Kase was a little worried by her morbid description, so he quickly jumped to the next cloud. "Look at that one," he said, pointing. "It looks like a volcano erupting. The lava is flowing magically into the air like a fiery water fountain."

Cali followed his finger. "That one looks more like a heart that someone stabbed with a giant knife, causing the blood to squirt out everywhere," she said, and sobbed a little harder.

Kase was really worried now. "Is there something you want to talk about?" he asked, hoping that he could somehow help.

Cali seemed to regain control and pointed to another cloud. "What about the one over there?" she asked.

"I think that one looks like a teacup pig," Kase replied. "It's the cutest, happiest teacup pig you've ever seen."

"I think it looks like a lost bulldog puppy," replied Cali. "It's the saddest, loneliest bulldog puppy in the history of the world." A tear rolled down her cheek.

"Look at that, we got the same thing!" said Kase. He felt Cali's pain, but tried to remain cheerful for her.

"What do you mean?" she asked with a sob.

"Well, you know what they say," Kase replied. "Bulldog puppies are the teacup pigs of the dog family!"

Cali chuckled. "That makes no sense, and nobody says that," she said. She wiped the tears away from her eyes. "Don't make me laugh; I want to be sad and moody right now."

"I understand," Kase said. He got up to leave.

As he sat up, he felt his sister's hand grab his. "Don't go," she said, still trying to hold back her tears.

He lay back down and clutched her hand in support. He didn't know what to say; he didn't know what was going through her mind, or weighing on her heart, but he wanted to be there for her. Whatever she needed him to do, he would do. Whatever she needed to say, he would listen. They lay in silence as the minutes ticked by.

"My life is over," Cali finally said bluntly. Although tears still slowly rolled down her cheeks, her voice was surprisingly calm.

Kase didn't know how to respond. He rolled onto his side to face her. "Cali, I ..."

"Niveous and I broke up," she said as she wiped another tear away.

"I'm sorry," Kase said, trying to sympathize. He felt powerless: he wanted to do something to help her. He wanted to take her pain away, and see her happy again. He wanted to break Niveous in half.

She turned her head towards him and laughed. "No, you're not." She smiled through her tears. Her hand clutched his a little tighter. "It's okay, though. Thanks for being here," she said, and another tear rolled down her face.

Kase lifted his thumb up and wiped it off. "What happened?" he asked.

Cali looked back up to the sky. "I don't even know where to start," she said. She took a deep breath. "Things haven't been good between us for a while. He's been busy. I've been busy. I didn't think it would actually come to this, but at the same time it doesn't seem that surprising. Ugh, I'm so stupid!" She closed her eyes in frustration. Kase waited patiently as she gathered her thoughts.

She took another deep breath, and then continued. "Niveous and I have been together since my first year at The Academy; we were part of the same study group, we became friends with the same people, and we did a lot of fun things together."

Kase squirmed. Were they talking about the same Niveous? He couldn't see it.

"We eventually became inseparable. It was refreshing for me to feel like I was a part of something: part of a family. With mom's death, dad leaving us at the farm, and then going to a school where I didn't know anybody, I felt so alone, and more than a little overwhelmed. Niveous made me feel safe and secure—really, he's the one who made me feel confident here. I finally felt like I was somewhere I belonged."

Kase thought about his own clique. Rocky made him feel important because of all the advice he asked for. A.J. helped him push a little harder with her competitiveness. And he felt like he could trust silent John with anything. He thought he could understand what Cali meant.

"For the first few semesters, we had all the same classes together. We were a good team, and we made each other better. We often had the top marks in the class, because we pushed each other to the limits. We picked the same electives so that we could be together; we even planned out our schedules so that we could major in the same subject area."

Cali wiped away a tear and waved a hand at the sky. "We talked about majoring in politics, with the idea that after The Academy, we could get jobs in public service. We could help change public policy, divert funds into the right programs, and really make a difference throughout the realm. It really felt like, as long as we had each other, we could do anything that we wanted to."

She sighed, and her voice got softer. "Last year, we decided to start taking a few different electives—so that we could diversify a little bit. We both agreed that it would help us round out our knowledge, to work better as a team, and pursue our goals after The Academy. We both got jobs working for the Sage Mirror Integration Group, but we were assigned to different project teams. Although we weren't spending all our time together like in our first few semesters, it didn't really feel like we were growing apart. But …"

Kase looked over when she stayed silent.

She ran her fingers through her hair, pulling it up away from her face, and flopped her arm down on the grass above her head. "But we weren't making time for each other anymore. It started to feel like we weren't connected, you know? I tried bringing it up, and Niveous said that if that was the way I felt, then maybe we weren't meant for each other anymore. I was confused. I had thought we were still on the same path … but maybe I was just oblivious and ignorant to it all."

She took a deep breath. "I said fine, then. It's over."

Cali sighed and closed her eyes. "To be honest, I'm not even that heartbroken. I thought I would be—I feel like I should be. But I don't want to get back with him at all. It's as if we were walking down a path at night. I didn't know where we were going, but he was beside me holding the light. As long as we were together, I knew that we were on the right path. Then the light went out. Now I'm standing on the dark path on my own. But I've realized: I don't actually need that light. All I need is to know where I'm going."

Kase knocked his shoulder into hers. "And you've got that together. More than anyone I know."

"Right now? I don't even know anymore. Did I pick the right specialty? Should I continue studying politics, or should I change? Do I want to go into public service after school, or do something else? How do I make friends? His friends were my friends. His dad was even someone important to me, and has given me a lot of advice over the years. Now it feels like I have nothing. I have no one."

"You have me!" Kase said.

Cali smiled sadly. "I know, brother, but I need more than you right now. This week is the registration week for the Q. I was supposed to be on Niveous's team with Sharaine and Gose, but now, I have nobody. If I can't do the Q, then I probably won't get a job in the area that I want; if I can't do the Q, my life is pretty much over."

"Do you mean the Quest Series? I'll be on your team!" exclaimed Kase.

"Yeah, and thanks, but it doesn't really work like that," Cali said with a smile. At least she wasn't crying anymore.

"Why not?" asked Kase.

"You're only in your first year. And besides, your team has to represent whatever castle you attend. Scholar teams are made up of scholars. Warrior teams are made up of warriors. So I need some other scholars for my team, but I don't know anyone who's available," she said, disheartened.

"I might know a scholar that can help you out," Kase said excitedly.

Cali laughed. "You know a scholar? Other than me?" She laughed again. "You're a real social butterfly. What's their name?"

"I might be the most popular guy at this school," Kase said jokingly. "You're lucky you know me." Cali laughed harder as Kase continued. "Her name is Talen Sparwood."

Cali's laughter stopped. She looked unimpressed. "I know who Talen is. She's a year younger than me, but she's in a couple of my advanced classes. She's very intelligent, but she seems a little … weird."

"I know for a fact that Niveous absolutely hates her," he replied.

Kase could see the anger flash across her eyes. "She's in," Cali said seriously.

"Great!" Kase replied excitedly. "I have to go to class now, but we'll go find her after!"

"She's actually in my last class of the day, World History. I can try talking to her, but if you want to meet up with us, then maybe we should all meet here?" Cali asked.

Kase agreed and got up to leave. Cali quickly got to her feet and gave her brother a tight hug. "Thank you, Kase. I feel a lot better right now," she said into his chest.

Kase remembered what Cali had said about feeling alone. "I know your old friends were like your family, but I *am* your family. I will always be there for you, Cali."

CHAPTER 7

Unity

Kase was focused. His hand position was perfect. He concentrated on moving his left one forward first, followed by his right. He felt his body wobble, and lost his balance. He went crashing to the ground.

"You need work on your handstand walks," Cali said as she and Talen approached.

Kase got up and scratched his head. A few blades of grass fell from his hair and onto the ground. "That doesn't usually happen," he said, his cheeks flushing.

"Sure, brother." Cali laughed. She lightly tapped Talen's arm with her elbow, looked over, and gave her a wink.

"Yeah, sure, Kase," Talen said in the same tone. She smiled brightly at Cali.

"No, no, no," he replied. "Don't agree with her. We were friends first. You should be on my side."

"Sorry, Kase, she's on my team." Cali put her arm around Talen. Talen's cheeks flushed this time.

"Oh," said Kase, surprised. "So you already asked her about the Q, then?"

Cali moved her arm back to her side. "Not quite." She turned to the other girl. "Sorry to spring this on you, Talen, but I brought you to Kase for a reason. We wanted to talk to you about the Quest Series."

Cali told Talen everything. She explained her break-up with Niveous, her future after The Academy, and her own exclusion from her original Q team. Cali was ready to start pleading, but Talen needed no more convincing.

"Sure, I'll be on your team," Talen responded simply.

"Oh, thank you, Talen!" Cali exclaimed. She wrapped her arms around her and gave her a big hug. Talen blushed again and gently returned the gesture. "Now all we need is two more team members," said Cali as she let go of her embrace.

"Don't we only need one member?" asked Talen. "I mean, you, Kase, and me makes three, right?"

"No." Kase shook his head. "Unfortunately, the rules state that each team has to be represented by the castle they attend. Since you and Cali are both scholars, you need to be on a scholar team."

Talen looked confused. "No, I've read the Quest Series rule book. Many of the examples given *imply* that all members are to be from the same castle, but there's nothing that states they have to be," she said confidently. "I think, traditionally, all teams have been made up of strictly scholars, wizards, or warriors, but there is nothing in the rule book that says you can't have it another way."

"But I thought each team must be sponsored by a professor from their castle in order to ensure that they're supervised throughout the Q," said Cali.

"Not exactly," replied Talen. "The rule book states that each team must be sponsored by a professor from *a* castle, not *their* castle. I think all we need to do is find a professor that is willing to break tradition and represent a team composed of different students."

Cali laughed. "So all we need to do is find a rebellious professor that is willing to bend the rules for the most highly regarded, traditional competition in The Academy? That might just be impossible!" She sighed.

The three teammates all sat in a moment of silence as they tried to think of something or someone that could help them.

"I've got it!" said Kase excitedly.

"You know a professor?" exclaimed Cali.

"No." Kase smiled. "But I know someone else who might be able to help us out."

"You really are a social butterfly, aren't you?" Cali clapped him on the shoulder.

Kase led Talen and Cali to the wizard castle, and explained his plan to ask Lenia to join their team. Even though Cali was a little reluctant to bring a wizard onto their team, she trusted his judgement. And Talen was willing to work with Lenia. So the two of them followed Kase. He didn't actually know where he was going, but he was confident they were going to find her. They had to find her.

After walking through a few halls, and climbing up and down a few stairwells, he saw her sitting at a table with another girl. She was moving her hands slowly over the top of a bowl, and a miniature fire tornado twirled to life underneath them. She angled her hands left, and the tornado moved softly to the right. She angled her hands right, and it moved back to the left. It was as if she was a fire puppeteer. Her bright smile was illuminated by the perfect firestorm.

Cali and Talen waited while Kase approached her on his own. As he walked up to the table, the girl sitting beside Lenia met his gaze, and jabbed Lenia in the side with her elbow. Lenia didn't look up, and seemed annoyed that her friend was trying to take her focus away.

Kase took a deep breath and leaned on the table.

"Hello, handsome," said Lenia's friend.

Kase noticed Lenia roll her eyes, but she still kept her focus on the fire.

"What's your name?" the friend asked as she twirled her hair.

"Kase Garrick," he replied.

The fire tornado disappeared from between Lenia's hands. She slowly looked up.

"Is that a new version of Flapdragon that you're playing?" he asked with a grin.

Lenia's friend let out an overdramatic, hysterical laugh. "Oh, don't mind her; she's just goofing around. My name is Aura. But I'm starting a study group to get down to some *real* magic. Want to join?"

Kase smiled politely in return. "I wish I could help you, but I'm actually here to see if Lenia can help me out." He leaned forward and spoke in a softer voice. "I mean, I'm hoping that you can help us out." He turned and pointed towards Cali and Talen.

Lenia followed Kase's finger. Cali smiled and waved, but Talen responded with a blank stare.

Out of the corner of his eye, Kase noticed Aura jab Lenia again. Lenia glared at her, but Aura had a smirk on her face, as if she had busted Lenia for keeping a secret, and was waiting for the story to unravel.

"I'll try," Lenia said as she turned back to Kase. "Let me come over to your friends and we can all talk about it together." Aura tried to pull on her arm to make her stay, but she shrugged it off as she stood up.

"Nice to meet you, Kase Garrick," said Aura.

"You too!" he replied politely.

Kase introduced Lenia to Cali, and then explained his sister's dilemma. He told her their plan to enter the Quest Series, and how they needed both the help of a professor and another student willing to bend the rules with them. "I was kinda hoping that you could be that fourth member of our team," he concluded.

"I'm honoured," Lenia replied. "But I really don't know what to say. I thought the Q was only for students in their final year?" she said cautiously.

Talen raised her hand, and then immediately answered. "The rules state that each team should consist of four current members of

The Academy. It does not specify what year the students should be in. Traditionally, students in their final year enter the Q in order to set themselves up for graduation."

"Well, I'm sure students in their final year do better because they're more experienced than the rest," added Lenia. "I'm only in my third year, and I don't want to be a burden to your team if I'm not ready to compete at that high of a level."

"You won't be a burden to us at all," replied Cali encouragingly. "From what my brother has told me, I think you would really add another dimension to our team."

"I'm sorry, I just don't know." Lenia looked up at Kase. He felt a pit start to grow in his stomach.

"I understand," Kase said to her. "I don't want to put pressure on you to join if you don't want to."

Lenia grabbed his hand. "I'm sorry, I'm not saying no," she replied. "I'm just not saying yes, yet. I actually think I might know a professor who can help you out, so why don't we go talk to her first?" He felt the emptiness disappear.

"That sounds like a great plan," he replied.

Lenia let go of his hand, went back to her table to gather her things, avoided some pointed looks from Aura, and then led the team to Professor Bright's Advanced Elements classroom.

On their way over, Lenia explained that Professor Bright had office hours every day after class, and was usually there marking exams, doing lesson plans, or experimenting. Lenia knew that if any one of her professors would be able to give them some insight into their tricky situation, it would be her most inspiring teacher.

They entered the room to find a professor standing at the head table with a glass of water in front of her. She looked up as the students approached.

"Hi, Professor Bright," said Lenia.

"Lenia!" she replied, exuberance marking her voice. "You're just in time! And you brought some new faces!"

"Yes, professor," Lenia said. "These are my friends: Cali, Talen, and Kase. I'm sorry if we're intruding, but we could really use your help."

"Hmmm," replied the professor as she studied the other three students. "Of course, of course. But first, let us conduct an experiment!" The professor grabbed the glass in front of her and took a sip of the water. She then placed the glass in the middle of the table. "Tell me, Kase," she said, "what do you see here?"

Kase focused on the glass, and then looked at it from different angles. He knew there was something suspicious going on, but he couldn't tell what it was. He shrugged his shoulders. "It looks like a glass half-filled with water," he said.

"That's a very optimistic observation," Professor Bright said with a wink. "And you are correct. It is a clear glass that is doing what it was meant to: hold water inside of it. Now Cali, if I removed the water, what would we have?"

"You would be left with an empty glass," Cali replied politely.

Professor Bright smiled. "Correct. Now, what if we went the other way. What if, instead of removing the water, we removed the glass. Talen, what would we have?"

Talen looked a little skeptical, but gave her usual logical response. "You would be left with a puddle of water."

Professor Bright smirked, as if she'd tricked Talen. "That is a good answer," she replied. "It is not a wrong answer, but it might not be entirely accurate in this instance. Yes, the water might form into a puddle on the table, but it also might not. It's more of a hard maybe." She turned to Kase and smiled. "Story of my life."

Kase was confused, which seemed to be exactly what Professor Bright was hoping for. He turned to Lenia for clarity, but she was staring at the glass excitedly.

"In my specialty," the professor continued, "I teach my students how to control the different elements. We understand that certain elements act a certain way. The glass in this experiment is a solid, and its shape is constant. On the other hand, water is a liquid, and its shape is fluid."

Professor Bright centred the glass in front of her, causing the water within to slosh side to side. "We can use the solid in order to hold the liquid, as you see here, because the water occupies the inside of the solid: the glass. If we take away the glass, the liquid will flow into the next shape that it finds, which would be the top of this table." She tapped the wood surface.

"That is what I presume Talen was thinking: the water would flow into a flat shape on the flat surface of the table, forming a puddle. Without the reliance of the solid glass, the water would be forced to take a new shape, because that is how water acts. That is what water is."

The professor waved her right hand over the half-filled glass of water. Kase watched intently.

"However," the professor continued, "if we know how to manipulate these elements, we can change how they would normally react. Sometimes a glass is just a glass, and sometimes water is just water." Professor Bright's hand started moving more swiftly over the top of the glass, and the students could see it start to crack.

"But sometimes, everything can be more than what it is!" The professor shot her hand up and held it high as the glass exploded into a fine dust. It rushed past the students like a blowing breeze, and flew to the sides of the room. Although the glass was extinguished, the water was left untouched; it didn't explode along with glass powder, and it didn't form into a puddle. The water was still in the shape of the glass, as if nothing had happened.

Kase, Cali, and Talen were all shocked with what they saw. Lenia was giddy at the professor's display.

"That is unbelievable." Kase reached out to touch the water. He stopped his hand just shy, and looked to the professor.

"Go ahead," she replied with a gentle smile.

Kase moved his right hand around the water. When the water was within his grip he clenched his hand, but his fingers went through it, as if they were entering a stream. Although the water had the shape of a glass, he couldn't grip it like one. It still acted like water.

"That is so cool!" Kase tried grabbing it again and again. He removed his hand after his fourth attempt, and stood back, amazed.

"Don't give up just yet, Kase," said the professor. "Try again. This time, I'll help you. Why don't you grab the water and drink it all down?"

He shrugged. "Okay."

He reached his hand out again, but this time he gripped the water. It gave a little under his fingers, but it held its shape. He picked it up, and the professor followed his movement with her hand. He moved the water to his lips and gulped it down.

"Refreshing!" he said when he was finished. Everyone laughed.

"That's a great experiment, Professor Bright!" said Lenia. "Are we going to try that in class?"

"Thanks, Lenia," replied the professor. "Unfortunately, it's not quite complete. I want to be able to bring the glass back into its original form, but I don't know exactly how to do that yet. Let me show you."

The professor extended her arms and lightly fluttered her fingers, as if she were tickling the air. The students watched as the sparkling dust at the edge of the room came back and reformed into the original glass shape.

"I can get all the pieces back, but I don't know how to make them all join together." She stopped moving her fingers. The pieces sank into a pile of glass dust. "I feel like I need to add something back, but I don't know what."

"Could you add an adhesive of some kind?" Cali tapped her chin in thought.

"Great suggestion," replied the professor. "I already tried that, though. I have to add an unreasonable amount, and it changes the shape of the glass. It becomes significantly bulkier, and it remains a little unstable, so unfortunately, it doesn't work."

Cali was already caught in her own mind map, so she quickly fired back with another possible solution. "What if you heat it up? I know that glass is made by quickly melting sand particles, among other things, so have you tried to reheat the dust in order to mold it back into its original shape?"

The professor seemed happy with Cali's persistence, but had some more disappointing news. "Yes, I've tried that as well. Unfortunately, I haven't had any luck melting the glass with conjured fire. I don't think the fire is hot enough in this setting."

A few moments passed as Cali and the professor tried to think of other ways to get the glass particles together.

Talen swiftly raised her hand. The professor looked a little confused, but she acknowledged the action. "Yes, Talen?"

"Thank you, Professor Bright," she said. "My answer comes in the form of a question. Have you tried purple glass?"

"No," replied the professor, tilting her head. "Why?"

"That's brilliant, Talen!" exclaimed Cali.

Kase and Lenia shared a look. The scholars seemed to be on the same page, but everyone else was waiting for an explanation.

Talen obliged. "Glass is made from a few different minerals, but the main ingredient is silica. Silica melts at a temperature of seventeen hundred and twenty-three degrees, and becomes an igneous liquid that is easy to form. When the liquid cools, the result is glass."

Professor Bright nodded slowly. She placed her hand on her chin and slowly tapped her finger on her lips as Talen continued.

"However, there is a mineral found in purple sand that is similar to silica, but not quite. It is called silico. Unlike silica, silico melts at a temperature of five hundred and ninety-three degrees. The resulting cooled compound is called purple glass.

"Purple glass is not commonly used because it is considerably more brittle. In this demonstration though, I don't think you're really worried so much about the strength of the glass, as much as the solid property that it represents."

Lenia poked at the soft pile of glass dust on the table. "But, is the fire still going to be hot enough?"

"I should think so. From what I've seen, the fire that you create produces temperatures anywhere between six and eleven hundred degrees. Although it fails to melt the silica in the regular material, it should be suitable enough to melt the silico in the purple sand."

This time, it was the professor's turn to be stunned. "Thanks, Talen; I'll have to give that a try." She shook her head slowly. Then, she stood erect and looked at Kase, Talen, and Cali with a curious eye. "Okay, who are all of you, and what kind of help do you need?"

The students took turns explaining their story. Lenia started with why she had brought her friends in, and then Cali took over with her own plea. Talen and Kase chimed in when they could.

After they finished, the professor had only one question. "Why haven't you joined the team yet, Lenia?"

The gnawing feeling began in Kase's stomach again.

Lenia shuffled her feet nervously. "I don't know," she started honestly. "I guess I didn't really want to get my hopes up, because we don't even have an official team yet."

"But what if I said yes," interrupted the professor. "What if I said I would represent your team, if it were to enter the Q. Would you want to be the final member?"

Lenia looked down at the floor. "I still don't know," she said. "I mean, I don't want to let anyone down. I … just don't know if I'm ready," she admitted.

"You won't let us down," Kase said, grabbing her hand.

"None of us are really ready," admitted Cali.

Talen raised her hand. "I'm ready," she said confidently. Everyone laughed.

"Don't worry, Lenia," said Professor Bright. She rested her arm gently on Lenia's shoulder. "Sometimes, it's not about being ready, or being in the perfect situation. Think back to the experiment that we just did together. A glass doesn't have to look, or act, like a glass. The water inside of it doesn't have to act like water. Sometimes, they are both a little more special than that. Sometimes, there is no glass."

Kase slowly reached a finger out towards the pile of glass. He wanted to poke the soft mound of dust, but Cali swatted his hand away. He turned his attention back to the professor.

Professor Bright removed her arm and addressed the rest of the group. "I know that we have just met, but I feel that this idea of yours can lead to something extraordinary. I've always strived to push the boundaries, and preferred to be the exception rather than the rule. I'm in!"

Cali gave a small cheer. Talen looked at Cali and smiled.

Kase clutched Lenia's hand and tried to meet her gaze, but she still looked at the floor. She let go.

Professor Bright lifted Lenia's chin so that she could look her in the eye. "The choice is up to you though, and you alone. I know you're special in your own way, Lenia, and I hope that you join us, but you have to make this decision for yourself."

Lenia nodded to the professor. She looked at Cali, who was still smiling. She turned to Talen, whose face was expressionless once again. She met Kase's gaze, and her eyes glimmered. She took a deep breath, and her shoulders relaxed.

"I'm in, too," she said.

CHAPTER 8

The Furnace

Kase raced across the common area. He danced and manoeuvred his way around the other students heading towards the great hall, many of whom were already gathered in their teams of four. He scanned the field for his own team, and spotted Lenia waving at him. He moved his hand behind his back. He wanted to keep his gift a surprise.

"I'm so excited!" exclaimed Cali as he approached.

"I can't wait for it to begin!" added Talen, albeit with a blank expression.

"Do you think everyone knows what we're doing?" Lenia asked Cali. Kase glanced around, and noticed some of the strange looks they were receiving.

"Who cares?" Cali replied. "Come on, let's go."

Cali led the group into the auditorium, but Kase tugged at Lenia's arm. "I got you something," he whispered. She followed his twinkling gaze down to his side. He presented her with a white dandelion. "Do you have a fire starter?" he asked. He smiled and looked to the right in a playful mimicry of her usual mischievous expression.

"Always," she whispered back. She fumbled with it when she yanked it out of her pocket, her excitement almost getting the better of her.

Kase held the dandelion as she sparked the flame. They both stopped walking in order to watch the miniature fireball take shape. It flashed with striking brilliance. They looked at each other and giggled.

"Come on, you two, pick it up." Cali's face showed her impatience, which made Kase feel a little guilty. It was worth it, though.

They all entered the main castle together. It was the first time Kase had been in the great hall, and he was overwhelmed by the size and beauty of it. The enormous room was one open area, with high, wooden rafters that stretched at least five storeys at its peak. Beautifully chiselled stone pillars ran the outer edges of the room, supporting the soaring ceiling. The closest ones that Kase could see sported delicate scrollwork along their lower edges. Above them, balconies lined the outer walls, and although they were empty at the moment, they had enough room to hold thousands of people.

Today, the great hall seemed pretty bare; only the students from the Quest Series were invited to the opening event. From the looks of things, all the scholars were together on the left side of the room, all the warriors were in the middle, and all the wizards were gathered on the right.

Cali led the team to the left edge of the room, not really standing with the scholars, but not noticeably on their own, either. All of the students were facing the stage, which filled the front length of the room; there, a giant, free-standing mirror was on display. The long edge of the rectangular mirror was resting on the stage, but it stood tall enough that it almost reached the ceiling. Kase wondered who, or what, was big enough to need a mirror that size.

Without warning, the words 'The Quest Series' appeared on the mirror's face, with the banners of each of The Academy's schools in the background. All the students were in awe, and some of them even cheered. Kase hadn't realized they could make a sage mirror that big.

"Good afternoon, competitors," said the Grand Master in a loud and reverberating voice as he took the stage. "Welcome to this year's Quest Series." The students all cheered, and he waited for the room to fall quiet before continuing with the formality of the assembly.

He enlightened everyone with the history of the competition, explained the format and rules within the game, and emphasized the importance of the challenges that awaited them. He stressed the significance of the Quest Series, which made Kase feel even more excited than when the Grand Master had first explained it to him weeks ago.

The assembly ended with a display of all the registered teams on the giant sage mirror. The Grand Master called each team up onto the stage for verification, and so their sponsoring professor could deliver their competition package. The package consisted of a regular-sized sage mirror and a portal token that would take them anywhere in the realm for free.

Each team was excited to go on stage, and the crowd was equally excited to cheer them on. There was a friendly competition between the different castles, and the sense of good gamesmanship echoed throughout the auditorium. Kase waited eagerly until his team was finally called.

"The Liberati!" the Grand Master said, with as much vigour as he had the first. Kase, Lenia, Talen, and Cali all let out a cheer, and at first the rest of the crowd followed suit. However, it quickly died off into quiet murmuring when the four of them took the stage. It was as if the other students didn't know how to react to the team of misfits, so they chose to do nothing.

As the Liberati awkwardly made their way across the stage, they were comforted by the positive nature of Professor Bright.

"Hi team!" Professor Bright smiled warmly. "Don't worry about this crowd. Here is your sage mirror and portal token." She handed each of the tools to Cali.

A loud and obnoxious student near the front spoke up. "Are they even allowed to be here?" he asked.

Kase recognized Niveous' voice. He clenched his fists as he scanned the room. He found Niveous' hateful eyes glaring at him. He glared straight back.

Niveous' accusation met with more murmurings from the crowd, and a few shouted agreements throughout the room.

The Grand Master raised his arms to call for quiet. "Even though, traditionally, the teams are formed within each school, it does not mean that the teams must be segregated as such. The world is constantly changing around us, and it is important for us to change and adapt to it as we move forward. Now, let's all give a warm welcome to The Liberati!" The Grand Master started to clap. He looked at the team and gave them a wink.

Slowly, the rest of the room started to clap along, and welcomed the diverse team half-heartedly. Kase wanted to jump off stage and put Niveous in his place, but Lenia grabbed his hand. The Liberati made their way off the stage and back to their position in the crowd.

"That concludes our opening assembly," said the Grand Master. "Once everyone has left the auditorium, the information for the first event will be available on your sage mirror! I commend you all for entering this year's Quest Series. Participation demonstrates initiative as you continue to look towards graduation and beyond the walls of The Academy. Good luck to all of you!"

The crowd let out a large cheer, and people quickly started to exit the great hall.

Like the rest of the competitors, the Liberati couldn't wait to start.

"Let's all go into the common area and check out the first event!" Cali exclaimed as she led them to the open grass outside. She held the sage mirror in front of her and made sure that everyone in the group could see it. "Mirror, mirror, show me the details of Quest Series Event One," she commanded.

Kase didn't know what to expect, and peered at the mirror anxiously. Its response appeared to be solely text.

Cali took control and read the information aloud. "In the southern part of the realm, past the tropical forests, beyond the steam pit fields, and underneath a perpetual smoky haze, lies a dormant volcano known as The Furnace. Although the lava churns with uneasiness and angst, its heat isn't as scalding as those from other volcanoes of its type. The molten rock is of a magical nature, and it is rumoured to have medicinal and miraculous properties. The wizard school is hoping to analyze these properties further, but is in need of worthy samples of this magical lava.

"In order to help the faculty of wizards, teams will need to find a way to gather samples of the lava and transport them back to The Academy. Each team will submit their samples to their sponsoring professor, who will verify the amount of lava gathered and submit it to the Grand Judges of the Quest Series. The team with the greatest sample size will be awarded the most points.

"Although the lava is hot and warming, be wary of the cold moon that rises fast at The Furnace."

When Cali finished, she looked at her other teammates. Her smile was bright as she waited for a response from the rest of the Liberati. To her dismay, they were all confused.

"Is that it?" Kase asked after a moment of silence.

Cali laughed. "What do you mean, 'is that it'?" she said. "There are so many levels to this event, you don't even know!"

"Like what?" Lenia asked cautiously.

"For example," replied Cali excitedly. "How are you going to hold the lava?"

"Umm ..." Kase searched for an answer. "In a cauldron?"

Cali's smile faded, and she considered his answer seriously. "I guess you're not entirely wrong," she said positively. "A regular cauldron would heat up, too hot to hold, and might even melt due to the heat, but a thicker cauldron made of a material with less conduction would probably work. I just don't know how we're going to carry it all that way."

"On a cart!" he replied more enthusiastically.

"All right, brother, but is that even plausible for where we have to go? The southern mountain regions are pretty rugged. Let me explain what I'm thinking about right now, and we'll see if we can get somewhere."

Lenia looked at Kase and shrugged.

Talen had raised her hand, but Cali continued on without waiting for any input. "There are three major problems ahead of us with this challenge. First, how are we going to contain the lava? Second, how long is the journey? And third, how are we going to keep the lava from cooling into solid rock before we can get back to The Academy?"

Cali paused, but then continued to talk as if she was having a conversation with herself. "For the first problem, I don't think we necessarily have to find the right object to hold the lava; what we need is the right material. Once we discover what can withstand the heat, but also doesn't let the heat transfer to the outside, we should be able to transport the lava with ease."

She started to pace back and forth. She was looking at the ground, and not paying attention to the rest of her teammates. Talen's hand slowly fell down to her side.

"For the second problem, we need to find a map of where we're going, and thus plan our travel for the most direct route. I know from my second year geography class that The Furnace is well beyond the southernmost gateway portal, and will likely be a day's travel no matter how we get there."

Talen raised her hand again, and stood on her tiptoes in order to try and get Cali's attention, but Cali was too focused to notice. "But by studying the terrain and gathering information on the different areas we encounter, we'll know what to expect. We can cut down on that time, at least a little bit."

"I think Talen has something to add," Lenia suggested.

Talen looked at Lenia and relaxed her hand, but Cali looked up at the sky, tapped her chin, and then continued. "This will not only help us avoid trouble areas, but also figure out the exact distance we need to travel."

Lenia turned to Kase and raised her eyebrows.

"Cali," Kase said, a little louder.

"Which brings us to our last problem." Cali held a finger up towards the group. Talen lowered her hand completely, and they all waited for Cali to finish. "Transporting the lava, without it cooling in that time, will be our trickiest challenge. I'm thinking that if we have a large enough sample, the outer edges might cool, but the centre will remain warm. We just need to know how long it takes for the lava to cool when contained, and then figure out how long it will take us to travel. Once we gather enough information, we should be able to estimate what our minimum sample size can be."

Cali turned on her heel, facing the scholar castle. "That only leaves one course of action—I'm heading to the library!" She started walking away.

"Do you need us to do anything?" Lenia asked.

Kase chuckled; he had been thinking the same thing. He was happy that Cali was so confident and taking the lead, but he was hoping he could help out in his own way, too.

Cali stopped mid-stride and laughed. "Sorry." She looked back at them all with a wide grin. "Let's all head to the library together!"

"There are other teams heading towards the gateway already." Talen pointed across the field, in the opposite direction. They weren't the only group of students trying to decide what to do. Some were arguing with each other. Others were sitting down and checking notebooks. Still more were running towards the portal.

"Yeah," Kase agreed. He pointed along with Talen. "There goes The Headsmen towards the gateway. Shouldn't we be worried about what they're doing?"

Cali's excitement faded as she glared in the direction of Niveous and the other friends who had abandoned her for the Q. "The Headsmen are definitely our number-one enemy in this competition," she replied in a firm, monotone voice.

Talen looked up, startled at the sudden animosity.

"But we can't be worried about what our enemies are doing. We need to focus on what we're doing: what our strategy is, and what our strengths are. If we start worrying too much about what they, or any other team, are doing, we'll end up just wasting our time."

"Can't we just head out and use our sage mirror along the way?" Lenia asked.

"I agree," Kase said in support. "I mean, even if we do something different, we don't want to fall behind."

"Look, Kase," said Cali sternly, "I know that warriors are people of action, but scholars know how to attack a problem and solve it efficiently. Talen, back me up here."

Talen closed her eyes, as if reciting something by rote. "The most effective means to solve a problem is to define it, lay out the variables that you are given, and identify the variables that you have yet to discover. Only from there can you hypothesize alternative solutions, agree on a final course of action, and then carry out the determined resolution."

Cali grasped her brother's arm. "We can still utilize the sage mirror, but it's only one tool that we can use for the Q. We can't rely on it completely."

"So you don't think the Headsmen are getting a head start?" asked Kase.

"Trust me, Kase." Cali gently pulled on his arm. "They aren't going to The Furnace tonight. I'll show you what I mean when we get to the library. Let's go!"

Talen and Cali started heading towards the scholar castle. Kase looked back at the other teams heading through the gateway portal, but he trusted his teammates' decision.

He turned back towards Lenia, who smiled and shrugged. "It makes sense," she said, before turning to follow.

※

The Liberati had taken over a table in the back corner of the library. It was littered with maps, books, and loose papers. Talen was busy copying a map of the southern part of the realm into her notebook. Cali was reading a book on metal properties, and was trying to find one with a high enough heat tolerance to hold the lava. Lenia was reading up on The Furnace and some of the other volcanoes within the realm.

Kase was leaning back on his chair, tossing grapes into the air one at a time, trying to see how high he could toss one up before catching it in his mouth. Just after he threw one high into the air, Lenia leaned over with her book to show him the mysteries of The Furnace.

"Hey, look at this," she whispered.

He lost his concentration for a split second and took his eyes off the grape. He quickly leaned back to get in the right position, but lost his balance. The chair tipped backwards, and he fell to the floor with a comical thud. He didn't want to look, but he heard Lenia giggle. He turned to her, finished chewing his grape, and grinned.

Talen was focused on her work, and Cali turned back to hers with a roll of her eyes, but Lenia couldn't stop giggling.

Kase got up and reset his chair. "What's that?" he asked, pointing at the picture she had offered of a creature that had bony limbs, pale skin, and a malicious glare.

"That's a banshee," she said in a soft voice. "Apparently, they made The Furnace their home because they lust over the magical power radiating from the lava."

"They look serious," he replied. "They have such sharp teeth and ... claws?" He tapped at the illustration of its long, narrow hands.

Lenia nodded.

"How are we going to get by them?"

"They only come out at night." Cali remained focused on her book, writing something out as she spoke. "That's what the last line in the Event description meant. 'Be wary of the cold moon that rises fast at The Furnace'. It's easy to lose track of the daylight under the dark cloud of the volcano, so we have to make sure that we have plenty of time left during the day to obtain the lava. That's also how I know that none of the teams will head there tonight."

"Okay." Kase shrugged and leaned back into his chair. He was getting ready to throw another grape when Lenia leaned over again with her book.

"Take a look at this one." She showed him a different page. "All the other volcanoes are black, but this one is green. It's covered in trees, but you can still see the lava at the top. It's called The Green Gem. It's so pretty."

He smiled back at her. "It almost looks like a giant green olive."

"Wait." Cali finally looked up from her writing. "A volcano? Let me see that."

Lenia handed the book over.

Cali's eyes grew wider. "You two are brilliant!" she exclaimed.

"We know," Kase said as he gently elbowed Lenia's arm. "Umm ... how?" he added sheepishly.

"When a volcano erupts, the lava clears out everything in its path," said Cali. "On an active volcano, the area around the peak is usually barren, because nothing survives the continual destruction. But on this volcano, the species of vegetation survives because it has found a way to continue life beyond the aftermath of the eruption.

"I'm guessing that there must be something that protects them from the lava's heat. Talen, do you know anything about this?"

Talen walked over to peer at the book. "Unfortunately, I don't," she admitted. She picked up the sage mirror and tried to get more information. "That's odd, there's nothing here," she said as she handed it to Cali.

"This information mustn't be entered into the system yet," said Cali. "Kase, I think I have a book on tree species in my dorm room. Would you be able to go get it for me?"

Kase quickly stood tall. "Finally, some action," he replied happily.

"I'll come with you." Lenia stood as well. "I could use a change of scenery."

"Excellent!" said Cali. "I'm confident our answer lies with that vegetation."

"I'll start mapping out a plan for us to head there." Talen grabbed her notebook once again.

Kase and Lenia quietly headed out of the library. Kase led the way to Cali's room, and tried to give Lenia a tour of the scholar castle as they went. He wanted to sound smart, but didn't know the names of all the rooms they passed. It didn't matter much, because Lenia couldn't stop laughing. He was glad she was enjoying their mini-adventure.

When they opened the door to Cali's room, they received a surprise. It was a mess. There were clothes on the bookshelves, books and notes on the bed, and bedding in the closet. Kase didn't know how she could sleep in this room.

Lenia looked past the mess and was drawn towards the window, which bathed the room in the lowering sun's red glow. "My dorm is on the ground floor. I used to sneak up to the roof of the wizard castle and watch the sunset. I've been so busy lately, I kind of forgot how wonderful and calming it is."

"Well," Kase said as he popped another grape in his mouth, "let's go up there now!"

"What about the book?" Lenia asked. She looked at the mess around the room. "It's going to take us forever to find it."

"Already got it," he said proudly as he showed it off. It was titled *An Encyclopaedia of Trees,* and had a picture on the cover of a great oak tree that looked almost like it had a human face on its trunk.

"That was fast," she said, surprised.

"I have eyes like a hawk," he said proudly. "In fact, some call me Hawk-eye." He was also used to Cali's lived-in mess. She hadn't changed much since they were kids.

Lenia smirked. "I know what you're doing." Her eyes twinkled.

"I don't know what you mean ..." He tried to keep his voice innocent, but he couldn't contain his smile.

"You can't make up your own nickname," she said. "Don't worry; I'll still come up with something cool for you."

Kase laughed and shook his head. "I thought I had it!" he admitted as they walked out of Cali's room. This time, Lenia led the way. Their direction was simple: all they had to do was head up.

They climbed the southern stairway to the top floor, but instead of entering the hallway, Lenia moved to the open window near the stairwell.

She poked her head out and peered around the edge. "Perfect!" she said happily.

"What?" he asked.

"Follow me," she said. She reached outside of the window and grabbed onto some of the wooden lattice on the outside wall. She shifted her body outside, and started climbing up to the roof.

"You're crazy," he said as he tucked the book into his belt. He reached out to the lattice and started climbing up after her. They both made their way onto the flat-topped roof with ease.

Once their feet were firmly planted, they made their way along the parapet to the western edge, to get a better look at the sunset. The common area for The Academy was below them. The orange sunlight bounced off the greenery of the park, producing a breathtaking view.

"So beautiful." Lenia rested her arms on a merlon and sighed.

"Want to see something cool?" Kase asked.

"Absolutely!" she replied with a smile.

"Take a look in the opposite direction," he said as he turned towards the eastern sky and pointed.

She followed his finger, but didn't focus on anything. "What am I looking for?" she asked hesitantly.

"About half an hour before the sun completely sets, you can see the eastern star come to life. Normally, it's harder to notice with all the other stars in the sky, but during the sunset, it's the only one that shines. When it comes into view, it almost looks like a firefly coming to life."

Just as he was explaining it, a flash of green appeared in the sky. It looked like a fire starter was in the sky, sparking a small, green candle in the shape of the star.

"You're right," she said happily. "That is really cool! How did you know that?"

"Well," he said confidently, "I'm actually a pretty smart guy. Some might say that I'm not just a great warrior, but that I'm also a little bit of a scholar, too."

Lenia laughed. "So you're a scholar-warrior? A schorrior?"

"I was thinking super warrior." He laughed. "But, yes."

Lenia smiled and turned back towards the sunset. "I'll take that into consideration for your nickname," she replied. As they continued to watch the late glow of the sun, her eyes faded down towards the common area. She let out a disgruntled sigh as she stared at the ground below.

"What was that?" Kase started eating grapes again.

"There's a guy in one of my classes that I just can't stand," she replied. "He's doing homework under that tree over there. It's not like he's a bad guy; I mean, he's actually pretty nice. It's just that every time I see him, he gives me a hug."

"What a jerk!" Kase said sarcastically as he popped another grape in his mouth.

"It's really annoying!" She giggled. "You're right, though, it's not that bad. I just don't want him touching me. I wish I could get back at him, somehow."

Kase checked how far away the hugger was, and grinned. "Would it cheer you up if I was able to hit him with this grape?" he said as he held up the small fruit.

Lenia giggled. "Don't tease me," she said. "There's no way that you could hit him from here."

"Something you might not know about me," Kase boasted, "is that I'm a grape throwing champion. Lots of people think they can throw a grape well, but they always forget about the fundamentals. It's all in the hips. Watch and learn."

He stood tall and took a step back from the edge. He licked his finger and held it up, as if trying to judge which way the wind was blowing.

Lenia covered her smile. His large frame stood confident in the orange glow of the early night, despite his ridiculous purpose.

He pulled his arm back, stepped forward, and followed through.

The grape's course was precise. Its aim was true. Its purpose brooked no room for mercy. It reached its destination with full force, and the grape splattered across the hugger's face.

His head jerked in surprise and impact. He shook it as he tried to figure out what had happened.

Kase quickly ducked behind the wall. "Get down!" he said with a chuckle.

Lenia quickly ducked behind the edge of the wall, rolled over, held her gut, and laughed uncontrollably. They both had to wipe away the tears from their eyes.

"That just made my day!" said Lenia. She still couldn't stop laughing. "What an impossible shot!"

"I told you!" he said with another laugh of his own. "I want to look to see what his reaction is, but I can't."

Lenia started to calm herself as best she could. "Okay, I'll do it." She got to her knees.

Before she could look back over, a pigeon landed on the merlon on the other side of Kase. Instead of checking on the hugger, Lenia quickly ducked back down with a squeak, and put her head behind his shoulder, as if to shield herself from the bird. She covered her face with her hands and tucked her knees in close.

Kase looked at her, then looked at the pigeon, then at her again. He stopped laughing. "You really don't like birds, do you?"

"I don't," Lenia murmured in a small voice. "It's going to claw my eyes out. Or worse, it might poop on me."

"It's okay," he replied in an exaggeratedly soft voice. "I won't let the pigeon poop on you."

Lenia giggled, then squeaked again when the bird cooed and flapped its wings. "Is it gone?" she asked.

"No," he replied.

She peeked through her fingers. The pigeon was no longer there. "Liar." She playfully slapped the shoulder that she was hiding behind. "We should probably head back now. It's getting a little cold out."

Kase nodded his head in agreement. They didn't even check on the hugger, just made their way back to the lattice, climbed down, reentered through the castle window, and headed back to the library.

"There you are!" Cali greeted them.

"You may want to think about tidying up your room more often," Kase teased as he handed her the book.

"Mm," Cali acknowledged, and she immediately flipped through the tome. "Here it is," she said excitedly. "'The skukum tree is native to the southeast volcanic region known as The Green Gem. Although its natural habitat is an active volcano, the tree has flourished over hundreds of years.'"

She quickly scanned the page. "Blah, blah, blah, grow to two hundred feet tall, yadda yadda, home of the goliath bird-eating tarantula, don't care ... Here! 'Although the seeds are soft, the immense heat of the lava can't destroy them. When the volcano erupts, the rest of the tree dies, but the seeds remain intact because of their protective outer shell. Once the ground cools, the seeds sprout, and the species survives.' This is it! This is what we need to hold the lava!"

"That's great!" exclaimed Kase in support. "Now what?" he asked.

"Well, while you two were gone, Talen and I finished the maps, and calculated travel and cooling times," Cali said happily. "We now have enough information to get us to The Furnace, and The Green Gem. Since it's the weekend, and we have two days off before next week's classes start, we basically have one to get the seeds from the skukum tree, and the other to grab our lava."

"It is inadvisable to travel on The Furnace at night, so it is imperative that we get there in two days' time," Talen put in.

"But it's definitely doable." Cali was almost jumping up and down. "This is so awesome!"

Cali's excitement was contagious, and soon the whole group couldn't contain themselves. They agreed to end their research for the night, and meet up the next morning in order to make their trek to The Green Gem. They happily packed up their belongings, quickly returned the books in the library to their rightful places, and then hopped back to their respective dorms.

Kase slept uneasily that night. He was both eager and apprehensive for the start of their journey the next day.

⁓

When they stepped through the gateway portal into the southernmost part of the realm, they were all amazed by the gorgeous tropical forest in front of them. The three portal doors at this gateway were set on top of a small hill, with a short clearing before the great brush of the jungle. Kase could hear small animal noises and the rustling of leaves as the wind blew gently.

Although they couldn't see any distance past the height of the great trees, Cali told them that to the left was The Green Gem, and to the right was The Furnace.

Cali looked at her map, and pointed easterly towards the forest. There was a small path that marked their way. She held her notebook while Talen and Lenia followed behind her. Kase brought up the rear. He carried a sac across his back that contained food, water, more books and notes, and some throwing knives. He also had a small axe in its sheath on his hip, in case he had to clear a path for them.

"Wait!" said Cali before they entered the tropical foliage. "Let's capture this moment on the sage mirror!" she said excitedly. She grabbed the mirror from her pocket, and the group huddled together. "Smile!" she said. "Mirror, mirror, capture image." A soft flash dashed across the mirror. "Store that image in the Liberati Event One collection."

"I think my eyes were closed," said Kase as the group separated.

"Too late," Cali said with a wink. She kept the mirror in her hand and continued on. She had estimated it would only take them a couple hours to make it to The Green Gem, so they were in no rush to get there.

None of them had been to the tropical forest before, so along the way they stopped in order to check out some of the other vegetation, small animals, and streams.

Talen was noticeably happy to be out and about with friends, and told them everything she knew about the inhabitants of tropical jungles. She revealed the secrets of the tiny Beedub butterflies that they saw flutter by. She found and caught a couple Ruby Red frogs, explaining what gave them their vibrant colour, before letting them back into their pond. She helped Lenia pick a beautiful Zebra Lily to put in Kase's hair. They all told him how pretty he was, and captured an image of him.

Kase was unimpressed, and refused to smile for the mirror, but everyone else seemed to enjoy it.

They reached a clearing in the forest, and took a moment to admire the wonderful monstrosity of The Green Gem in front of them. Light smoke drifted from the top of the volcano, and a small flash of red could occasionally be seen. They all agreed that it was tragically beautiful.

It didn't take long before they started to notice the difference in vegetation. The trees seemed to grow exponentially. The skukum trees were a lot taller than the rest of the plant life, with wide trunks, heavy branches, and triangular leaves. The group approached the base of the first one they saw, and stared straight up in awe.

"How tall do you think it is?" asked Kase. He tried to see where the top of it ended.

"According to my notes, skukum trees can grow to be two hundred feet tall," said Cali as she looked down at her book.

"This one looks only one hundred and sixty," said Talen. She leaned back farther, craning her neck. "Maybe one hundred and seventy."

"Only?" Kase asked sarcastically. "How far up are the seeds?"

"They're right at the top!" Cali exclaimed confidently. "Good luck!" she said to Kase. Neither she, Talen, nor Lenia were going to attempt to climb the tree.

"All right!" shouted Kase. "Finally, it's my time to shine!" He quickly removed the sac from his back, and emptied all the items. "What do the seeds look like, and how many do I need to get?" He slung the empty sac over his shoulder.

"They look like a purple watermelon," Cali replied. "Kinda brownish, but not quite; maybe more like puce. We need five of them."

Kase didn't know what 'puce' meant, but he nodded in agreement. He was pretty sure he would recognize them when he saw them.

He looked up to the first branch of this tree, too high to easily reach, and decided to try one of the others. He found a suitable one, with its first branches not much higher than his head. The rest of his team set up their blanket next to the trunk and took a seat.

"Watch out for spiders," Cali said casually.

He nodded, jumped, and held on to the lowest branch, swinging himself up to a standing position. He was about to continue his ascent when a glint of light caught his eye from the direction of the group.

Lenia was holding the sage mirror towards him. He smiled at her, and reached for the next branch with an extra flourish. He quickly made his way up the tree.

After a few minutes, he checked to see how far he was from the ground. All he saw were branches and leaves. When he turned his head back up, he noticed a small, fluttering bird. It wasn't perched on the tree, but rather looked like its feet were caught on the branch. It tried to fly away from him, but couldn't get up into the air. He reached out to help the bird, but he hesitated.

He pulled his hand back. "I'd love to help you out, friend, but you might poop on Lenia, so sorry."

He continued his climb, and before he knew it, he was at the top of the tree. There must have been hundreds of brownish-pink seeds, which reflected the light trickling through the green leaves above. They glowed like starlight underneath the top level of foliage. He wished he had the sage mirror so that he could capture an image and show the rest of his team.

He reached up with both hands and plucked the first seed. He placed it in his sac gently, and then continued until he had five. The seeds weren't very heavy, but they filled the sac and formed an awkward bulge. He knew that he would have to be careful on the way down the tree, so that he wouldn't crush any of them accidentally on the branches. He started his descent slowly, and then got a little faster as he regained his rhythm.

He was about halfway down when he noted that his left hand stuck to the branch it was holding. He pulled it off and saw a white, gooey substance peel away with his hand.

"Gross!" he said aloud. He tried to brush his hand off on his clothes, but it just kept sticking everywhere. He looked again at the branch he was holding, and saw two bird legs next to where his hand had been.

"That's strange," he muttered. He went in for a closer look. It looked like a bird had been perched there, and got ripped away while its feet stayed secured to the branch. It was disgusting, and yet he couldn't take his eyes off it.

His attention was caught by a low, hissing noise to his right. He slowly turned his head and was face-to-face with the biggest spider he had ever seen. Its legs were at least a foot long on either side of its ugly, hairy body, and it was perched next to his arm.

He didn't want to stick around for an extra look, so he quickly jumped down to the next branch. He felt something heavy on his right arm. He panicked, clutched the hairy thing with his left hand, and side-armed it away as hard as he could.

He heard another hissing noise from above him, so he quickly climbed down to the next branch. He didn't know how many spiders there were, but he didn't want to find out. He could hear their soft, menacing noises, and could feel them graze his arms and legs, but he kept his head down and raced down the tree as fast as he could.

With this extra challenge, he became more focused than he ever had in class. His movements were precise. His action was less of a climb, and more of an elegant dance. He was able to twist and turn so the sac wouldn't hit the branches, and still keep his swift pace ahead of the pack of hairy, ugly, giant spiders. He stepped left, grabbed right, swung back, threw a spider off him, stepped right, swung down, and ducked.

The ground came up swiftly below him. Instead of carefully swinging to the last available branch, he leapt for the ground.

While in the air, he swung the sac from his back to his front, and cradled it. As he hit the ground, he rolled onto his shoulder to break his fall, and protected the seeds with his body. Instead of rolling to a stop, he quickly bounced to his feet.

"Run!" he screamed as he glanced back at the rest of his team.

Lenia, Cali, and Talen all looked at him, confused, then burst out laughing after a moment of silence.

"I'm serious!" he said, bouncing from foot to foot as he looked back up the tree. He put the bag down on the ground and drew his small axe, gesturing for his partners to move away from the trunk. He was ready to attack anything that had followed him down. He couldn't see any spiders between the branches, so he checked the ground around the tree.

"Put that away before you hurt yourself," Cali said as she got up.

"But the spiders," Kase said as he pointed up at the tree. "The spiders were—"

"I told you they were big. Don't worry; they stay in the trees. They were probably just chasing you away from their nest. Now, let's see the seeds!" She was tugging at the sac in excitement.

Kase took one last look at the branches and gave a satisfied sigh. "I'm pretty good with this thing, you know," he said as he put his axe away.

"I know," Cali said with a wink. She looked in the bag and clapped her hands in joy. She took one of the seeds out in order to inspect it, and then put it back. "Mission accomplished!" she said.

The team all cheered in excitement, relishing the minor victory. Without spending too much extra time, they packed up the rest of their items and started their trek back to the portal door. It was a small step for them in the grand scheme of things, but they were all happy with the result nonetheless.

᠅

Their mood was more serious for their journey to The Furnace the next day. Instead of watching the meandering flight of Beedub butterflies, they studied the maps intently. Instead of stopping to eat on their blanket, they snacked while walking. They were focused.

Kase carried the sac with their supplies, including the seeds that were going to hold the lava. The night before, Cali and Lenia had cut them open and hollowed them out. Four of the seeds would be used for storage, while one of them was to be used as a scoop to fill them. Each member of the team would have to carry one of the vessels, but they were all up to the challenge.

The path to The Furnace was a little more traveled than the one for The Green Gem. There were a lot of other teams on the quest, some taking the trek slowly and cautiously, and others running as fast as they could. It was interesting to see some of the other strategies, but as they had agreed, it wasn't something they allowed themselves to focus on.

The trek through the jungle was long and tiresome. The sunshine disappeared behind the black smoke from The Furnace in the skies above. Although the path was darker, the Liberati seemed to gain some extra energy when they could see the tip of the volcano through the trees.

"We're almost there!" exclaimed Cali. She pointed down the path excitedly.

Kase expected to see a clearing ahead, but instead he saw four warriors running towards them. There were two of them on each edge of the path as they carried a large, square cauldron. Their arms were raised high overhead as they each gripped a protrustion on their respective corner. "Move!" one of the warriors shouted.

There was barely enough room for the warriors to get by, so Cali stepped to the side of the path, and the rest of the Liberati followed suit. They stopped walking, and leaned as far as they could against the brush next to them so the warriors could pass.

"Move!" the warrior shouted again, but the Liberati had nowhere else to go.

Kase leaned a little farther, but as soon as the warriors ran by him, he heard a loud crash. He turned to see all of them strewn about the path, their cauldron tipped over, and a pool of lava flowing from its brim.

"The lava!" shouted the warrior closest to Kase. He jumped to his feet, grabbed one of the handles of the cauldron, and leaned back. He righted the cauldron so that the top of it was pointing to the sky once again. He scrambled for the lid, and placed it on top.

"What happened?" shouted another angrily.

"Shea tripped," one of them said. He pointed at the warrior sitting on the ground, rubbing his shin.

"I had to step to the side when we passed that group," Shea replied. He put his hand on a tree on the edge of the path and stood up. He shook out his leg gingerly, and then limped around in a circle. "I must have hit a rock or something."

"This is your fault!" the largest warrior said as he pointed at Kase and took a few steps forward.

Kase puffed up his chest and stood in front of the Liberati. He stretched out his arms to shield them. "I ..."

"Tarkin," said the warrior who lifted the cauldron. "There's a crack here."

Tarkin turned his attention back towards the cauldron and looked at it closely. "How much lava is left?" he asked.

The warrior lifted the lid and peeked inside. "About half," he answered. "We should try to get this back to The Academy as fast as possible so we don't lose more."

"Dragoon," the others answered.

Tarkin turned back to Kase and stared at him. Kase stared back. "You better watch where you're going," he said threateningly.

He lowered his hand and walked backwards towards the cauldron. "And watch your back."

The four warriors each grabbed a corner of the cauldron, lifted it high above their head, and started running again, leaving the Liberati and a small pool of lava behind. The lava was already starting to harden as it cooled. Kase lowered his arms when they were a safe distance away.

"What just happened?" Lenia asked.

"I don't know," Cali admitted. "But that lava looks so cool! Let's keep going!"

The Liberati shrugged off their encounter with the warriors, and continued down the path until they finally reached the end. The only challenge left before they were at the volcano was the barren land of the steam pits.

There were seemingly random streams spraying out of the ground of the pits. Some of them were shallow and sharp, while others were tall and fierce. There was a bridge that extended over the fountains of steam on the other side of the volcano, but the hike to it was an extra hour each way. Luckily, Cali and Talen had a different plan.

"Are you sure this is going to work?" Kase asked skeptically. He could already feel the warmth of the spouts ahead of them.

"Don't worry," said Cali. "Talen's got her map." She nudged Talen with her elbow, gesturing for her to take the lead. Talen hesitated, but then smiled and opened her notebook to show off her sketch.

"The locations of the steam spouts have been well-documented over time," said Talen. "Although seemingly random, if you take a large enough sample size, you can begin to see patterns in the field." Her map basically displayed hundreds of dots, but there were distinguishable clear areas. Within those, Talen had traced a path.

Kase stared at the map, then back out at the steam pits.

"That's amazing." Lenia shook her head in disbelief.

"Follow me," said Talen encouragingly. "But make sure you follow *exactly* behind me. Make the same steps that I make, and we'll get through this field in no time!"

As other teams were taking the long way around, the Liberati slowly and methodically followed their shortcut. Talen led the way, turning left, zig-zagging, turning right, side-stepping, and turning again. It almost seemed like the four of them were dancing their way across, but Talen had it all planned out to perfection.

The team quickly navigated through the pits without getting hit by any steam, and they found themselves at the base of the massive volcano in a quarter of the time, warm and damp from the pits' humid atmosphere.

Not too far away, there was a stream of lava flowing out of the mouth of the volcano. All the other students were trying to collect lava by using various types of thick vessels. Some of the teams' vessels were bigger than others. Others wore protective clothing in order to carry them. None of the other teams were using a puce-coloured skukum tree seed.

The Liberati made their way to the hot river and unpacked their tools. Cali grabbed one of the seeds, along with the scoop, and got as close to the lava as possible.

"Here goes nothing," she said. She dipped one side into the stream to collect her sample. She held the scoop for a few seconds to see what would happen. It didn't change shape at all. Cali couldn't contain her excitement. She increased her pace and filled the seed in no time.

"It works!" she exclaimed. "I mean, I knew it would work, but ... it actually works!" The group cheered, but they did it softly so they wouldn't draw attention to themselves.

Cali filled the first seed, and then put the top back on. She handed the seed to Kase, who held it close. He was amazed that he couldn't feel any heat, but was careful with the vessel nonetheless.

Cali filled the other three seeds, and the team members cradled them gently, like a baby.

As they started their trek back to the portal door, they couldn't help but see the other teams looking on at them in wonder. Instead of being nervous about the strange glances, Kase felt proud of his team, confidently carrying their unorthodox vessels. No other team came forward to question the group of misfits, but he knew they wanted to.

They made their way back through the steam pits with caution and ease, and out into the tropical forest.

After hiking for a few more hours, fatigue from the long trek started to sink in for three of the four members. They were still about an hour away from the portal gateway by Cali's calculation, so they decided to stop, rest, and have something to eat. Kase sat next to Lenia, and leaned against the tree behind them.

"We're so close to being done the first event!" he said excitedly.

"And judging from what the other teams were doing, I bet we have one of the best sample sizes!" chimed in Talen.

"The last few days have been so incredible." Cali smiled. "Thank you all so much for all your hard work." She removed the top of one of the seeds to look at the lava. Since they had kept them enclosed, it seemed like it hadn't cooled at all.

"It's so beautiful out today, too," Lenia said. She took a deep breath, looked up at the sun peeking through the leaves, and then closed her eyes. "I can even smell the lavender from the forest!" She rested her head on Kase's shoulder. He was enjoying the day, too.

"That's strange," Talen said. "Lavender isn't native to this region."

"It smells good nonetheless," Cali said as she lay out on the blanket. Kase closed his eyes. It smelled lovely, but it was making him tired. Maybe they did deserve the rest.

***

"What happened!?"

Lenia's exclamation woke Kase up. He opened his eyes. He felt rejuvenated, as if he had taken a quick nap. He turned towards her and smiled. She looked like she was in a panic. His smile disappeared.

Talen and Cali were both sprawled out on the blanket, eyes closed. He knew something was wrong. "Cali!" He reached over and nudged her.

"The seeds!" Lenia shouted. She got up and frantically ran around the tree they had stopped beside.

Kase jumped to his feet, finally noticing what she had: all four of the seeds had tipped, spilling their precious contents. Already, a thick crust had formed over the spill.

"Cali!" he yelled again. His voice cracked this time in panic.

Talen shook her head. She propped herself up and tried to open her eyes. "What happened?" she asked in a dreamy state. She seemed disoriented.

"Where am I?" asked Cali as she rolled over. She looked up at Kase and smiled. "Hi Kase; what are you doing here?" She looked past him and smiled at Lenia too. "Hey girl!" she said happily.

Kase was dumbfounded by Cali's reaction, but her smile quickly faded. "Oh no." Her voice quavered in disbelief. "What happened?"

Cali scrambled to her feet, but abruptly stopped moving when she saw the mess. "What happened to the seeds!" she yelled.

Talen got to her feet too, and started to rub her head.

Lenia was trying to scoop up what she could of the cooled lava, but the seed she used mostly just scraped over the newly-formed stone.

Cali ran over to the patch of burned grass and rapidly-cooling rock that was all that was left of their efforts. "No. No, no, no!" She, too, tried to reclaim some of the magical lava. Most of the skukum seeds were trapped under the mottled stone. Kase tried adding his strength to the efforts, and Lenia tried reheating the lava with her own fire, but to no avail.

Cali was the first to give up. Her shoulders sagged in hopelessness. "It's over." Her voice quivered. She sat on the ground, and put her head in her hands.

"No, it's not!" Kase said reassuringly. "We can't give up! We still have a few days left. We can get some more seeds, get back to The Furnace—"

Cali cut him off with an angry sweep of her arm. "It's over!" She jerkily wiped tears off her cheeks. "We've lost. We don't have time to do this again. Not with classes, too. Not if we want to even have a chance at the finals. We had one shot at this whole thing, and we almost made it, but we lost. I don't even want to think about it anymore. I failed."

Cali got up and started to head back to the portal door. She didn't gather up her books or maps, and she didn't look at any of her team members. She just kept her head down and walked away.

The other three Liberati looked at each other, speechless. They didn't know what to do. Their leader had given up.

CHAPTER 9

Can't Stop, Won't Stop

Kase sprinted through the tropical forest. His legs were strong. His steps were sure. He didn't need Talen's geographical knowledge, because he remembered the way. He didn't need Cali to explain what had to be done, because he already knew. He didn't need Lenia by his side, though he wished she were. All he needed was to be the fastest he could be. He wanted to be faster.

He jumped over a tree branch that had fallen across the path, and felt the skukum seeds shift in his sac. He reached behind him and steadied them as he kept sprinting. He had acquired them the night before, and didn't have time to get any more. He had to get to the lava. It was the last day before Event One was over.

He followed the path around the last bend, and found himself at the edge of the steam pits. He stopped so that he could catch his breath. It also gave him time to focus. He pulled out the dotted map of the steam pits that he had taken from Talen's notebook. She, too, seemed to have given up hope of succeeding in the quest. Kase, though a little nervous, still felt the chance was worth the risk.

He looked up from the map. The sky was getting darker. He'd started his run immediately after his last class of the day, but even so, he didn't have much daylight left. He needed to keep moving. Get through the steam pits.

He could feel the heat of the steam spouting randomly from the ground, and wished he had more time, so that he could take the long way around.

He took a deep breath and another step forward. He stopped. There was a noise he could barely make out behind him, but it was getting louder. It sounded like … the beating of wings.

No sooner had he identified it than it stopped. He heard a snort.

Kase slowly turned. Turanus was standing at the edge of the forest, his wings held out wide. Kase's jaw dropped. Turanus' presence was impressive, but Lenia sitting on top of him was even more so.

Lenia shook her head as if she was waking from a trance. "Kase?" she asked. Turanus knelt down, and Lenia dismounted. She paused, and put her hand on the unicorn's mane. "Thank you, friend. That was more than I could think to ask for." As she had with Luna, she pulled a loose hair to remember him by. She looked at it for half a second, and by the time she looked up, Turanus was gone.

"Where'd he go?" She looked around.

"He's not much of one for good-byes," Kase said as he walked over. "I'm so jealous of you right now! You *rode* him? How many people get to say they've ridden a unicorn? How was it?"

"It felt …" Lenia paused, and then met his gaze and smiled. "Like a dream. Just seeing him was spectacular, and when he knelt down in front of me, I knew that he wanted to take me somewhere special …" She shook her head again as she snapped back to reality. "Wait a minute. What are *you* doing here? Why did Turanus bring me here?"

Kase turned back towards the steam pit field and to The Furnace beyond. "I'm going after the lava," he said confidently.

"I thought we were done," Lenia said. "I mean, I admire the effort, but I thought we weren't supposed to be here after nightfall. Isn't it dangerous?"

"I'm not willing to give up," he said. "I refuse. We were so close before, and we still have a chance, because it's not over yet. I know it could be dangerous, but that just means that we need to hurry."

111

"What about the maps? What about the steam field? We don't have anything." Lenia started to panic. Kase reached out and touched her arm.

"I have everything we need," he replied confidently. "Just try and keep up," he said with a wink.

"Well, you might not know this about me," she replied with a wry smile. "But even though I'm a wizard, I'm pretty strong and fast. In fact, I'm kind of like a wizard warrior."

Kase laughed. "So you're a warriard? A wizarrior?"

"I was thinking more of a super wizard, but both of those work." They giggled. Kase relaxed, and felt more confident in their endeavour.

He started jogging through the steam field, following the exact route that Talen had led them just days before. Lenia raced on after him. Knowing that a mistake would not only hurt him, but Lenia too, made him focus a little harder.

They were through the steam pits quickly, and he picked up the pace to the lava stream.

Lenia tried to keep up as best she could, but he was a little too fast for her. She was running pretty well for a wizard, though.

He removed two skukum tree seeds from his sac, and a third that he had fashioned into a scoop. After he filled the first one, Lenia finally caught up to him. "You're crazy!" was all she could muster as she tried to catch her breath. "It's admirable, but you're crazy!"

Kase put the top back onto the first seed, then took out an extra container from his pocket. There was a white, gooey substance inside that he used to seal the lid. As Lenia listened in amazement, he told her about his journey.

A couple days after Cali had given up hope, he decided that he wasn't going to give up, too. He was strong enough to run the route instead of hike it. He remembered everything they had undergone in the quest, and what they had done to succeed. It seemed to him like a waste to throw that away, with Event One not being over yet.

The day before, he had made his way through the gateway portal, and sprinted to the skukum tree. He climbed the tree as fast as he could, avoided the goliath spiders, and even collected some of their webbing to use as an adhesive. He had made it back to The Academy before nightfall.

He knew that the trek to The Furnace was a little longer, but he believed in himself, and knew he had to at least try. He easily ran through the tropical forest, not stopping until he made it to the steam pits. As he finished his story, he also finished filling and sealing the second seed. He picked up both seeds and handed one to Lenia.

Lenia took it carefully. "That's amazing, Kase!" she said. "You're amazing! Your idea is going to save our team!"

Kase blushed. "I just knew in my heart that I couldn't give up," he replied. "Not on something that means so much to Cali."

Lenia smiled back, the expression warming her features. The light from the lava made her eyes look like they were on fire. They moved to the left, but when she refocused, her expression became fearful.

Kase knew what was next. He spun around, and met the evil glare of a white banshee. It looked a lot scarier than the ones in the books they had read. It was lean, and had burn marks all over its body. The skin it did have was stretched taut over bone. It looked like a ghost, barely hovering above the rock of the volcano only a few hundred yards away. Its empty, black eyes were locked on the duo. It let out an ear-piercing scream.

"What do we do?" yelled Lenia, as she took a few steps back and covered her ears.

An instant passed, and then it seemed like hundreds of banshees were rounding the edge of the volcano beyond the first one. Kase turned back around and simply yelled, "Run!"

Lenia didn't move. She was frozen with fear. Luckily for her, Kase was already in mid stride. In one swift move, he turned her by the shoulders and grabbed the hand not holding the precious seed, pulling her into motion.

They made their way across the edge of the volcano. Lenia looked over her shoulder, and he couldn't help but look, too. The banshees hovered just over the ground, but they could fly like lightning. They twisted and turned like a chaotic pack of hungry hyenas, fixated on their prey. Lenia ducked her head down and scrunched her eyes nearly closed, still running.

Kase was focused on his run. His steps were strong and precise. Lenia opened her eyes when she could hear the spouts of steam. Although the world was moving fast around them, Kase still managed to run the path that Talen had taken them on, hardly glancing at the map. He dodged left, and then went right. He zig-zagged, and went left again, pulling Lenia along the trail behind him. He could feel the steam shoot up all around them, and then he felt a sharp pain on his side. He gasped and turned. There was a banshee beside them, swiping at him violently.

He hobbled for one step, then kept going. He dodged left, and made another move to avoid the steam, but the banshee was not as lucky. The steam hit it in the belly, and it screamed in pain. Lenia screamed, too, hands held up near her face. Her hair fluttered with the closeness of the steam jet.

Afraid she would drop the seed, Kase pulled her ahead of him, shielding her back. He guided her by the shoulders, moving slower now with the pain jabbing him in the side with every step. She kept going, shoulders hunched, gasping now with the length of their run.

He looked back, worried, and noticed that most of the banshees had stopped at the edge of the field. Some of them were brave, and were circling around the area that they had entered. The deeper they got, the less the banshees tried to chase them. Once they were halfway across the steam field, they had escaped the banshees completely.

Even so, it wasn't until they made their way to the edge of the tropical forest that they stopped for a rest. Darkness had fallen over the land, so only the light from the volcano could be seen.

"We're safe," Kase said as he tried to catch his breath. Lenia stood hunched over, but was still clutching her seed with a death grip.

"I can't believe ... we just did that!" she said, still trying to gasp for air. She put her seed down on the ground, reached into her pocket, and grabbed her fire starter. She found a stick and lit it like a torch, using her magic to keep the flame bright.

Kase rested against a tree, and then slid to the ground. He could feel that sharp pain on his side, and covered it with his free hand. His shirt was wet, and he could feel his blood slowly pumping out. He tried to apply pressure to the wound, but it didn't do much for the pain.

Lenia moved closer to him, and moved her torch down towards his wound. "Are you okay?" she asked softly.

"I'm fine," he replied through clenched teeth. "It's just a slash; I can get it checked once we're back at The Academy."

"Can I look at it?" she said as she moved closer to him.

"I'll be fine," he said in a softer voice, but she was going to check out his injury anyway.

She stuck the torch into the ground next to the tree, and knelt down beside him. She moved his hand aside, and gently rolled up the blood-soaked shirt to reveal the heavy gash in his side.

"You're right," she said with a smile. "You're fine."

He laughed and then felt a sharper pain. His body shuddered. "Don't make me laugh," he said.

Lenia put her hand over his wound and closed her eyes.

"What are you doing?"

Lenia opened her eyes and met his gaze. "It's okay," she replied with a warm smile. "I'm going to heal you."

"How?" he asked. Her touch soothed him.

115

"I come from a family of healers," she replied as a warm glow shone from her hand. It reminded him of his uncle's magic. "I learned from my mother and father when I was little. I don't do it often, though. The only way to heal another person's wound is to absorb their pain; to transfer it to my own body, and then use my power to diminish it from within." She closed her eyes, took a deep breath, and readied herself for the challenge.

"Wait." He grabbed her wrist. "You're going to take on my pain? I don't want you to be hurt, too."

"Don't worry." She peeked one eye open and smiled. "I'm strong, remember? I'm a super wizard."

He let go of her wrist. She was right. She was strong, and powerful: the strongest person he had ever met.

Lenia moved her hand in a circle. Her arms shook for a second as the pain entered her body. Her eyebrows furrowed in concentration. She shifted, and Kase could tell that she felt the pain in the same side as he did. However, as she did so, his pain lessened. It flowed out of him like a cool stream.

As his pain decreased, her face became more exaggerated. It scrunched up, but then relaxed. It scrunched up again, but once again relaxed. It seemed like she was in a chaotic battle—one that she was winning. His pain diminished. The wound healed.

As she finished, she threw her hands back and jerked backwards. She fell to the ground and clutched her throat.

"Lenia!" Kase exclaimed. He scrambled, and then kneeled over her. She was out of breath, but stared directly at him. She still clutched at her throat, but her breathing had already started to steady itself out.

"That was strange," she said as she calmed down. "I knew that the pain would transfer to my side, but I don't know why I felt it in my throat, too."

"Are you okay?" Kase lifted her into a sitting position.

"Yes," she said with a reassuring nod.

Kase helped her up and they checked his wound again. There wasn't even a scar. "You're a really good, super wizard," he admitted. "Are you going to be a healer when you're done at The Academy?"

Lenia laughed. "Thanks, but a healer is the last thing that I want to be. Healers are important, and they do wonderful work, but I don't want to be anything like my parents."

She reached down and grabbed the torch. She held it high as she peered into the tropical forest. "I don't really know what road I'm headed down, but I know that I'm destined for something different. Something more." She looked back at him and smiled.

"I know exactly what you mean," Kase said as he thought about his own goals. He felt his heart warm, and wondered if it was an effect of the healing process.

Lenia handed him the torch and grabbed the seeds. "I'm ready when you are."

"I'm pretty strong too, so I can carry one of those." He gestured towards the seeds.

"No, I'll hold onto these," she replied, and pulled them close. "I think I've earned it, super warrior."

Kase laughed. "Anything for you, super wizard."

CHAPTER 10

Sandcastles

"There they are!" exclaimed Lenia. She pointed across the common area. Cali and Talen were lying on the grass together, pointing up to the sky. "What are they doing?"

"They're playing the cloud game," Kase replied solemnly. "Cali must be depressed."

"Good thing she has us to cheer her up," Lenia said with a smile. "They're going to be so excited when we tell them what happened!"

Kase couldn't help but smile, too. She was right. They rushed over to join the rest of the Liberati.

"That one looks like a couple of best friends enjoying a day swimming at the beach, but underneath them is a giant man-eating shark that is lurking and ready to feast," said Cali as they approached.

"I knew we'd find you here," Kase said. He and Lenia stopped beside Cali.

"I love sharks," responded Talen in a sad tone. She ignored Kase completely. "I wish I had a pet shark that could eat whoever I wanted it to." They both sighed.

"Me too." Cali also ignored Kase. "I think I'd name mine Death Hammer."

"That's a pretty name," said Talen. "I would name mine Carl."

"It looks like our team is in thirty-third place!" Kase held the sage mirror towards Cali.

"Threes!" exclaimed Lenia in support.

Cali stared in disbelief. "What? But how?" She snatched the sage mirror from Kase's hand. She turned it towards Talen so that she could read the list of all the competitors, too.

As they looked at the mirror in awe, Kase explained how he and Lenia were able to collect the lava from The Furnace using a new set of seeds that he had grabbed from the skukum tree. He told them about their escape from the gaggle of banshees, and how Lenia had healed his wound. He also told them how they made it back in time for Professor Bright to submit their sample, and how impressed she was with the usable sample size. She had wanted to sneak some of the magical lava away for herself in order to conduct her own experiments, but they promised to get her some more after the Q was over.

When he finished, he noticed that Cali was crying. His excited smile vanished. It wasn't the reaction he was expecting.

He knelt down and reached out to touch her, but she pushed him away. "You're such an idiot for going to The Furnace at night. It's so dangerous!" Her voice quivered through the tears. She grabbed his arm and pulled him in for a hug. "Thank you so much."

She let him go, and wiped the tears from her eyes. He helped her to her feet, and then helped Talen. Talen was expressionless, as usual.

"I guess there's only one thing left to do," Cali said. She looked at the rest of the Liberati. "It's the first day—let's get going on Event Two! Kase, would you do the honours?" she said with a smile.

He took the sage mirror back and held it down as they all huddled around. "Mirror, mirror, show me the details of Quest Series Event Two," he said confidently.

They watched as a cloud filled the face of the mirror. When Event Two was revealed, he read it aloud.

"Over two thousand years ago, an ancient civilization known as the Eidola lived peacefully in the western desert. Unfortunately for them, they lived in a time of great violence and plunder, and soon suffered the same fate as many other civilizations at that time. Although they were conquered, and the majority of their kingdom destroyed, their history lives on in the three towers that survived, known as the Sandcastles of the Eidola."

"It's pronounced Eye-dola," corrected Cali. "Not E-I-dola."

"Sorry." Kase cleared his throat and continued. "It is believed that the sandcastles acted as guard towers. Positioned geographically in a perfect triangle in the middle of the desert, each tower was used by the Eidola to guard a key: a key to their final, secret tower, which acted as a vault for all of their knowledge, history, and precious artefacts. Although the civilization was conquered in an effort to uncover this treasure, and the keys were collected from the towers by their enemies, this fourth, secret tower was never found. To this day, it acts as a tomb for the their treasures."

"Ooh, treasure," Lenia murmered.

"In order to preserve the history of this ancient civilization, The Academy has restored all of the Sandcastles of the Eidola. Students are to venture to each of the three towers and find the new keystones that The Academy has placed inside each one. In order to confirm the discovery, teams are to use the sage mirror in order to capture an image. Points will be given for each image, but only if all team members are in it with the keystone.

"Each sandcastle takes a certain set of skills in order to obtain entry, and certain groups may have advantages over others. However, it should be noted that in certain situations, your adversaries can be your allies."

After he finished reading Event Two, he returned the mirror back to Cali and shrugged. "So, what's next?"

Kase, Talen, and Lenia all looked at Cali for advice, but she still seemed a little reluctant to lead the team. "I don't really know," she started. "They have this event every Quest Series. The only problem is, they change the sandcastles from year to year. Even though they're similar, each one is modified to present a new set of challenges. The only thing I know for sure is that one castle will favour the scholars, one will favour the wizards, and one will favour the warriors."

"That's perfect!" exclaimed Kase. "We have a group member from each school. We have the best team for this event!"

"Not exactly," said Cali hesitantly. "Each group member has to enter the castle and make it to the keystone. That means that each one of us will be tested at each castle. There might not be a guarantee that we all can enter. For example, only wizards might be able to enter the wizard castle, or it might take the strength of four warriors to enter the warrior castle. Our diversity might be a hazard more than a benefit."

"Well," said Lenia, "there's only one way to find out, isn't there?"

Kase felt as confident as Lenia, but he was worried how Cali would react.

Cali forced a smile. She took a moment to look at Talen and Lenia, who were both looking brightly at her. "Let's go to the library!" she exclaimed.

⚶

The next morning, they all gathered extra early and walked through the portal gateway into the western desert. They didn't see any of the other teams making the journey yet, so they were all hoping that they had gotten a head start. By Cali's calculations on her map, they had about an hour's walk before they would get to their first challenge. They had all decided that they should start with the scholar's sandcastle, since they had two scholars on their team.

Cali and Talen led the way, while Kase and Lenia followed behind. Kase thought the walk was boring compared to the first event. There were no tropical trees to hike through, no Zebra Lilies to smell, and no beautifully tragic volcanoes to look at. There was only sand, sky, sun, and the soft footprints they left behind them as they trudged through the desert.

He felt Lenia tug on his arm. "So, super-warrior. Know any good stories?"

He met her gaze with a smug smile. "Once upon a time," he started.

"Oh good, a classic." Lenia grabbed onto his arm with both hands.

He stopped for a moment while she got comfortable, and then continued. "Once upon a time, there lived the most beautiful princess in all the land."

"Is it ever anything different?" Lenia laughed softly.

Kase held up a staying hand. "One day," he said, "as she was riding the public carriage through the forest, an evil flock of wild birds came along."

"Okay, I don't like this story anymore." Lenia laughed again, at her own expense this time, and grabbed his arm a little tighter.

"These birds were not ordinary, terrifying birds," he continued. "They were at least ... what's a fair number ... a hundred, a thousand times more terrifying! Their feathers were as black as the darkest night. Their blood was as cold as the arctic breeze. Their claws were as sharp as a hard maybe."

"How are 'hard maybe's sharp?" interrupted Lenia.

"I don't know." Kase chuckled. "I heard Professor Bright mention it a few times. Anyway, they were soulless birds, and they had one thing on their minds: to terrorize the princess!"

Lenia giggled. "Continue," she said.

"The birds hovered around the carriage, just waiting for all the other passengers to leave." He lowered his voice for effect. "They knew that even though the princess told everyone she lived in the heart of the kingdom, she really lived nowhere close. As the last passengers exited, the birds decided to make their move.

"The birds thought they were being so smart, and so sneaky. They thought they had the princess pinned, but little did they know that she had a sixth sense about birds, and knew trouble was aloft. The first bird swooped down to claw the princess's eyes out, or worse, poop on her.

"She stood up and looked the bird in one of its tiny, lifeless eyes. 'Woooo!' she yelled. At the same time, she grabbed one of the magic fireballs that she always carried with her and threw it. The bird burned to a crisp, like a white, aging dandelion.

"The other birds saw their comrade perish, so they all turned and flew away. The princess rode the carriage all the way to her house in peace, tipped her hat to the carriage driver, even though he was no help earlier, and went inside to bed. That night, she had the best dreams ever. The end."

Lenia laughed. "I love that story." She let go of his arm. He was a little disappointed that they separated. She pointed towards the first sandcastle in the distance. "There it is!" she said excitedly.

The Liberati approached the sandcastle, and Kase was struck by the grand beauty of the ancient architecture. Each massive block interlocked with the others, but so seamlessly that he saw no cracks or signs of mortar.

They approached a corner of the perfectly square building, and decided to walk along the right face of it. There were detailed markings that covered the sandstone wall from base to roof, all in the ancient language of the Eidola. They reached the middle of the wall, where an open, framed doorway stood. They stopped in front of it to peer into the castle, but all they saw was darkness.

"Is this the entrance?" asked Kase. "I thought it was going to be a challenge to gain entry?"

Cali was about to answer, but a large, dark blue eye appeared above the doorway. "Hello there," said a voice, coming from the apparition. The eye wasn't set in the sandstone, but was almost like a glimmer on top of the doorway. It was contained within a light blue triangle, and was looking around at each member of the Liberati in turn. All of the students were awestruck as they watched the creepy blue eye studying their movement.

"I am The Eye of the Eidola," said the voice. "Who might you be?"

Cali pointed to each member of the group. "My name is Cali," she said confidently. "This is Talen, Lenia, and Kase." The eye's gaze followed her pointing perfectly.

"It is very nice to meet you," said The Eye. "What brings you here today, Cali?" it asked.

"We're here on a quest to find the keystones of the Eidola," Cali replied honestly.

"I know exactly what you are referring to," responded The Eye. "Unfortunately, this is not the correct door to enter." It started to fade away, and then disappeared from view.

"Which door should we enter?" asked Cali, but no response came.

"Where is there another door?" asked Kase. He didn't know exactly what was going on, but he was intrigued. He turned to Lenia, but all he got was a shrug in response.

"Maybe on the other side of the building?" Cali said, but she seemed unsure. "Talen, did you see anything like this in your research?"

"I've never read, seen, or even heard of a talking eye before," answered Talen. She stared at the doorway. "I don't know what to do, but the answer has to be here somewhere."

"Maybe we should try walking around the building," suggested Lenia. "There could be another door. Maybe it has a talking nose or armpit," she joked. Kase couldn't help but chuckle.

"Good idea, Lenia," said Cali seriously. "Let's make our way around and see what we can find."

The Liberati walked along the right side wall, and turned the corner to the next side of the square building. They didn't notice anything different about this wall compared to the last. There were markings from base to roof in an ancient language, and a doorway in the middle of the wall. They approached the door, and were not surprised to see anything but darkness.

"Is this the right door?" Kase asked.

Again, The Eye appeared. It moved around and looked at each member of the Liberati, and then responded, "I'm sorry, Kase, but this is not the correct door, either."

The Liberati frowned at each other, then kept moving towards the next wall. "Or is it?" a voice said from behind.

The group stopped and all looked at each other. "What was that?" Kase asked.

"I don't know," said Cali. "What should we do?"

"I think we should walk around the whole building, and make sure we know all of our options before we make a decision on what to do next," suggested Talen. The rest of the Liberati agreed, so they continued on.

When they got to the third side, they saw the same markings, the same doorway in the middle of the wall, and received the same message from The Eye. When they walked around the final side of the building, they saw something worse.

"Well, if it isn't the Liberati," Niveous said with a cocky grin. "Are you trying to spy on us and see how the number-one team in the Quest Series is going to handle this challenge?" He gestured towards the rest of his team, and they all laughed.

Kase clenched his fists and stepped towards them.

"Kase, don't." Cali reached out for him, but he shrugged her off.

Niveous stared at him as he walked forward. Kase stared back.

"Are you going to try and hurt me again, warrior?" Niveous puffed up his chest. "Do you want to get kicked out of The Academy this time?"

Kase stopped a few feet in front of Niveous and extended his hand. "Good luck to you and your team," he said calmly. "You may be number one now, but we're coming for you."

Niveous laughed. The rest of the Headsmen laughed. He didn't shake Kase's hand, but walked towards the doorway instead. "We're not worried about you, or your team," he said. "You shouldn't even be in this competition. You're nothing."

The Headsmen entered the sandcastle, and didn't look back. They disappeared into the darkness.

It took everything Kase had to not run after them. He took a deep breath and turned back to the Liberati. They were all right behind him, staring at the doorway.

"So, I'm 'nothing' to him now?" Cali huffed, an injured expression on her face. "How could he think … and Sharaine … ooh, I want to win this event so badly now."

"Let's crush the Headsmen," Talen said.

"Does that mean we should enter this door?" Lenia asked.

"Absolutely," Cali said. "Right now, we don't know what's on the other side, but we do know that the other doors appear identical. If this is the wrong door, then we'll just come back out and choose another one. I'm not too worried about the Headsmen, but I have a feeling that there's a game going on between us and The Eye. I just don't know how it all plays out yet. We have to try, though."

The Liberati all agreed with Cali's logic, and decided to follow the Headsmen through the door. The team took a few steps into the welcoming blackness.

Two eyes glowed in front of them. They were similar to The Eye on the outside wall, but one was coloured red, and the other was yellow. They lit up the room, revealing to the students a small hallway.

The hallway walls were the same colour of sandstone as the exterior, but with no markings on them at all. There were two doors at the end of the hallway, directly opposite the door they had just entered through, with one eye above each.

The Liberati walked cautiously towards the end of the hall. Cali and Talen were side by side, with Lenia and Kase right behind them.

As they were walking, Kase heard a whisper. "This is the wrong way." He heard the laughter of the Headsmen bounce off the walls.

He turned towards Lenia. "Did you say something?" he asked softly.

"No?" Lenia replied in a confused tone.

"You're nothing," said another voice. It sounded like Niveous, but he wasn't in the room.

"I think we're going the wrong way," Kase said aloud. Cali and Talen looked at him, but a voice from the front of the room drew their attention away.

"You're going the right way," said the yellow eye. "In fact, you should enter this door next."

"No, you should enter this door next," said the red-coloured eye.

"I don't like any of this." Kase started to take a step back. "I heard a voice say that this isn't the right way; I think we should leave."

"You *should* leave," said a whispering voice. Every member of the Liberati heard that warning, and all looked at each other.

"Let's get out of here and regroup. I need some air." Lenia covered her ears. Kase and Lenia started to backpedal towards their entrance door.

"Wait!" exclaimed Talen, but it was too late. They had already left. But instead of stepping outside onto the warm sand of the desert, they walked again into the same room with the red and yellow eyes. Talen and Cali were both staring at them in amazement.

"Wait, how did we ..." Lenia looked at Kase in fear.

"I thought we just left this room," he added, and scratched his head.

Talen sighed. "I think I know what's going on." She took a deep breath.

"She's just saying that," said the whisper. "She doesn't really know."

"Kase, I *do* know what's going on," said Talen confidently. "We're in an infinite trap. It's basically a large maze. The idea is to keep wandering through the maze, door by door. If we choose the right door, we continue on through the maze; but if we choose the wrong door, we end up back at the beginning. I'm guessing that this room is the beginning of the maze."

"What do you mean?" Kase was starting to get a little freaked out, and more than a little confused.

"Let's say we go through a few doors, and then end up back in a room that looks exactly like this one. It may *seem* like we're just in another room that is similar, but it actually means that we have come back to this exact room. Therefore, if we choose the wrong path, we have to start over."

"We can't leave?" Lenia's voice squeaked.

"This maze is meant to trap people into continuously wandering through the rooms, ultimately containing them in a perpetual state of being lost," Talen explained. "All we have to do is keep track of which doors we enter, and where they lead. Once we are able to walk through the maze by picking all the right doors, we will end up at the end, and find our keystone."

Talen opened her notebook, and drew a box the same shape as the room they were in. "I will make a map of this castle, and make notes on which doors lead where. This may take a while, but as long as we stay focused and keep track of our path, we will eventually get to the end. The only thing we have to make sure we do is stay together. If we split up, there may be no way to find each other again until the end."

Kase, Lenia, and Cali all nodded in agreement. "Do most infinite traps have talking eyes and creepy whispers?" Cali asked her.

Talen looked at the eyes above the doors, and blinked a few times while studying them. "I think The Eye was created by The Academy in order to bring another element into the trap. I read that the Eidola were masters at mental games, so I think that The Eye is supposed to represent an extra challenge within this castle. With all the messages we're getting from it, it seems like it exists only to cause confusion and doubt."

"Then we have to make sure not to listen to it." Lenia glared up at the now-silent eyes above the doorways.

"Correct," Talen said. "We have to trust in ourselves. If we get caught up in listening too much, it might force us to lose focus and choose incorrectly."

"You are a very smart girl, Talen," said the yellow eye. "As a reward for your intelligence, I will inform you that this door is the first one that will lead you to solving the infinite trap."

"Correct," chimed in the red eye. "That is the correct door."

"What should we do?" Cali asked Talen.

"I think The Eye is trying to gain our trust back. It doesn't really matter at this point," said Talen. "Let's just pick a door and start documenting our path." She led the group through the door underneath the yellow eye.

They walked through the door and came upon a new room, this time with five doors at the end of the hallway. A red eye, two green eyes, a purple eye, and a blue eye marked them, and all were staring at the group as they entered.

"You have chosen wisely," said a whisper. "But what now?"

"I don't understand this at all," admitted Kase. The group had paused so Talen could draw the room in her notebook.

Lenia turned to Kase and put her hands over her ears. "Just like me, Kase," she said in a soft voice. "Sometimes you have to have faith in your own path, even when you don't understand it. Talen is right; we have to trust each other more than we trust the magic of this castle. All you have to do is focus. Focus on our team; we can do this."

Kase felt warm and relaxed. "You're right," he said with a smile. "I trust you. All of you." He covered his ears with his own hands. "Let's continue!" he yelled.

Lenia, Cali, and Talen all laughed, but were glad that he was figuring out his own way to deal with the trickiness of the sandcastle.

Cali, Lenia, and Talen all talked and pointed at the doors. They nodded in agreement, and then Cali and Lenia put their hands over their ears too. They trusted Talen to guide them through. She couldn't contain her smile.

Talen led the rest of the team through the purple doorway. Once they passed through, they came into a hallway with twenty doors. They were lined up along all three walls of the hallway, each sporting a different-coloured eye above. As soon as they entered, it seemed like every eye was trying to talk to them at once.

Talen completed her map of the room, and led the team through a random door. When they walked through the doorway, they found two doors at the end of a small hallway. One door had a yellow eye above it; the other had a red eye.

Talen made a note, and then led the team through the yellow-eyed door again. She continued on with the journey for a couple hours, with the rest of the Liberati following unquestioningly behind her.

The path was long and boring and filled with constant mistakes, but the team pushed on. The Eye continuously bombarded Talen with insults and misguided information, but she kept ignoring it. Her patience and meticulous attention to detail helped draw out a path.

They made their way through what seemed like hundreds of rooms, until they eventually found themselves in a hallway with a single door at the end of it. This door had a gold-coloured eye above it, but it wasn't a glimmer or a cunningly insulting image; it was made of solid gold, and was imbedded in the sandstone.

They all stared at the door, and knew that this was the end. However, Cali, Lenia, and Kase all kept their hands over their ears. Talen reached over to Cali, tugged at her arm, and gave her a smile.

"We're here!" Talen said excitedly as Cali's arms came down.

Kase and Lenia followed suit. Though happy that they had found the end of the infinite trap, Kase was even more relieved that they heard no more voices.

"Well done, Tal!" exclaimed Kase.

"Outstanding!" Lenia said.

"You're the best!" Cali winked at Talen.

"Thanks." Talen blushed. "Now, let's go!" She led them towards the final door.

They walked through, and came into a large room that looked like an ancient tomb. The walls of the room were filled with markings and tapestries. There were valuable artefacts on display, which glimmered from a ray of sunlight that shone through the high ceiling and illuminated the room. Although the room was beautiful, the greatest marvel was in the middle of it: the golden keystone, in all of its glory.

The four of them excitedly walked up to the keystone and studied it. It was as tall as Kase was, and had a midnight owl engraved on its face. 'The Path' was etched underneath the branch that the owl was resting on. In front of the keystone was a small stand, shaped perfectly to hold a sage mirror.

Cali put the sage mirror on the ledge, and the group gathered around the keystone for their image. "Talen, would you please do the honours." Cali gestured towards the mirror.

Talen beamed with pride. Her smile was almost bigger than her face. "Mirror, mirror," she said excitedly. "Capture image."

All of the students smiled as the mirror flashed and gave them what they needed to prove that they had successfully made it through the first Sandcastle of the Eidola.

After they were done, they headed back through the only door of the room, and were returned immediately to the outside of the sandcastle.

※

After leaving Kase in line, the rest of the Liberati moved closer to get a better view of the obstacle along the outside of the second sandcastle. Even though they were now able to see it in more detail, it was still pretty hard to decipher it all. Talen was amazed there were so many even trying.

Kase was standing in line with some more warriors, waiting for his turn. Everyone's eyes were fixated on the female warrior falling from about twenty feet in the air. She landed on the soft ground with a 'whumph' and a spray of sand.

"Ooooohhhh," groaned the crowd, as the fallen warrior got back up to her feet. She had nearly made it to the top. She gingerly made her way back to the group of warriors and smiled as she accepted a few high fives for her effort. She went to the back of the line, and awaited her next attempt.

Kase's focus returned to the top of the obstacle in front of him. The entire structure was made of sandstone, and it was hard to know which parts were where. There were stationary platforms on part of it, moving ones on another, and random posts moving in and out. It looked like there were fifteen different levels in total, with the top level being about twenty-five to thirty feet from the ground. With everything the same colour, and the heat making it all look like a mirage, he couldn't figure out how he, or any of the warriors, were going to climb it.

Kase watched as the next warrior took his turn. He timed his jump so that he could grab a sandstone coloured rope that was hanging on the second level. He tried to climb it, but part of the obstacle course moved and jabbed him in the ribs. He let go and fell to the ground.

"Oooooohhhh," the crowd intoned again as this warrior got up and also made his way back to the line. Kase admired both fallen warriors' strength and persistence.

A number of warriors tried and failed the climb. So far, the highest he had seen a warrior make it was the twelfth level. It almost seemed like the obstacle was a random event; some warriors would make the same move as their fellow comrades, but came tumbling to the ground.

There had to be some sort of pattern, Kase thought, but it wasn't obvious just yet.

Before he could witness any more warriors try, he was at the front of the line.

He took a deep breath and started his own ascent. He jumped on the first platform and then swung up on some kind of ledge. He ducked out of the way of a moving post, but then felt a small rod jam into his side and push him off. He flew towards the ground and landed hard.

"Oooooohhhh," said the crowd as he gathered himself. "Good try," said one of the other warriors.

"You'll get it next time," said A.J. She chucked him on the shoulder with a stiff grin. She had joined with an older team this year too, and had been a little disappointed when Kase had said he was already a part of another one.

Although they were all competing against each other, there was still a sense of camaraderie between all the warriors. Kase walked back to the end of the line and waited his turn for another chance at the obstacle.

The hours went by. The warriors continued to try and climb to the top; just when some of them became worn out by the constant failure, one would succeed, boosting morale. Successful members would wait at the top for the rest of their team. Some were waiting for a long time.

Kase had gotten close a few times, and once made it as far as the thirteenth level, but in the end he suffered the same fate as the rest of his attempts. Instead of standing in line again, he limped over to where the rest of his team were sitting and watching. His arms clutched his ribs, and sweat dripped off his long hair. He felt exhausted.

He sat beside Lenia.

"How are you feeling, super warrior?"

Kase just groaned.

"Maybe you should eat something, Kase," said Talen. "It might give you the boost you need to get past the thirteenth level."

"How many times have you fallen?" asked Cali. She was busy reading a book and sunbathing.

"Eighteen," said Kase and Talen at the same time.

"Well, I lost," said Cali.

"You lost what?" asked Kase, a little confused. He reached for some water to quench his thirst. "Are you betting on me?"

"Don't worry about it." Lenia laughed. "Now, eat something and go try again!" she said encouragingly. She reached for a banana and held it towards him.

"You guys are going to have to do this soon, too, you know." He reluctantly took the banana, unpeeled it, and shoved it in his mouth. When he was finished, he got up, turned back to the obstacle, and strutted towards it with confidence. He tossed the banana peel over his shoulder. It landed in Lenia's lap.

"Hey!" she yelled. Kase turned back and grinned.

As soon as he returned to the obstacle base, the crowd roared. One of their comrades had made it to the top. That team was nearly complete: only one left to go. The final member started his run, but began having trouble with the moving obstacles about halfway up. His team members noticed his difficulty, and one began jumping back down through the platforms to reach him.

"Is she allowed to do that?" Two warriors muttered with one another.

"Nothing in the rules says she can't." Talen had walked up closer to watch the action. She was staring intently at the platforms, watching their seemingly random movements.

That was met with a few more excited conversations. With his comrade's help, the final warrior made it to the top to join his team. The rest of the warriors kept taking turns, and a few others succeeded, but Kase kept coming up short.

The rest of the afternoon flew by, and it soon became close to sundown.

All the other warriors had either succeeded or quit for the night, but Kase was determined to make it to the top. Talen started shouting advice to him whenever she noticed a pattern within the platforms. As he fell for a thirty-fifth time, the rest of the Liberati approached the base of the wall.

"It seems like everyone else has left," said Cali. "Should we go home too, and try again tomorrow?"

"I actually think I have it this time," Kase said as he looked back up. "How much time do I have left to try?"

"You can have one more attempt, but then we'll have to start heading back," said Cali.

"Perfect!" Kase got himself ready. He danced around and shook his arms a little as a burst of energy hit him.

He jumped up to the first platform, and started scaling the obstacle like a squirrel. He would jump up a level, dodge an obstacle, and swing up to another one. He even retreated down a level a couple of times in order to get his timing right for the next burst. He was starting to get the hang of the obstacle's patterns, and this climb felt different.

With one final leap, he reached up and grabbed the top edge of the wall. He lifted himself up in triumph, and then threw his arms up as he danced around. "Wooooo!" he screamed.

"Way to go, Kase!" cheered his team from the base of the obstacle.

"I did it!" he yelled back down to them.

"We knew you would!" replied Cali, "Now, come back down and help us do it!"

Kase took a deep breath and then raced back down the obstacle. He was more confident now because he had finally conquered it, but he knew that guiding three non-warriors was going to be more challenging. He retraced his steps and made note of which levels needed quick movements, and which ones they would be able to rest on.

Before their ascent, Kase and the rest of the Liberati discussed their strategy. He was surprised at how much they had paid attention, and was happy with their enthusiasm. It reminded him of when he helped his warrior brethren in class. The Liberati may not have been as strong as Rocky, John, or A.J., but they were catching on a lot faster.

Lenia volunteered first and raced up the first few levels. Kase climbed with her, and had her back every step of the way. Her instincts were on point, but she still had to rely on Kase's advice. They dodged the jutting pillars, patiently waited for their next move, and then jumped up a few platforms. Before they knew it, they were at the top.

"We did it!" Lenia exclaimed once they made it to the top. She danced around while Kase leaned over and caught his breath. He was a lot more tired this time.

"No time to dawdle, super warrior," Lenia shoved his shoulder. "Get back down there and do it again!"

Kase met her gaze and grinned. He was too tired to think of a comeback, so he just nodded. "Yes, super wizard," he said before he descended again.

Cali was up next, and then Talen followed suit. Although their climbs were a lot slower, their strategy and patience paid off. Cali and Kase worked well together, she understanding exactly what he needed her to do almost before he even said it.

By this point, Talen had memorized many of the platform's obstacles, but Kase had to carry her on his back for the last bit of the climb, because she tired a lot faster than Cali and Lenia.

When he reached the top for the final time, Kase collapsed on the ledge. Talen rolled off his back, got up, and jumped around in joy. Kase sprawled out, and tried to regain his strength.

Cali placed the sage mirror in the holder in front of the keystone, and they gathered around to capture the image of them in the fading light. This time the golden keystone had a dragon engraved on its face, with the words 'Of Destiny' inscribed underneath.

"Kase, get up. You need to do the honours," said Cali as she readied herself.

Kase peeled himself off the ground and slowly walked over to the keystone. He wiped the sweat from his brow and tried to focus, but he was a little dazed. He felt a splash of water hit his face.

"Does that help?" Lenia giggled.

Kase took a deep breath and used his shirt to wipe the water away. The cool water felt refreshing on his hot skin. "Yes, actually," he said with a smile.

"I've got your back," Lenia said. She raised her arm up and put it around his shoulder as he huddled with the group.

"Mirror, mirror," Kase said. "Capture image." They all smiled into the mirror as one. They had successfully made it through the second Sandcastle of the Eidola.

"Store that image in the Liberati Event Two collection."

Lenia looked at the setting sun. "Looks like we better get moving if we want to make it back before the sun is completely gone," she said. Then, she quickly turned around and pointed.

"You remembered," Kase said. He looked out at the star with her. It glowed like a firefly.

"Of course I did, schorrior." Lenia laughed. Kase joined her. Cali and Talen exchanged confused looks.

☀

The next day started out like the previous one. The team gathered extra early, and headed out to the desert in pursuit of conquering the third Sandcastle of the Eidola. Cali and Talen led the way, while Kase and Lenia followed behind.

"I like your braid," Kase said as they walked.

Lenia grabbed it with both hands. "You know, I can do this to your hair too, if you'd like," she said as she looked up at him.

"I don't think my hair is long enough." Kase jokingly ran his hands through his hair. "I've seen some people around The Academy with their hair wrapped in a bun. Can you do something like that for me?"

"Absolutely!" She giggled. "Let's do it right now!"

Kase laughed. "There's no way we can do it now; I mean, we don't even have any unicorn hairs to put in."

Cali stopped and turned around to look at Kase. "Unicorn hair?" Her mouth opened wide.

"It's a long story," Kase said. He ignored Cali and focused on Lenia. "How about after the Q is done?" he said with a wry smile.

"Deal!" Lenia said excitedly. "You're so fun," she added.

"You're telling me that story when the Q is done too." Cali rolled her eyes and started walking again.

In the distance, they all saw a small tornado twirling, picking up sand and debris. Cali stopped and looked at her map. "It looks like that tornado is close to where we have to go for the final sandcastle," she said. "Should we keep going, or wait to see if it moves somewhere else?"

"I think that tornado is the third sandcastle," Lenia said softly as she stared at the horizon.

"Are you sure?" Cali twisted her book around, trying to see something different on her map.

"Yes," Lenia said assuredly. "Trust me."

The Liberati kept moving, and as they got closer they realized that the tornado wasn't going anywhere. The swirling wind was dark, but they could all see something glimmer in the eye of the windstorm. Although they weren't close enough to feel the effects of the great wind, they took caution and stopped walking.

"What do we do now?" asked Kase.

"I think Lenia knows what to do," Cali said confidently. Talen nodded in agreement.

"I do know what to do," replied Lenia nervously. "I've just never dealt with this kind of phenomenal, natural power before. In my elements class, the one that Professor Bright teaches actually, we've learned to control elements such as water, fire, and earth by creating little tornadoes in the lab. We've never tried to control something of this magnitude. It's probably something that would take four wizards to control."

"Is there anything we can do?" asked Kase.

"Yes." Lenia took a deep breath and closed her eyes. "Follow directly behind me, and stay as close as you can. I'm going to try and create a passageway for us."

Lenia led the way, with Kase, Talen, and Cali following behind. The wind picked up as they walked towards the tornado. It blew their clothes around as they walked.

At this point, Lenia focused her power and started her own spell to control the winds. "Great desert wind, don't be wild; create a path, calm and mild."

As soon as she completed the words of her spell, Kase felt the wind around him diminish. The path that the Liberati walked was calm, a tunnel of air that cut through the tornado. A golden keystone stood tall at the end of the tunnel.

The Liberati kept walking, and Lenia kept the winds from altering their trek. With each step that they took, Lenia seemed to quiver, but she didn't break. She concentrated harder as they made their way across the sand and towards the keystone.

They were approximately fifty feet from the entrance when they felt a slight breeze. They started walking faster, but this caused the breeze to grow stronger the closer they got to the keystone. Cali wrapped an arm around Kase to try and keep up. Her other hand held Talen.

"I don't think I can hold this much longer!" Lenia yelled so everyone could hear her.

"Of course you can!" Kase said. Some of the sand was blowing into their path, but not enough to dissuade them. "Have faith in your own path, even if you don't understand it. All you have to do is focus. Focus on our team; we can do this." He put his hands on her shoulders, and felt something stir inside of him. The path became calm again.

"You've got this, Lenia!" Talen said reassuringly.

"We're almost there!" Cali said. "Try angling with the wind— like swimming *with* a river instead of across it."

They made their way past the edge of the swirling wind, and felt the calm of the eye around them. When they were all safe, Lenia collapsed onto the ground.

"Lenia!" Kase knelt down beside her.

"You did it!" Cali said as she also rushed to Lenia's side. She gripped her by the shoulder. Talen joined her excitedly.

Lenia took a deep breath and smiled. "We did it," she said. Kase helped her up. She hugged him and buried her face into his chest. "That was amazing!"

"You really are a super wizard," he said as he held her tight.

"I know," she said. They both giggled.

They joined the rest of the team at the keystone, which had the symbol of the unicorn. The words 'Trust In' were written below it.

Cali put the sage mirror on the stand in front of it. "Lenia, would you like to do the honours?" she said as they got ready for the reflection to be captured.

"Mirror, mirror," Lenia said excitedly, "capture image." Their frozen reflection shone back at them. They had successfully made it through all three Sandcastles of the Eidola.

CHAPTER 11

Cold Blooded

Kase, Cali, and Talen were waiting for Lenia in their usual spot in the common area so they could all uncover Event Three together. Cali was looking at the sage mirror, reading the overall standings after the first two events of the Quest Series. "We've moved into eleventh place!" she said excitedly.

"Ones!" said Kase. He looked again for Lenia, knowing that she would have appreciated his comment, but he didn't see her yet. Instead, he saw the Headsmen coming with a team of warriors. They were the same warriors who had the lava accident in Event One. "Here comes Niveous," he said in an unimpressed tone.

"Who cares?" Cali kept her eyes on the sage mirror.

Kase tried to avoid looking at Niveous's thin, cocky, face, but he couldn't help but glare as the Headsmen approached them. Out of respect for his other teammates, he decided not to act on the thoughts racing through his mind.

"Well, if it isn't the luckiest team in the history of the Q," said Niveous condescendingly as he approached. "You all must feel pretty special knowing that you were the only ones to conquer all three Sandcastles of the Eidola."

"We have a good team," responded Cali, refusing to look at Niveous. "Now, please leave us alone so we can focus on beating you again in the next event."

Niveous laughed. The rest of the group all laughed along, trying to get under the skin of the Liberati. "Come on, Cali," said Niveous. "I'm just trying to show some good gamesmanship. You and your brother should try it; you might make some new friends, like we have with Ninety-Nine Problems," he gestured to the four warriors that were with his team.

"Dragoon!" they responded in unison.

"They helped us with the obstacle course, and we helped them solve the maze." Niveous' attention was still all on Cali. "I think from here on out, we'll be helping each other in other ways, too."

Kase noticed Tarkin staring at him. Instead of staring back this time, he turned to Niveous. "I think Cali asked you nicely to leave," he said in a stern voice. "So you should move along."

Niveous stepped towards Kase and looked up at him. He moved his head closer to Kase's. "What are you going to do about it? Are you going to try and hurt me, like the last time you wanted me to leave?"

Two of the warriors frowned, and glared at Kase.

"Or are you just going to try and intimidate us again, like in front of the sandcastles?"

One of the Headsmen, Sharaine, chuckled.

Kase looked Niveous in the eye, and held out his hand. "I would like to wish you good luck, and safe travels as you continue on with your quest," he replied politely.

Niveous took a step back and looked at Kase's hand. "This again?" He laughed. He shook his head, turned his back to Kase, and walked towards his teammates and new friends.

"Your turn." Kase could just barely catch Niveous' comment to the biggest warrior.

"Don't worry, we've got this." Tarkin nodded to two of his teammates.

"Good. Then the rest of us will go and plan for the next event. Come on." Niveous gestured to the rest of his team, as well as the final member of Ninety-Nine Problems, and kept walking.

The Liberati watched as the five of them left. However, three of the Ninety-Nine Problems team remained.

Tarkin walked up towards Kase, who was still holding his hand out to be shaken.

"Wrong move." Tarkin reached out for Kase's hand, but he didn't shake it. Instead, he made a fist and swung up into the middle of Kase's stomach. Kase hunched over in pain.

"What are you doing!" shouted Cali. She took a step towards the warrior, but Kase quickly stuck his arm out, stopping her before she moved farther.

He stood straight up and looked his fellow warrior in the eye. "I would like to wish you good luck, and safe travels as you continue on your quest," he said again, more polite than he had previously. He kept his expression pleasant, but his eyes were fierce. He stuck his hand out again.

Tarkin smiled grimly, and struck him again in the stomach.

"Kase!" Cali put her hands on her brother's back, still doubled-over. "Stop hurting him!"

Tarkin took a step towards her. "Out of the way." He pushed her shoulder. He didn't have to push hard to send her flying. She screamed, and hit the ground hard.

Kase was still bent over, but he saw Cali fall from the corner of his eye. His blood boiled with rage. He couldn't control it anymore. Before the thought had entered his mind, he came up swinging. An uppercut hit the warrior square in the jaw. The warrior's head snapped straight back, and he fell to the ground, dazed by Kase's blow.

The other two members of Ninety-Nine Problems clenched their fists and walked towards Kase. He brought his hands up to defend his face, shifted his stance so his left foot was leading, and got ready for battle.

The warriors split up, and tried to get to Kase from different angles. One of them charged and took a swing.

Kase quickly ducked under the moving fist, and braced himself as the warrior's body moved over the top of his. In one fluid motion, he grabbed the warrior's upper arm and shoulder, and flipped the warrior over his back, sending him flying. The warrior landed with a thud.

"Everyone stop!" yelled Talen. Nobody listened to her.

Kase straightened up. The other warrior had gotten in close, and struck him in the face with a quick jab.

Kase's head snapped back, but he regained his focus, crouched down, and buried his head into the warrior. He tackled him to the ground. They rolled around together for a moment, but Kase was able to get on top with a quick move that Rocky had shown him in class. Kase started pummelling the warrior with a barrage of punches.

The warrior that Kase had flipped onto the ground had gotten to his feet, and was ready to run over to help his comrade.

His attention quickly changed because Cali had jumped onto his back. "Stop it!" Cali screamed as she held on tightly. The warrior started swinging his arms wildly, trying to grab Cali and get her off his back. He was stumbling from side to side. He stopped moving and looked down at Talen clutching his leg, trying to hinder his walking.

"Everybody stop fighting!" yelled a strong, deep voice. This time, everything stopped. Kase recognized the voice. He sheepishly turned to meet Professor Tusk's disappointed glare.

Kase and the warrior he was wrestling with got to their feet, while Cali, Talen, and the other warrior all stopped what they were doing and stood still.

"Fighting is not tolerated at The Academy," said Professor Tusk angrily. "I'm disappointed in all of you. Especially you, Kase."

Kase looked down at the ground. He didn't want to meet the professor's gaze again.

"Everyone follow me to the Grand Master's office immediately!" Professor Tusk instructed.

None of the students argued with the professor. No words had to be spoken. Kase, Cali, and Talen gathered their things and started walking towards the administration castle. The two warriors had propped up their dazed friend and were helping him to the administration building as well.

As they walked across the grass in a group, Kase noticed a lot of other students looking on. Some of them had excited looks on their faces, while others had looks of confusion. Kase made eye contact with Niveous and the Headsmen, who watched from afar. They all had satisfied grins on their faces that he wished he could wipe off.

Kase turned his head in the other direction, trying to ignore the hate that was building inside of him. He noticed Lenia coming towards them.

"What's happening?" she asked, but Kase wasn't able to answer.

"Please step away, young lady." Professor Tusk held out his hand. "These students are on their way to be punished by the Grand Master for fighting."

Lenia stopped with a worried look.

Kase turned his head back to her. "Follow us," he mouthed. She waited until they were all a safe distance away, and then proceeded towards the administration building.

⁂

"We've been sentenced to three days of detainment," said a dispirited Cali. The Liberati were standing in a circle outside of the Grand Master's office, trying to make sense of it all.

"For what?" Lenia asked as she searched for details. "Wrong place, wrong time?"

Kase recognized that she was trying to make a joke to ease the tension, but he was too focused on his anger to appreciate it. "I want to crush Niveous," he muttered.

146

"Calm down, brother." Cali put her hand on his shoulder. "There's nothing we can do now." Kase shrugged her off and walked down the hall. He needed some space. Cali turned to Lenia and explained what had happened.

Lenia looked on in amazement. Cali was humble with her description, but Talen was grinning as she danced around and shadowboxed.

"I wish I could have been there to help," Lenia said, watching Kase pace.

"We're actually lucky you weren't there," Cali said. "Our team still has a chance in the third event!"

"What do you mean?" Lenia said nervously.

"The Grand Master decided that this was an Academy altercation, and didn't happen within the Quest Series," Cali explained. "Therefore, we haven't been disqualified from the competition; just disciplined within the rules of the administration. We have to serve our sentence over the next three days, but you can attempt the event all by yourself!"

Lenia seemed anxious. She looked down at the ground. "I don't think I can," she admitted.

"You've got this." Kase had returned to the group and put his hand on her shoulder.

"You've got this." Talen imitated Kase and put her hand on Lenia's other shoulder. The entire team laughed together.

"We don't have to report to the Administration Disciplinary Room for another hour," Cali said as she extended the sage mirror to Lenia. "That means we can at least help you get ready for the event. Would you like to do the honours?"

Lenia took a deep breath and tried to relax. She seemed jittery as she took the sage mirror. "Mirror, mirror, show me the details of Quest Series Event Three," she said. The team let out a little cheer as the cloud filled the face of the mirror.

When Event Three was revealed, she read it out loud. "From the shores along the beaches, to the shallow coral reefs, to the deepest and darkest corners of the ocean floor, the sea is a peaceful home to all underwater creatures. The reason so many species benefit is because of the care and protection that is offered by the most majestic of sea creatures: the mermaids.

"With a seemingly invisible hand, they keep peace throughout the ocean using many different strategies, laws, and tools. One of those tools is called a trident. Handcrafted by the mermaid that wields it, the trident's magical power is an extension of themselves, and therefore is as unique as each mermaid.

"Each team will venture to the home of the mermaids and construct their own trident. They will present the trident to the Mermaid Queen, who will validate it. Points for this event will be scored based on the time it takes to construct the trident and present it to the Queen.

"There is no map that leads you to the home of the mermaids, for they move around the sea at will. However, the doors that mark the entrance always remain the same. The key to open them is closer than you think."

"Mermaids?" exclaimed Cali excitedly. "Mermaids! I love mermaids!" Cali's joy turned to sadness as reality set in. "I'm so jealous," she admitted.

"I don't know what to do." Lenia kept staring at the mirror. "I don't know where to start. I don't know where to go. I don't know anything."

"You might not have us along with you for this wonderful journey," Kase replied with a warm smile. "But you have us in spirit. I believe in you. We all believe in you. We have your back, no matter what."

Lenia's eyes softened. She looked at Talen and Cali, who were smiling in support of her as well. "Well, let's go to the library and see how much of this stuff we can figure out!"

CHAPTER 12

The Black Trident

L enia woke up before dawn. She wanted to get a jump on the day, and make sure she had the most daylight available for her journey. She quickly got dressed, but spent some time braiding her hair. She wanted to keep the hair from Turanus with her for good luck.

She had a sac with some water, food, some notes about mermaids, and a map that Talen had made for her. In her pockets she had the sage mirror, the portal token, and her favourite fire starter. She was ready for her solo adventure.

The sun was just peeking over the horizon as she walked through the common area towards the gateway portals. The fire was bright, the grass was dewy, the morning smelled fresh and alive, but shadows still lurked from the night before. Lenia moved through the grass alone, until she noticed some of the shadows move towards her.

"Aren't you up early," said Niveous as he cut off her path.

She stopped, but didn't say anything. She was thinking about how he had treated her teammates, and knew he couldn't be up to any good. She noticed the rest of the Headsmen and a lone warrior gather around her.

"Is it too early for you to talk?" Niveous said mockingly. "Maybe you should go back to sleep," he whispered.

Lenia held her breath. She didn't have to look around to find out who had blown the dust towards her, because she could feel it. It was floating through the air on her left, but she didn't move, blink, or breathe.

Instead of moving towards Lenia's face, the dust hung in the air. She tilted her head and raised her eyebrow at Niveous. She could see the fear and confusion written all over his face.

With her practice of controlling the elements, and her experience with the sandstorm in Event Two, it was easy for her to manipulate the dust particles that were flying through the air, even without casting a spell. She brought both her hands up under her chin, and made a small shelf with her face-up palms. The dust swirled in the air, and collected on the tips of her fingers, forming a small pile. The Headsmen froze in shock.

She could feel every particle on her hands, and calmly blew the pile back at Niveous and the Headsmen. The dust soared through the air and into the lungs of the wicked. Its magical power started to go to work.

"No," said Niveous in disbelief, his eyes opened wide.

"Don't mess with the Liberati," Lenia said with a smirk. She watched her adversaries collapse into a deep slumber, falling under the sleeping effects of the powder. She gently stepped over their bodies, strewn out awkwardly on the ground, and continued on her way towards the gateway portals.

"Today is going to be a good day," she said to herself as the warm sunshine gently touched her smile.

⁂

Lenia swam up to the surface and gasped for air. The water around her was ice cold, and she shivered as her body tried to stay warm. She took a few breaths and tried to figure out where she was. She had followed Talen's map perfectly, but the cavern she was in didn't look very mermaid-like. She didn't know what she expected.

The water was glowing green, which slightly illuminated the cave. She looked up to see where she had fallen from, but there was

150

only jagged, black rock above her. She glanced around the water's surface. Her eyes suddenly grew wide with fear as she realized that she wasn't alone.

A sharp, black fin was circling around her. It was large, and she could only imagine the size of the beast that owned it. She felt helpless, and watched as the fin dove beneath the surface. She was a sitting duck.

She felt a tug at her leg, and then she was pulled underwater. She screamed. She kept screaming as she was dragged down. "Stop it!" she yelled, and then she realized that she was speaking underwater.

"Wait, what?" she asked. Instead of drowning or choking, she was breathing normally. The coldness of the water even seemed to disappear. The pulling stopped, and merely held her in place beneath the surface.

"Hi," said the creature. Lenia looked down and saw a beautiful young mermaid staring back at her with sapphire eyes. Small, silvery scales covered half her body, from the fin on her tail all the way to her upper torso. She had long, copper hair that flowed gracefully in the open, green water.

"Hello?" Lenia touched her lips. She still didn't know how to explain what was going on.

The mermaid laughed. "Here, grab this." She lifted her gold trident towards Lenia's face.

Lenia wrapped her fingers around the shaft.

The mermaid let go of her leg, but kept her hand on the trident and swam up so that they were face to face. "If I touch you, or if you touch my trident while I'm holding it, you will feel some of my power flow through you," the mermaid instructed. "You will be able to speak, breathe, and your body will adapt to the pressure and temperature of the water because of our connection. If we break that connection, you will drown."

She slapped Lenia's hand away, and ice-cold water filled her lungs. The mermaid grabbed Lenia, and the magic returned.

"That's crazy," said Lenia in disbelief. She coughed. "Wonderful, but crazy."

"My name is Anastasia," replied the mermaid. She smiled. "You're a special one, aren't you? What's your name?"

"I'm Lenia," said the wizard. "Sorry, I'm … I'm just glad I'm alive. I thought you were a shark or something!"

"I was," giggled Anastasia as she turned her head to study Lenia.

"What?" Lenia's jaw dropped.

Anastasia giggled again. "You don't really know much about mermaids, do you?"

"You can change into different animals?" Lenia said in disbelief.

"Kind of," Anastasia replied. "It's more of a disguise than anything. I don't turn into a shark; I just look like one. I can make myself look like a lot of different creatures. As mermaids, our purpose is to keep peace among all life under the sea. Sometimes we have to disguise ourselves in order to learn about other sea creatures, or about different species on land that affect the sea."

"Like an illusion," Lenia said as she tried to relate it to her own classes.

Anastasia smiled and nodded. "All the information we can gather helps us do our part in maintaining the balance of the ocean. Education is important, whether we're learning things ourselves or teaching others. That's one of the ideas that drives our relationship with The Academy, and why we've decided to become involved with the Quest Series. It gives us an opportunity to learn something new about the world above, and helps teach others about the world below. Is there anything new you can tell me about?"

Lenia loved everything that Anastasia had told her, and was completely fascinated by the magic she had already seen. She wanted to share some of that wonder. She reached into her pocket and pulled out the sage mirror. "Have you seen one of these before?" she asked.

"Of course!" said Anastasia excitedly. She took the mirror and looked into it. She combed her hand through her hair, and then moved it closer to her face. She turned her head from side to side. "Ugh, I'm getting old," she complained.

Lenia laughed. "How old are you, twenty-one?" she joked.

Anastasia blushed. "You're too kind," she replied. "I turn four hundred and twenty-nine this year."

Lenia's mouth opened wide. "But you look so young. That is awesome!" she admitted.

Anastasia laughed. "I like you," she said as she gave the sage mirror back to Lenia.

"No, wait," Lenia said. "This is a sage mirror; have you not used one of these before?"

"What's a sage mirror?" asked Anastasia.

"It's a tool that connects us to a world of information," replied Lenia. "All you have to do is speak into it, and it shows you what you need to know. Like this. Mirror, mirror, show me information on mermaids."

Lenia turned the mirror so that Anastasia could look into it again. They both watched as a cloud appeared, followed by a sketch of a mermaid. Lenia used her finger to scroll to the information written under the sketch.

"How astonishing!" Anastasia said. She read the mermaid description. This time, her jaw was the one left open. "What a marvelous contraption. This tool can help educate anyone about topics they can't be there to see! Oh wait," she said as she kept reading. "That's wrong; I can't do that; that's right; that's wrong. Who's in charge of putting information in this thing?" she asked.

"I think the scholars at The Academy transferred information from book sources," replied Lenia, a little confused about Anastasia's contradicting attitude.

"Well, sometimes experience outweighs book knowledge," Anastasia handed the mirror back. "I'm sure you've read a little already. Would you like me to *show* you what it's like to be a mermaid?" she asked.

"Absolutely!" replied Lenia. "But wait; one last thing. I'm going to hold this mirror up, and I need you to look into it with me."

Anastasia moved her head closer to Lenia's. "Like this?"

"Yes, now smile," Lenia said as she smiled too. "Mirror, mirror, capture image." The mirror flashed, and the image of Lenia and Anastasia was shown. "Store the image in the Liberati Event Three collection."

Anastasia waved back and forth in the water, creating swirls with her tail. "That is remarkable! I need one of these!" She moved her trident so that it was perpendicular to her and Lenia. "Well, now it's my turn to show you something extraordinary. Are you ready to go for a ride?" she asked wickedly.

"Yes?" Lenia asked as she gripped the trident hard, knowing she was in for something strange and delightful.

"Okay, get ready." Anastasia looked straight ahead. Lenia focused in front of her, but before she could blink, think, or take a breath, her eyes fell upon a great coral reef. There was a multitude of fish and sea life scurrying about.

"We're here!" said Anastasia with a wry smile.

"How did we …" Lenia started, looking around at all the sea creatures around her.

"One thing that wasn't shown in that mirror of yours is that we mermaids can move about the sea instantly. In the blink of an eye, we can go from one corner of the open ocean to the other. That's how we're able to watch over everything. If someone drops into the ocean from a secret doorway, or if someone sticks her finger in the base of a waterfall, we know about it." Anastasia smiled at Lenia.

Lenia was amazed at the power and knowledge of the older woman. She thought about the journey that led her to the cavern, and how quickly Anastasia had found her. "So you saw me in the cave right away?" asked Lenia.

"I did," admitted Anastasia. "It made me wonder about why you were on a journey by yourself, while all the other students that are coming to the sea are in groups."

Lenia looked away. She felt her cheeks heat up. "The rest of my team got into some trouble, so I'm trying to do this event by myself. I don't really know what I'm supposed to be doing, but I'm here. I'm here to try and save our team. I don't know if I'm going to be able to do it by myself, but I do know that I'm going to try,"

"You're a good friend," Anastasia replied with a smile. "You're smart, strong, passionate, and your heart is true. You'll be able to succeed at this event, and your team will be proud of you. And don't worry; you're not on your own. You have me."

"So you can help me make a trident?" said Lenia. Her eyes lit up with excitement.

"Of course I can!" said Anastasia encouragingly. "In fact, tridents are pretty easy to make. There is a steam cove at the bottom of the ocean that all mermaids use. There are cauldrons there that contain all of the necessary elements of the trident core, and we add that mixture in a magical trident mould. The only things we have to include are the personal items that make our trident unique.

"There's not really a limit to what else gets included, but at a minimum there are three things that we need to add: a piece of the ocean, a piece that we adore, and a piece of ourselves. The piece of the ocean can be anything: a rock, a fish, or a plant. This helps the trident connect to the wonderful life of the sea. The piece that we adore is a personal item that we have attached meaning to. This helps the trident connect to our own admirations and intentions, so that it knows what we want to do with it. The piece of ourselves can be a drop of blood, an eyelash, or a piece of hair. This helps strengthen the bond from us to the trident. All we have to do is gather these items and head to the cove."

"That sounds pretty easy," said Lenia. "Where should we start?"

"Well, we're here at this beautiful coral reef." Anastasia waved her hand in front of her. "Why don't you pick something from it?"

Anastasia led Lenia to the reef's edge. Lenia was amazed at all the little creatures scurrying about. There were blue fish, orange fish, and fish with coloured stripes. There was red coral, purple coral, and transparent coral, too. There were miniature sea horses, pink crabs, and rainbow mantis shrimp. It was like looking at a tiny city, with a multi-cultural array of beautiful species.

"I love all the sea creatures here," Lenia said, her eyes filled with wonder. "But I don't want to hurt any of them by making a trident. Can I just pick a piece of coral to put in?" she asked.

Anastasia smiled compassionately. "Of course you can take a piece of coral. Here, let us find a piece that is suitable."

Anastasia swam them down near the base, where the colours weren't quite as vibrant. She aimed her trident at some soft, reddish-green coral, and the tip of it started to glow. A slender beam of light shone and hit the coral, causing a small clump to jettison from the outcropping. Anastasia opened her hand, and the clump came floating towards it.

When it reached her, she gently gave it to Lenia. "This was once a part of the living reef, but has since passed on, leaving this delicate piece behind to serve as home to other creatures, and support for the rest of the coral colony. And now, it will help serve you."

"Thank you," said Lenia as she accepted the gift. She noticed some markings on Anastasia's arm. "Who's Tiberiu?" she asked.

Anastasia lifted up her forearm. The name had some artistic designs and colour around it on her skin. A soft expression touched her face. "Tiberiu is someone that used to mean a lot to me. I decided to permanently mark his name on my arm using the ink from the four-eyed octopus, to honour his memory."

"It looks really cool," said Lenia, as she looked at the marking a little further. The colours used were remarkably vibrant, and seemed to glimmer when they caught the light. Anastasia moved her arm so Lenia could see it better.

"Do you want one?" asked Anastasia.

"I don't know anyone named Tiberiu," said Lenia sarcastically.

Anastasia laughed. "I could write a different name if you want, or I could make a design of something else, if you prefer."

"I don't really know," said Lenia hesitantly. "That is really pretty, and I definitely want one, I just don't know what to get. Do you know anyone else with one?"

"The last girl I made one for was a pimple-faced teen named Ali. She wanted a crow on her shoulder. Would you like something like that?" asked Anastasia.

Lenia's smile instantly turned into a frown. "Gross," replied Lenia. "I hate birds."

Anastasia laughed again. "Me too!" she exclaimed. "Whenever I go to the surface, I have to look around for seagulls, because I don't want them near me. Their squawks are annoying, they're dirty, and don't even get me started on how difficult it is to get bird poop out of my hair. I like to think that all creatures in the world are equally special and wonderful, but birds and I do not get along. Sometimes, I don't go to the surface if I know that there are avians lurking."

Lenia and Anastasia both started laughing uncontrollably. Lenia couldn't believe that there was someone else who felt as strongly about birds as she did, let alone a confident, wise mermaid. "You're amazing!" admitted Lenia after the two girls finished giggling together.

"You actually remind me of someone," said Anastasia as she settled down. "She was a wizard competing in the Quest Series about thirty years ago. She was caring, smart, slightly sarcastic, and incredibly talented. She was blown away by the power of my trident, and was fascinated by my ability to control the element of water. She wanted a whirlpool drawn on her shoulder blade. She was overjoyed by how it turned out, and her smile lit up the sea like an electric eel. Your smile and laugh remind me of hers."

Lenia was flattered by Anastasia's story, and was drawn in more by her charm. "A whirlpool? Well, I'm sure it was beautiful!"

"Would you like something like that?" asked Anastasia.

"I don't think so," said Lenia. "I'm having a wonderful time in the sea with you, and I kind of want something that reminds me of our adventure together." Lenia looked down at the reef. Her eyes were drawn to a few baby sea turtles that were making their way towards her. She stuck out her hand, and cradled one of them. "Can you use this in your design?"

"Absolutely! I love that idea!" exclaimed Anastasia. Before Lenia could take another breath, Anastasia took her to a different part of the sea, where they found themselves face to face with a four-eyed octopus.

"Hey, Trixie." Anastasia put her hand on its face. Trixie seemed overjoyed to see Anastasia, and Lenia knew that they had a special connection. Anastasia started to tickle Trixie under one of her tentacles, which made her chuckle. Lenia didn't know that octopi could laugh, and she couldn't help but giggle along with the strange creature.

As Trixie laughed harder, Lenia could see a few blasts of black ink enter the water beneath the tentacle. "Who's a good girl?" Anastasia stopped tickling Trixie and pet her. The octopus swam away happily, and left the two friends with their ink.

"Where would you like the design?" Anastasia asked. "On your forearm?"

"I don't really want it overly visible," replied Lenia. "How about on my ankle?"

"Perfect!" replied Anastasia. They worked together to roll up Lenia's pant leg. Lenia held the trident as Anastasia swam down and put her hand on Lenia's calf. Anastasia moved her hand around in a circular motion, creating a design with the watery cloud of ink.

"How does that look?" asked Anastasia as she completed it.

"I like it, but is it going to remain black like that?" Lenia asked. "Can I have it coloured, like yours?"

"This is just the design." Anastasia patted her leg. "Once I use my trident to complete it, it will release the colour within the ink. I must warn you though, this may sting a bit."

Lenia handed back the trident to Anastasia. The mermaid placed the middle prong of the trident over the design. A small glow radiated from the trident, and Lenia could feel her skin start to get hot. It felt like she was being burned with a hot plate around the area of the design.

The glow quickly became brighter and hotter, and then disappeared instantly. Anastasia removed the trident from Lenia's leg and checked out her handiwork.

"It's lovely!" exclaimed Anastasia. "I think it's my best one yet! A special design for a special girl," she added with a wink.

Lenia checked her ankle, and was blown away by how colourful it was. It shined brilliantly with all the colours of the coral reef. The contrasting lines that shaped the sea turtle were clean and precise. It was the most beautiful image she had ever seen.

"I love it!" said Lenia. She reached out and gave Anastasia a big hug. "Thank you so much!"

"You're welcome," replied Anastasia. She held Lenia tight. "Now, let's get going on that trident again."

"Okay," Lenia said as she disengaged. "What do we have to do next?"

"We have a piece of the ocean," replied Anastasia. "And we have a piece of yourself already. All we need is a piece that you adore. Do you have an item that means a lot to you?"

Lenia reached into her pocket. "Will this work?" she asked, pulling out her fire starter.

"That depends," replied Anastasia skeptically. "Is there a story behind it?"

Lenia stared at the fire starter in her hand. It was made out of blackish-green metal. The outside of it was scaled, like a dragon's back. It was old, sleek, and beautiful. "My family once went to the Domini Promenade for a street festival," Lenia began. "There were many different people, from many different lands, coming to sell knick-knacks, entertain locals, and spread cheer in the city. One of the entertainers was a wizard, who loved manipulating fire for the crowd.

"I was only nine at the time, but I remember the spectacle vividly. The wizard was making flames dance, shooting fire up in the sky, and juggling small orbs. I didn't know how he was able to hold the small balls of fire in his hands with such grace, but it was beautiful. I was standing in the front row, and I think the wizard noticed how amazed I was. At the end of the show, he flipped me his fire starter and told me to keep it as a souvenir. He not only gave me the power of fire, but he inspired my love for controlling it as well." Lenia closed her hand around the fire starter and held it tight.

"That will work," Anastasia said with a smile. "Thank you for sharing that story with me. I feel like I know a little more about the world above."

"Perfect!" Lenia was relieved that it would work as an ingredient for her trident. "So, what do we do next?" she asked.

"Now we can go to the steam cove to make the trident!" said Anastasia.

Before Lenia had a chance to think, she saw a cauldron in front of them.

"Whoa." Lenia moved back a little bit in the water, one hand on Anastasia's shoulder. "I'm still not really used to that yet," she said with a laugh.

When she was able to focus, she noticed that they were in a large cavern. There were multiple cauldrons all around the room, with the mould of a trident in the rock underneath each one. Steam was coming from the moulds, and heating the cauldrons from below.

Anastasia laughed too. "Sorry, I should have warned you," she said. "The cauldron is ready for you; all you have to do is put in the ingredients. I would suggest using a piece of your hair in the cauldron, but some people insist on putting in other weird things. The pimple-faced girl popped a pimple into it, which I found to be quite disgusting. Some people like to use their blood, but a hair will work just the same."

Lenia nodded in agreement. Anastasia kept a hand on Lenia's back, so she could have both hands free.

First, she put the piece of coral in the cauldron, and watched as the gold colour of the liquid turned reddish-green. She put the fire starter in next and saw the liquid turn greener still. Finally, she undid her braid and pulled a hair from her head. She also took the black hair from Turanus' mane out and held it with her strand of hair. Considering his involvement with her adventures in the Quest thus far, it felt right to include it as well.

She put both hairs into the cauldron, and steam rushed out from the top of it. The liquid turned gold again, and then became pitch-black.

"Is it done?" Lenia asked.

Anastasia looked over her shoulder. "That's odd," said Anastasia as she looked in wonder at the cauldron. "I have never seen the liquid turn black before! This is so exciting!"

Anastasia moved her hand, and the cauldron turned upside down. The liquid inside the cauldron went into the mould below, and filled it perfectly. After a few moments, the mould started to vibrate, and the steam tried to escape. "Let's move back a little bit," Anastasia said, pulling Lenia with her.

Lenia kept her eyes on the mould as it vibrated harder. A small light came from the centre, and then it began to pulsate. Soon, the entire mould glowed so brightly that she had to cover her eyes with her hand. With one final pulse, the light disappeared, and a smooth, black trident floated up in the water before her, spinning slowly on its axis.

"A black trident?" exclaimed Anastasia. "I've never seen a black trident before! That is incredible! You are incredible!" She shook Lenia's shoulder gently.

Lenia didn't know what to say. It was definitely cool-looking, and she was excited because Anastasia was excited, but she didn't know how to respond.

They moved over to the trident together. She gently wrapped her fingers around it. It was warm to the touch, and she could feel it slowly beat in time to her steady heart.

"Let's see what it can do," said Anastasia excitedly.

"How does it work?" asked Lenia, as she looked at the sleek, black trident in wonder.

"Try focusing on the power within you," replied the mermaid. "We're taught that the key to controlling the trident is openness. Just as your eyes see more when they're open, and your heart feels more when it's vulnerable, your power works best when you open yourself up to it."

Lenia couldn't help but smile; the words reminded her of Professor Bright's usual lecture. "I know exactly what you mean," she said as she relaxed.

She looked at the forks of the trident and they began to glow. Instead of a bright, white glow like she had seen on Anastasia's trident, this glow was red and orange. It sparked into flame right before their eyes. The fire burned like it would on the surface, despite the fact that they were underwater. She could feel the heat from the fire as its flame boiled the water directly around it.

"That's impossible," said Anastasia in wonder.

"I've been talking, breathing, and moving through the sea in the blink of an eye. Nothing is impossible," Lenia replied. She was happy to see Anastasia's excitement.

"We need to go to the Queen," Anastasia said. Before Lenia could think of how to respond, a golden city appeared. She looked at the black trident; the flame had gone out.

"Is this the City of the Mermaids?" asked Lenia. Anastasia was slowly leading her along a long path, laid out in mother-of-pearl, which led to a golden, square building.

"Not exactly," said Anastasia. "Mermaids don't really have a definitive city to live in. We live in the sea, and move around as the sea permits. These structures have been labelled as the City of the Mermaids, but it's just a bunch of storage units, and a great hall that the Queen uses for gatherings and celebrations."

She gestured to a large, spiral structure ahead of them. "We store information about our activities, powers, and traditions here, and use the great hall to communicate everything to the Queen. The location is known only to mermaids, and its secrecy is imperative to our lifestyle and the life of the sea."

When they got to the door of the hall, Anastasia tapped it with her golden trident. The door slowly opened, and the two entered respectfully. At the front of the hall was a beautiful mermaid with white hair, whom Lenia assumed was the Queen. Her attention was focused on The Headsmen in front of her.

Niveous and his team were all holding hands together with a black-haired mermaid. Lenia realized that there was a second mermaid among them, this one keeping hold of a singular student. She thought she recognized him as the lone warrior from their group this morning.

Niveous gestured to the warrior, who nervously swam up to the throne with his mermaid's help, clutching his trident.

"What is your name, and what team are you representing?" the Queen asked him.

"My name is Brutus," he replied. "I am representing the team Ninety-Nine Problems."

The Queen smiled elegantly. "Welcome, Brutus. Let us hope that creating a working trident is not one of your problems," she said jokingly. "Please, show me your trident."

Brutus raised up his silver trident and yelled, "Dragoon!" He brought the trident back down, and his mermaid companion placed her hand on it as well. It seemed like he needed help activating its power.

Both Brutus and the mermaid leaned back as the head of the trident shot off the stem, hitting the roof of the great hall. It clanged loudly as it bounced off the polished ceiling, and hung still in the water. The head disappeared, and then reappeared on the stem in front of Brutus.

"Congratulations, Brutus, yours is the seventh team to successfully create and exhibit your trident," said the Queen. "Your team, Ninety-Nine Problems, will receive the seventh highest amount of points for this event. Good luck in the rest of the Quest Series, and with your graduation from The Academy."

Brutus was led away and back towards the entrance of the great hall. He didn't seem to care that Lenia was behind him, and was more overjoyed with his own accomplishment. His smile was beaming.

Niveous then swam forward, holding a glowing, coppery-green trident. His team introduced themselves as a chorus, and the Queen bid them continue with their demonstration. Niveous held it aloft. The trident grew bright, and then became dim as his brief display was over.

"Congratulations, Headsmen. You are the eighth team to successfully create and exhibit your trident," said the Queen. "Your team will receive the eighth highest amount of points for this event. Good luck in the rest of the Quest Series, and with your graduation from the Academy."

The black-haired mermaid led Niveous and the Headsmen past Lenia as they exited the hall. She paid no attention to him as they passed. It was her turn.

"What is your name, and what team are you representing?" the Queen asked.

"My name is Lenia," she replied politely. "I am representing the Liberati."

The Queen smiled demurely. "Welcome, Lenia. That is a very nice design on your ankle. Anastasia must really like you." She nodded to Anastasia.

Lenia looked down at her rolled-up pant leg, and then glanced at her friend. Anastasia smiled and bowed gracefully to the Queen.

"Please, show me your trident."

Just as she did before, Lenia held her black trident and opened herself up. The head sparked with a radiant flame.

The Queen's face lit up in wonder. "What magic is this?" She swam towards Lenia to get a closer look. She moved her hand towards the flame and felt its warmth. She looked at Lenia with an inquisitive eye, and touched her shoulder gently.

The fire went out, and Lenia's mind started spinning. She could feel the Queen's power in a white flash that rushed through her. The Queen released her hand and moved gently back towards her perch at the front of the hall.

"It is my honour to meet you, Lenia Rie." The Queen bowed gracefully. "Your power is new to me, and I am grateful for your display. I do not believe anyone has ever thought of creating a trident like that before." Her eyes twinkled, and Lenia wondered if she knew what she had added to the trident, just as she knew her name.

"I can tell that you have a kind soul, so I am not fearful that your power is a threat to our life under the sea. In fact, I would like to embrace it as something great and new, rather than something fearful and different."

Lenia fiddled with the haft of the trident nervously.

"In terms of the Quest Series, you are the ninth person to create and successfully display your trident. Your team, the Liberati, will receive the ninth highest amount of points for Event Three. However, because you have demonstrated a new power for us, I would like to extend a gesture of peace and tranquility. I would like to make you one of my appointed ambassadors between the surface and the sea. Will you accept this great honour?"

Lenia felt excited, but she didn't know how to react. She looked over at Anastasia, who smiled and nodded proudly, as if to guide her answer.

"Thank you very much," said Lenia. She bowed in acknowledgement to the Queen. "I am humbled by your request, and it would make me very proud to accept."

"Very well." The Queen smiled. She raised her hand, and Lenia felt her trident warm beneath her hand. She looked up at the head of the trident and saw a soft, white glow pulse three times, and then disappear.

"Thank you for showcasing your magic in this event. Good luck in the rest of the Quest Series, and with your graduation from The Academy. I hope that we get a chance to develop our relationship in the future."

Anastasia led Lenia away from the Queen and back out of the golden hall. They swam down the path and outside of the ornate, coral entry arch.

Once away from the city, Anastasia couldn't hold her excitement in any longer. "An ambassador!" she exclaimed. "That's so wonderful!"

Lenia smiled in return. "I know, right?" she said excitedly. "What does that mean, exactly?"

Anastasia giggled. "It means that you have been granted some of the power of the mermaids," she said. She knocked Lenia's hand away from her golden trident, and swam backwards.

Lenia reached for her throat, expecting to drown, but she was still breathing normally. "That's amazing!" Lenia exclaimed. She held her own trident and watched the fire burn on the end of it once again. "This doesn't happen to everybody?" she asked.

"An official envoy has only been appointed once before in my lifetime," replied Anastasia. "It truly is a great honour to be accepted into our culture. When the Queen touched you, she searched your soul for its true intention. She must have been satisfied by the good nature of your being, and has offered you the respect of our species as a token of peace. You truly yield a great power, and we hope that our bond with you remains strong in this turbulent world that we live in."

"So I can come back again?"

"Anytime. Every other student will see the power of their trident disappear as soon as they break their connection with their mermaid counterpart, but your power will remain. As you keep your trident beyond the sea, use its power wisely. Whenever you return to the sea, you will have the respect of not only the Queen and myself, but of all mermaids within our kingdom. It truly is a great privilege to have met you, Lenia, and I hope that we can remain friends in the future."

"Absolutely!" Lenia reached for a hug with Anastasia. She still couldn't swim like the mermaids, so she didn't move forward at all. Anastasia swam forward and embraced her. Before she could blink, think or breathe, Anastasia had already taken her to the shore.

Lenia felt the ground underneath her feet, so she stood tall. Her head reached above the water, and she breathed in some fresh air for the first time in hours. She looked around and saw a gentle beach stretch before her. "Where are we?" she asked.

Anastasia's head was above the water as well, but her tail was still moving swimmingly. "We are at Oyster Beach. This is the drop-off point for all students from The Academy. There is a portal door just beyond the sand and line of trees there."

She pointed up the beach, then grasped Lenia's hand. "Please come back and visit me soon. Just remember: once you make contact with the sea, I will be able to find you, no matter where you are."

"Thank you so much," Lenia replied. She didn't want to say goodbye to her new friend, but she knew she had to continue on and return to The Academy. "You don't know how much you've inspired and influenced me. I'll definitely visit you again soon." The two friends embraced again before Anastasia left.

Lenia walked up to the beach and looked at the hot sun. It was late afternoon, and the sunshine felt warm on her skin. She walked along the sand and stopped just before the tree line. A rustling got her attention.

Niveous, the Headsmen, and Brutus walked out of the brush. "Well, well, well," started Niveous cockily. "We meet again."

Lenia glared at him, and didn't respond. She didn't back down. She simply stared at her adversaries.

"Not much of a talker, are you," Niveous said with a grin. "Don't worry; we're not here to harm you. The event is over, and we've already beaten you. We waited here to offer you a truce." He extended his right hand, as if he expected her to shake it.

She grinned more wickedly than he had. "I don't think so," she replied. "Event Three might be over, but you're not a trustworthy, or compassionate, adversary. I don't accept your truce. I don't accept an apology. In fact, I don't expect anything from you. Just don't mess with me or my team at all; or else."

Niveous looked at his fellows surrounding her and laughed. "Or else what?"

Lenia slammed her trident into the ground, and felt the power of it surge through her, just as it had with Anastasia. The head of the trident glowed, and then burst into flames.

Niveous, the Headsmen, and Brutus looked on in shock, and then looked at their two powerless tridents. They turned and ran away.

Lenia stopped the fire and focused her attention back to the sun. She tilted her head back, closed her eyes, and let the warm light caress her skin.

"Today was a good day," she said aloud to herself.

CHAPTER 13

Selfless

K ase took a step backward. He turned his head to get a better angle. "That's the coolest thing I've ever seen," he said.

"I know, right?" Lenia smiled and showed off her trident. "I was told that no mermaid has ever seen a black one before, let alone one that has the power to light fire underwater!"

"It's just a trident," he replied as he stared at her leg. "I was talking about your sea turtle design. Did it hurt? Can I get one?" He noticed her unimpressed expression. "I mean, yeah, your trident is really cool."

Lenia laughed. "It hurt a little bit, but I could handle it. You might cry if you had to go through it, though," she said playfully.

"I think I want one on my neck," he said. He pretended to ignore her comment. "I'd want people to see it as soon as they looked at me. I'd want something that strikes fear in them, like a deadly, terrifying pigeon or something."

"Gross!" Lenia laughed. "That would be the most unattractive design ever."

"Do you think you could come up with something better?" he asked.

"Absolutely!" she replied. "I'll have to think about it, but I'll definitely design something for you. Are you sure you want it on your neck, though? Maybe we should put it on your face or butt, to make it extra unique."

Kase laughed. "I never thought about that!" he said jokingly. "Okay, you make the design; I'll decide where it should go. Deal?"

"Deal," Lenia said with a smile. He couldn't wait for her ideas.

"Here comes Talen." Cali interrupted the flirting of the other Liberati members.

Talen arrived, her face expressionless. "I wasn't able to find anything," she admitted solemnly. Since their detainment, Cali, Talen, and Kase had been trying to collect proof of Niveous's involvement. Once Lenia told them how The Headsmen and Ninety-Nine Problems were both out to get her, they were all determined to have them banned from the Q.

"In order to disqualify a team from the Quest Series, their guilt needs to be proven beyond a reasonable doubt," Talen said disappointingly. "Since we don't have any evidence, any witnesses, or an admission of guilt, we cannot accuse them of interfering with our team. Any testimony we provide would all seem like hearsay; our word against theirs. If we really want to get them disqualified, we need a better plan."

"What if we get the other team, Ninety-Nine Problems, to go against the Headsmen? They were also in detainment with you; maybe they're harbouring some resentment?" said Lenia hopefully.

"I don't think that would work," Talen replied. "Ninety-Nine Problems would be admitting their own guilt and would probably get disqualified, too. We have to treat the Headsmen and Ninety-Nine Problems as one group; one common enemy."

"Is there any proof in the other events?" asked Lenia. "Maybe we could single out the Headsmen before their alliance?"

"I already checked all of the submittals," said Cali as she handed the sage mirror to Lenia. "There's no proof. Talen and I already discussed it at length while we were serving our punishment."

Lenia flipped through the images, but didn't find anything useful.

"What if we set a trap for them?" asked Talen. Her face still didn't show her thoughts, but Kase could tell she was planning something wicked.

171

"Like what?" asked Cali cautiously.

"I know what kind of dust they used to try and send me to sleep," replied Lenia. "It's called Sweet Dreams. Maybe we can use some on them, or use some on ourselves with other people watching?"

"That seems a little soft," replied Cali with a shrug. "Let's figure out something that can hurt them!" She sneered.

"Let's feed them to sharks!" exclaimed Talen. "Maybe Lenia can summon some with her magical black trident."

"I don't think that's how it works," admitted Lenia. "The only thing I know it can do is start a fire. Should we light them on fire?" she asked hopefully.

"Enough," Kase said sternly. He put his hand out for the rest of the Liberati to stop talking. Talen, Cali, and Lenia all looked surprised, but they fell silent and awaited his command.

"Haven't we learned anything from our last encounter?" Kase was thinking about all the times he had gotten involved with Niveous, and the talks he'd had with the Grand Master because of them. "When are we going to stop making the same mistakes? When are we going to stop stooping to their level?"

Talen frowned to hear her own words coming back at her. Cali shuffled her feet guiltily.

"I'll admit, I definitely want to take another round out of the guy that pushed Cali, but I can't help but think that there has to be something beyond revenge; something that makes us better than them. We've already overcome their attempts to bury us. In the first event, we came back and delivered the lava on the last day. In the third event, Lenia stepped up and dominated it all by herself."

"Yeah I did," Lenia stated proudly, admiring her trident once more.

"Their attempts to stop us prove that they fear us. They are worried about losing to us. They made the mistake of showing us how they're trying to stop us, and we'll be ready for them the next time they try something devious."

He stepped forward and grabbed first Cali around the shoulders, then Lenia. He nodded for Talen to come in close. "We belong in the Quest Series. We belong with each other. We belong at the top of the leaderboard. In the end, we owe it to ourselves to keep focus on what we do best: sticking together. By staying strong as a group, we will become champions not because we outsmarted the tricksters with more tricks, but because we earned the position of number one."

Cali slowly shook her head and smiled. "Well said, brother," she said proudly. "Does everyone agree?"

Talen and Lenia both nodded slowly.

"Let's find out what the next event is, then." Kase reached his hand out to Lenia for the mirror. "Mirror, mirror, show us the details of Quest Series Event Four." When it was revealed, Kase read it out loud.

"The Academy prides itself on being a school for the elite: a school for the gifted, for the leaders of tomorrow. As leaders of the realm, it is important for us to recognize that there are different creatures throughout the world that don't have the same benefits or luxuries that others have in their lands, cities, or schools. There are creatures that have hardships that surpass their own efforts and skills, which in turn makes it difficult for them to survive.

"One group in need is the Satyrs of Skyland. They have suffered greatly over the last few years, and it's been a goal of many to help them through these difficult times. Donations of food, clothing, and labour have been common aid to the Satyrs, and The Academy is one of the many institutions to offer relief.

"Teams will travel to Skyland for the weekend and volunteer their time to the Satyrs. Baby G will be the point of contact, and he will designate projects and log the volunteer hours of each individual. Teams will be awarded points for the hours worked by all team members, but extra points will be awarded for delivering a sac of warm clothing. The clothing donations can be picked up in the main auditorium.

"Sometimes the best thing you can do in life is to give without expecting anything in return." When Kase finished, he gave the sage mirror to Cali. "What's a Satyr?" he asked.

"Dragons," said Talen under her breath.

"What?" Cali looked at Talen in confusion.

"Sorry." Talen shook her head. "A Satyr is a creature that is half goat, half human. They are one of the many creatures that make their home on Skyland, but another native to that region is the dragon. They are violent predators, and their presence is one of the reasons that the Satyrs are facing hard times."

"Oh no." Lenia gripped her trident a little tighter.

"Awesome!" said Kase. He had always wanted to see a colourful, fierce, fire-breathing dragon, and was hoping that he would get a chance.

The rest of the Liberati all looked at him as if waiting for something. "Well—to the library!"

Like the previous events, the Liberati got up early the next day in order to gain advantage with the fresh daylight. Cali and Talen had made a map of where they needed to go, while Kase and Lenia had grabbed one of the clothing sacs from the auditorium, and added some water and snacks for the journey. Kase brought a sword and dagger in case he had to tame any dragons, while Lenia brought her beautiful black trident along. She wouldn't be without her new favourite fire starter.

As the Liberati walked towards the portal gateway, they could see at least twenty teams making the same trek. "Looks like everyone is trying to get a jump on the day," said Kase, searching for the Headsmen.

"This is the first event where there's only one way, and time, to go," said Cali as she looked at her map. "It seems like we can all just travel together."

They followed the other teams through the portal door, and to the base of the Skyland Grind.

As soon as Kase walked out through the portal, he was mesmerized by all of the tiny islands that floated in the air like a stairway, all leading to a giant landmass that rested magically above the clouds. The purple jagged rocks of the floating islands shined as the morning sunshine bounced off of them.

Climbing the Grind was almost like scaling a mountain, but was easier because of the alterations made throughout the centuries. The islands were joined by vines, ladders, bridges, and man-made stairs. Although the climb was not overly difficult, they all knew it would take some time to make it to the top.

"Wanna race?" Kase playfully poked Lenia with his elbow.

"To the top? Are you crazy?" she said with a laugh. "It's going to be like a two hour hike."

"Based on our pace and the challenges ahead, I'd say it's going to take two hours, six minutes, and thirty-three seconds," said Talen. She looked up to the sky.

"Threes!" exclaimed Kase and Lenia together.

"Let's just keep pace with the crowd," said Cali with a roll of her eyes. "We don't want to be alone with certain teams on this adventure, so we should stay with the group as much as we can."

The Liberati all agreed and began their trek up the Grind in earnest. There were other teams that were going faster and passed them swiftly, as well as teams that were irritatingly slow. Vines were climbed, ladders were scaled, and steps were trod.

When they were high above the ground, Lenia moved to the edge of the tiny island they were on and stared blankly off into the distance.

"What are you looking at?" Kase asked.

"I think my parents' house is that way." She peered into the distance.

"I think I can see it!" he said jokingly, since all he could see were trees and fields. "Do you miss it?" he asked.

"No," she admitted. "I would rather jump off this island in the sky than go back home. It's just funny how a person can look and see the whole world, and know that they're happy exactly where they are." She grabbed his hand and held it as she walked up the stairs to the next island.

The Liberati reached the cloud cover and knew they were close to the top of the Grind. They kept stepping and climbing, and it didn't take them long to get out of the wet, opaque mist. They soon found themselves overlooking the fluffy white clouds. It looked like they were on top of a sea of pillows. With a couple more steps, they were looking at the vast landscape of Skyland.

"This is not what I expected," said Cali as she took in the barren landscape. The grass in front of them was dead, and the trees were all burned to the ground.

"It looks like a forest fire started in this area; it stops at the edge of the field over there." Talen pointed to the left, at the forest past the brown grass. The other teams were heading there, which looked a lot more promising. There was a rainbow high in the sky above the pathway, while to the right lay a dark forest with black, stone caves in the distance.

"Why does it smell like bacon?" asked Kase. "I love this place!"

"I could really go for some bacon and pancakes right about now," agreed Lenia with a smile.

"Come on, let's keep moving," Cali said in a serious tone.

The Liberati followed the other teams across the field and through the forest. It seemed like any other forest down on the mainland, until they saw some of the creatures that inhabited it.

"Look at the size of that pig!" Kase exclaimed as he pointed to the left of the path. It was feeding on some mushrooms.

"It's the size of an elephant!" Talen added.

The giant hog ignored the noisy students, and continued eating. As the Liberati passed by, its tail started moving wildly. It let out some rancid gas.

"Gross!" yelled Cali as she pinched her nose with her fingers. She got out the sage mirror and captured an image of them all covering their noses, with the hog in the background. They laughed together before continuing on.

A little farther down, to the right of the main path, they saw the Headsmen making their way into the woods.

"What are they doing now?" Lenia asked, hand on her hip.

"Who cares?" Cali said. "Worrying about us, remember?"

"But if we are forewarned of their mischief, we might be able to do something to prevent it," Talen pointed out. "Or at the very least, we'll know what to expect."

They all looked to Kase.

"Fine—just so we know what they're up to."

The Liberati were led to a clearing that opened to a calm, misty lake. The water was almost black with the mist settling on the top of it, blocking all the sunshine from touching the surface. The Headsmen and Ninety-Nine Problems were walking towards a giant skeleton that was lying at the edge of the water.

The Liberati stopped at the edge of the forest to remain hidden.

"Look at how cool this dead hog looks!" said Niveous as he walked up to its skull. "Quick, Sharaine, capture this image for me!"

The Liberati sighed. It seemed like the Headsmen and Ninety-Nine Problems were just taking a break to have a little fun, and all took turns posing and mocking the skeleton.

But as their attention was on the bones of the dead, there was a living monster that was lurking in the water behind them. Kase couldn't quite see what it was. It looked like a reptile's nose sticking out of the water: almost like an alligator, but bigger.

"What is that?" He pointed.

Talen followed his gaze. "Dragon!" she yelled in a frightful tone.

The Headsmen and Ninety-Nine Problems all looked towards the forest line. They slowly turned their attention back towards the water as the dark, purple head and neck of the great dragon slowly revealed itself from the misty water's edge.

The dragon spread its wings out wide, dripping with water from the lake. It stood powerful and strong, and looked at least thirty feet tall. Its wingspan seemed to stretch to the corners of the small beach shoreline. It roared terribly as it studied its new prey. The grueling sound echoed loudly off the small waves that formed in the water.

"Everyone stand your ground!" shouted the largest warrior of Ninety-Nine Problems. He had been carrying a shield on his back, and in one motion shifted it to his left arm, while he unsheathed his sword with his right. The other warriors followed suit, focusing all their attention on the killer beast.

Instead of listening to their comrades, the Headsmen all turned and ran.

"Stand your ground!" shouted the warrior again, but the Headsmen ignored them. Their legs moved quickly in fear, and they made it away from the shore and to the safety of the trees beyond the beach.

At the sudden movement, the dragon started snapping at the warriors, but didn't try to strike any of them yet. It seemed like it was testing their speed, evaluating whether they would run or offer a threat.

"Dragoon, huddle!" said the warrior. All four of the warriors came together to form a strong front. They stood shoulder-to-shoulder, with their shields together and their swords ready.

"What are they doing?" Kase mumbled to himself in a concerned tone.

"I hope the dragon eats them," said Cali wickedly.

"I hope the dragon lights them on fire," said Lenia.

"Is it over yet?" Talen had covered her eyes with her hands.

The dragon extended its long neck, and then leaned its head back. When its mouth opened, its throat glowed bright with an orange flame. The warriors all hid behind their shields and got ready for the attack.

The dragon lowered its head, and flame burst out in a stream, covering the warriors with a hot spray. Although the fire hit them directly, their strong shields protected them.

The fire stopped, and the dragon leaned back in satisfaction, until the warriors popped up from behind their shields. The dragon tilted its head.

"Fall back!" yelled the leader. The warriors all started moving slowly, keeping their eyes focused on their enemy.

The dragon opened its mouth again. Its throat glowed bright once more. The warriors stopped moving, hid behind their shields, and got ready for another attack.

Instead of blowing fire again, the dragon turned around and swung its tail at the warriors. The tail whip sent them flying, and their swords and shields scattered about. They all landed in different places, but the biggest warrior seemed to be almost right at the dragon's feet. As the dragon turned, it focused its attention on its closest prey.

"He's actually going to get burned!" exclaimed Lenia as she reached for Kase's hand in fear. All she grabbed was air. He had left their group and was sprinting towards the beach.

"Kase!" she yelled.

His legs carried him swiftly across the beach. He hardly heard Lenia's call; his mind was focused on the ferocious dragon.

It leaned its head back and opened its mouth. Its throat glowed bright orange. Kase grabbed one of the shields on the ground, tucked and rolled in front of the fallen warrior, and protected them both. The flame covered the two warriors with a hot spray.

The dragon kept its head lowered, ready to feast on its warm dinner. Before it had a chance to satisfy its appetite, Kase dropped the shield. In one fluid motion, he gripped the dagger he had in his belt, pulled his arm back, and threw it at the dragon's wide-toothed face.

The dagger tore through the air with effortless celerity. Its course was precise. Its aim was true. Its purpose brooked no room for mercy. The deadly projectile was in pursuit of perfection, and would not accept anything less than total victory. It reached its destination with full force, and plunged its tip into the eye of the hungry dragon.

The dragon shot its head back and let out a painful roar. Its head wobbled back and forth. It turned away from Kase, and dove back into the mist from which it came, retreating in agony. Its painful cries could be heard echoing off the water as it escaped.

Kase watched the dragon flee, and he couldn't help but grin at the trail of swirling mist that it left behind. For a moment, all was silent.

He turned back towards the beach, and was about to rejoin the rest of his team, but the fallen warriors were all kneeling in the way in front of him, heads down.

"You saved us, brother," said Tarkin. "We owe you our lives."

"Dragoon!" replied the others.

"Please, stand," replied Kase in a firm voice. The warriors all stood tall and met his gaze. "Thank you for your gesture, but I was just doing what anyone would have done."

"Nonsense," replied Tarkin. "Our fellow comrades ran away in cowardice. You showed us honour and respect, even though we treated you poorly in the past. Please forgive us for our, and my, wrongdoings. We were aligned with the wrong people."

Kase was overjoyed with the turn of events. "I accept your apology." He forced himself to remain calm. "I think you owe one to the rest of my team as well," he added upon seeing them walk up the beach.

The warriors turned, dropped to one knee again, and bowed to the rest of the Liberati as they approached.

Before Cali, Talen, or Lenia could say anything, Tarkin addressed them sincerely. "We're sorry for how we treated you earlier. We acted out, and we were wrong. Please forgive us," he said.

"Dragoon!" replied the others.

Cali looked at Kase in awe and wonder. Kase shrugged in response.

"Apology accepted," she said casually.

The warriors all stood. "Thank you for your forgiveness," said Tarkin. "We don't deserve it. My name is Tarkin. This is Malekai, Brutus, and Shea."

"It's nice to meet you all." Cali introduced the rest of the Liberati. "I guess we should probably keep moving on with the quest, in case the dragon decides to return."

"I'm not concerned about the dragon," said Tarkin. "We have the Dragon Slayer with us."

Kase couldn't help but smile with pride.

"May we join you for the rest of the journey?"

"What about the Headsmen?" asked Cali with sharp concern.

"They have shown their true colours," replied Tarkin. "They are cowards, and don't deserve our respect. They mean nothing to us now."

"It looks like they took our sacs of clothing with them as they escaped." Malekai pointed to where their supplies had been.

"Figures," said Tarkin.

Cali finally smiled. "You may absolutely join us then." With that, she turned towards the forest.

Cali, Talen, and Ninety-Nine Problems crossed the beach and headed back to the main path. Before Kase could join them, Lenia rushed over and gave him a big hug.

"This is a surprise," Kase said as he wrapped his arms around her.

Lenia laughed. "Well, you're a Dragon Slayer now. I think you deserve one," she replied innocently. She grabbed his hand, and they caught up to the rest of their team together.

The two teams walked steadily through the forest, until they came upon a wooden fence with a large gate. There was a sign above it that read 'Welcome Quest Series Students'.

"This must be it!" Cali pushed the gate open.

They walked down the narrow path, and were soon overwhelmed by the hustle and bustle of the small community. There were straw mud huts at the base of some of the trees in front of them. There were tiny wooden houses above, with vines, ladders, and bridges dangling from the tree limbs.

There were Satyrs rushing around chaotically, carrying different tools, supplies, clothing, and food. There were kids playing about, running around and chasing each other innocently.

As the group kept to the path, they soon came to the centre of the community. A long line-up of students stood before them, with a large Satyr at the front giving orders.

The line moved quickly, and the students were sent away for their volunteer assignments. "Next!" yelled Baby G. The Liberati stepped forward. "Names?" He held a quill and looked at a piece of paper in front of him.

Now that they were up close, Kase could see that he was even shorter than Talen, but stood on a wide stool to make up the difference. He had long, scrawny arms that had patches of hair everywhere. It seemed as though the rough, stringy hair was trying to escape his body: it stood straight from his head, spilled out of his ears, and fell off his chin. The rest of his hair was kept at bay by the brown leather vest that reached from his human shoulders down to below his goat knees. His hooves were dark grey, and shifted as he kept his balance on the stool.

"Our team name is The Liberati," replied Cali. "My name is Cali, this is Talen, Lenia, and Kase."

"Do you have a clothing donation?" he asked as he scribbled on the paper haphazardly.

Cali looked at Kase, and he turned to grab the sac. He had set it down, but it wasn't there. Instead, Tarkin was holding it in his outstretched hand.

For a second, the Liberati all shared the same thought as they looked skeptically at Ninety-Nine Problems. They wondered if their new friends were going to take credit for the clothing that they had brought.

"Here is the sac of clothing for the Liberati." Tarkin handed the donation to Baby G. He smiled at Cali, giving her reassurance that their new alliance was, in fact, genuine. Cali smiled sheepishly back.

"Very well," said Baby G as he scribbled on the paper. He took the sac and gave it to a young Satyr behind him. "Are you warriors, scholars, or wizards?" he asked.

"We're a mixture," replied Cali proudly.

Baby G looked confused. He studied the Liberati, and then continued with his assignments. "Very well," he said again with a shrug. "All warriors are being put on fence duty, so whoever is a warrior can make their way to the left and to the fields. They are to report to Peeps, the fence builder." He pointed down one path.

"The scholars are all on seed duty, so they can make their way to the right, on to the storage barn. They are to report to Manny, the seed master." He pointed down the other path.

"The wizards are on manure and mud-hut building duty. They can make their way down the path behind me, and report to Tweeg, the manure expert. Next!" He looked back at his paper.

183

Kase shrugged his shoulders and walked down the left path. He watched Lenia as they went their separate ways. He wished he could have spent the day with her, and the rest of the Liberati.

In the end, he had such a good time that the rest of the day flew by anyway. He met with Peeps in the open field, and helped move lumber all afternoon with the other warriors. The Satyrs were building the fences, but the warriors were the labourers helping them move around their supplies. It was a streamlined operation, and the efficiency showed; they were able to fence in multiple acres of land. At one point, Kase thought about how easier life would have been on the farm if this operation could build fences on his aunt and uncle's land.

As he moved around the field, so did the legend of the Dragon Slayer. It seemed like Tarkin and the rest of Ninety-Nine Problems were telling everyone about his heroics. The warriors were impressed, the Satyrs were thrilled, and even the Satyr kids were excited.

The workday ended, and all of the Satyrs and warriors headed back to the main village for dinner. It was dressed up like a giant, outdoor party instead of just a dinner gathering. There were students and Satyrs everywhere, all joined together to eat.

"Attention!" yelled Baby G from the other side of the gathering. He was standing on a stool once again, addressing the crowd.

Kase tried to look for the Liberati, but he couldn't find them.

"I would like to thank each and every one of you today, from the students, to the organizers, to even the young kids who helped out."

There were small cheers around the assembly.

"From the bottom of my heart, your effort is greatly appreciated. Please accept this food as a token of our gratitude. There are blankets beside the food table, and there are sleeping areas all over the village for students to gain cover for the night. Please get some rest, before we move ahead with more projects tomorrow. Thank you again, and enjoy the entertainment of the Pan-Flute Band!"

As soon as Baby G finished his speech, the band started to play some lively jigs in piping tones. There were five members, all ranging in size and subsequent pitch. Their music electrified the air with a touch of excitement as the rest of the crowd ate and mingled.

Kase kept looking for the Liberati, but the energetic Satyr kids were slowing him down. Their excitement was contagious, and he couldn't help but play with them.

"I'm the Dragon Slayer!" yelled one little kid excitedly.

"Be warned, Dragon Slayer," said Kase in a deep, monstrous voice, "because I am going to eat you!" He roared and chased the young kid. There were four children that were all playing with him: running, screaming, and pretending to battle the dragon. He had his arms extended over his head as if he were showing off his wings.

He chased the kids around and around the small area until one of them stabbed him with an imaginary sword. "I got you, dragon, I got you!" she said excitedly.

"Oh no." Kase clutched his heart. He spun around in a circle and fell to the ground. He closed his eyes, and pretended to die.

The kid knelt down beside him and stroked his messy hair. "Don't die dragon, I didn't mean to hurt you," she said innocently.

Kase rolled over and stood up while the kids giggled and got ready to battle again. "Oh, I'm not dead!" he said as he lifted his arms up again. "But this time, I am going to get you!"

They all screamed playfully and laughed as Kase ran about.

When he noticed Lenia watching them, he quickly stopped what he was doing. He ran his fingers through his hair. "Hey," he said casually, trying not to be embarrassed by his actions.

Two of the kids slammed into him, and clutched at his legs as Lenia approached. "We got you again, dragon." They giggled.

Lenia covered her mouth with her hand. Her eyes darted away to the right. Kase could tell she was enjoying his game, and he couldn't help but smile back as he shrugged innocently.

"Come on, Dragon Slayer," said the one kid. "Let's keep playing."

"I think I need to leave you for now." He shook his head and smirked at Lenia. "We'll play this game again tomorrow, okay?" He looked down at the kids and touched their hair gently, avoiding their small horns.

"Okay," the kids said sadly together. They backed away from Kase, and then giggled as they skipped together, yelling 'Dragon Slayer' on their way.

"That was so adorable!" Lenia said as he walked over.

"Those kids love the Dragon Slayer story." He laughed. "They're pretty cute though, don't you think?"

"You're cute." Lenia grabbed his hand again. She led him over to a table, where they met up with Cali and Talen, gathered some bread, fruit, nuts, and a couple blankets, and then found a spot outside of the crowded area to eat.

They all sat at the base of a tree that was in between a couple of mud huts and decided that it would be a good spot to grab some rest. They could still see the crowd and listen to the pan flutes. There were other groups of students that gathered in the same area, but each team kept to themselves.

As they ate, they all chatted about the events of the day. Kase told them of the fence-building project, and how Ninety-Nine Problems couldn't stop talking about the Dragon Slayer.

Lenia took some time talking about how she had snuck off with Cali, Talen, and the other scholars and sorted seeds, instead of building mud huts. She had used her trident in order to heat up some of the seeds and make popcorn.

They all laughed and joked about who would put Satyr butter on their popcorn, or even eat it at all. Kase was grossed out even thinking where Satyr butter came from, but he was excited to try some of the dry popcorn.

"I brought some extra seeds for you." Lenia grabbed her trident. She concentrated until the head was red hot, but not burning. She placed the seeds on top and waited until they transformed into white kernels. She caught them in her hand and gave them to Kase to try.

"Delicious!" he said after tasting the soft treat. "They probably would be better with butter though," he said jokingly. The Liberati all laughed. Lenia kept popping more seeds. They ate their popcorn happily, and when they were finished, decided to get some rest.

They used one blanket as a base, and then used the other to cover themselves. Lenia rested her head on Kase's chest. He put his arm around her to make her more comfortable, and held her gently.

He closed his eyes, smiled to himself, and fell asleep happily.

⁂

The next day was a lot like the first. Kase joined the warrior group with more fence building, and then helped with tilling the fields for seeding. The rest of the Liberati helped the seed maker by gathering the seeds they had picked the day before, and spreading them about.

It took everyone all morning, but the Satyrs and all the volunteers worked together to complete the projects the students had volunteered for.

After a late lunch, the Satyrs all thanked the students again and sent everyone on their way. With the hours logged for their team, the Liberati had officially completed Event Four.

"I'm a Dragon Slayer," yelled one of the kids. Kase was playing one last round of slay the dragon with his new friends, and was doing a good job of chasing them around the main area of the village.

The kid thrust his imaginary sword into Kase's leg. He fell down to the ground. "You got me again," he said as he tumbled.

"All right, Kase, we should probably get going," Cali was watching the last few groups leave the village of the Satyrs.

"Come on, Dragon Slayer," said Tarkin. His team was waiting for the Liberati to join them. "We need you by our side for the journey."

"Don't go, Dragon Slayer," said the cutest of the kids, tugging at his shirt. She looked at him with big, sad eyes. "Stay with us forever and protect us from the dragons."

Kase felt his heart melt. He looked down at her, then at the other kids gazing at him forlornly. He wished he didn't have to go. "I'm sure you can fight the dragons without me." Kase knelt down and put his hand on the kid's shoulder. "Here, take this to help you." He unhooked his sword from his belt. He held it in both hands and presented it to the young girl.

The kid's eyes grew wide, and her smile even wider. "You're giving me your sword?" she said excitedly.

"Make sure you take good care of it," Kase said with a smile. He let the kid take the sheathed weapon from his hands.

"The sword of the Dragon Slayer!" She held it in the air for all to see. The other kids gathered around and looked at it in wonder. She brought it back down and gave Kase a hug. He felt her arms clutch him with incredible strength, and knew that she was overjoyed with the gift. She held the sword high and ran off giggling, followed by all of her friends.

Kase stood up and sighed. "Goodbye," he said to no one in particular. He waved to the kid's retreating backs. He turned around to follow the rest of his team, but realized they were all standing there, staring at him.

"That was wonderful." Lenia put her hand over her heart and smiled.

Kase laughed. "It's not that big of a deal." He tried to avoid their heartfelt looks. "Sometimes, when you make a connection with another being, you have to let them go." He paused. "It can be hard. I just thought that would help."

"That's the most beautiful thing I've ever seen," admitted Tarkin. "You got me, Dragon Slayer. You got me good," he whispered.

The Liberati and Ninety-Nine Problems all headed back through the forest. They were sure to avoid the misty beach on the way to the barren land before the Skyland Grind. The warriors were the first to descend the Grind, followed by Cali and Talen, but Lenia stopped Kase before they continued farther. She grabbed both of his hands and looked up at him.

"This entire weekend was really wonderful," Lenia said. Her pretty green eyes met his. "Kase, there's been something I've wanted to tell you for a while." She looked down bashfully.

He could tell she was uncomfortable, so he tried to liven up the mood. "You have a neck design ready for me?" he said jokingly. He tried to make eye contact with her again.

"No." She chuckled, but kept her gaze down.

"You have a nickname for me? I mean, Dragon Slayer is pretty cool. I don't know how you're going to top it." He turned his head to get a better angle.

"No." She laughed some more.

He removed his hand from her grasp and gently nudged her chin up. She looked away, but her expression had changed. Kase didn't understand what was going on. All he saw was the fear in her eyes, and he wondered what had shocked her.

Before he had time to think about anything else, a dragon landed in the barren space beside them. A light dust puffed up from the ground in the impact of its landing.

It leaned its head down, spread its wings, and let out a low growl. One of its eyes was scabbed shut. There was no dagger, but rather fresh claw marks surrounding it instead. It looked like the dragon had removed it.

"Go," Kase said to Lenia. He kept his eyes on the dragon. He instinctively reached for his sword, but all he grabbed was empty space.

"Take this." Lenia handed him her black trident.

He looked her in the eyes as he accepted the weapon. "Go," he said, calmly and sternly.

She backed away steadily down the Skyland Grind, and he heard her calling for the other warriors.

He turned back towards the dragon, holding the trident in both hands. The dragon was snarling at him, studying him, waiting for him to move. The trident felt warm, and he felt it pulse in time with his heartbeat.

He lifted his head and stared back at the dragon. He took a step forward.

CHAPTER 14

Dragon Slayer

Everything was amplified. The air was crisper as it entered his lungs. The sunshine felt warmer. He stared at the dragon. His heart was beating hard, but slowly at the same time. Everything was slower.

The dragon took a snap at him, but Kase casually moved to the side. The dragon moved sluggishly, and he moved like lightning. It snapped at him again, but he easily slid to its other side. He could see the dragon start to breathe faster. He knew it was getting angrier.

The dragon reared its head back in frustration. It opened its mouth wide, and an orange glow formed in its throat. Instead of moving out of the way, Kase stood still and held the trident in front of him. He thought of Lenia, and how she made the fire dance on the first day they met. A large spray of fire came hurling out towards him.

Like a shield, the trident protected him from the hot flame. He stood his ground, and the fire flowed around him. The trident started to glow a hot white, and he could feel a greater heat grow inside of himself. It was strange, but comfortable. It felt like something he had known his whole life. The dragon stopped, but when it saw that Kase was unharmed, it became even more enraged.

It looked confused and angry. Kase pointed the glowing trident towards it, and a surge of light was released. The light hit the dragon in the chest and burned its scales. The dragon writhed in pain.

He fired another surge of light, and it backed away. He fired a third time, and it backed off even farther.

Instead of moving towards him, the dragon flapped its powerful wings and rose above the ground. Kase aimed the trident and fired another beam of light, but the dragon easily maneuvered around it. It was more agile in the air, and had a better advantage. It was ready for its counter attack. With a high swoop and a powerful thrust, it hurled itself towards Kase. It opened its mouth and screamed.

Kase stood his ground again and aimed the trident at the charging beast. A more powerful surge of light shot from the trident, and hit the dragon square.

Its eyes closed, and it went crashing to the ground, but its momentum carried its body forward. Kase didn't have anywhere to go. The dragon's body drove into him with enough bruising force to knock his breath away.

Both he and the dragon flew over the edge of Skyland.

They were tumbling through the air. The clouds were thick, but it wasn't long before Kase escaped them. He stared at the ground below. It looked like a quilt. There were green patches, yellow patches, and blue patches. It was getting closer. It wasn't going to be soft.

He turned his head and tried to find the Skyland Grind. He couldn't focus on a single island; he was moving too fast. He thought he might be able to reach one of them, but he was too far away. He turned to the other side. The dragon was tumbling and rolling through the air. He turned back to the ground. It was getting closer.

He closed his eyes. He felt calm, even though he was headed towards his demise. He thought about Cali, and how he wished he could have said goodbye. He thought about Talen, and how much she hid behind her blank expression. He thought about Lenia, and the fire in her beautiful, green eyes. He gripped the trident with both hands, and held it close to his heart. He wished he could see those eyes one last time.

He felt the wind disappear from around him. He opened his eyes, still looking down. He was standing, upright, on solid ground.

He wiggled his toes. He blinked a couple of times. His heart was still racing up in his throat.

"Dragon Slayer!" Tarkin yelled. He was leaning over the opposite edge of the island they were standing on. All of Ninety-Nine Problems and the rest of the Liberati were peering over the edge with their backs to Kase.

"Kase!" yelled Lenia. She took a step back and stared at the horizon. "Kase." She moved her hands to her face.

Kase didn't know if he was dreaming, or if he was dead already. He touched his body. It felt real. He wiggled his toes again. He blinked a few more times.

"He's not ..." said Cali in disbelief.

All was silent. Kase wanted to say something, but he couldn't find his voice.

"He can't be ..." Cali knelt down and leaned over the edge. "There's just no way ..."

"The odds of someone defeating a dragon, combined with enduring a drop from this kind of height are ..." Talen paused as she tried to figure out the probability.

"Shut up, Talen." Cali's voice quivered.

Kase gripped the trident and studied it. He couldn't explain the magic and power of it, but he could feel it. He felt stronger, confident, connected to everything around him.

"Of course he's not," said Tarkin reassuringly. He placed his hand on Cali's shoulder, who started to sob. "He's the Dragon Slayer." He kept looking at the ground below.

"It's all my fault," said Lenia in a soft voice. She cradled her head in her hands.

Kase felt his heart drop. He tested his legs, and when they didn't give beneath him, he took a few steps forwards. He knelt in front of her.

Slowly, she looked up and met his gaze. Tears streaked down her cheeks.

He held the trident out in front of him, and finally found his voice. "I think this belongs to you."

"Dragon Slayer!" Tarkin said as he turned.

"Dragoon!" the rest of Ninety-Nine Problems shouted.

Instead of accepting the trident, Lenia launched forward and wrapped her arms around him. He fell backwards to the ground. She held on tight and buried her head into his chest. She had him pinned, but he didn't mind.

"Kase, you idiot!" Cali exclaimed as she wiped her tears away. "How did you ..." she looked over the edge, then turned back to him. "Didn't you fall? What happened?"

Kase opened his eyes, but he wasn't ready to let go of his hug. "It all happened so fast," he replied. "Can you give me a minute?" he asked.

"Of course," Cali smiled.

"Let's go check out the dragon!" Tarkin nudged Brutus. Ninety-Nine Problems left the island and continued their descent of the Skyland Grind.

"C'mon, Talen." Cali gave Kase a wink. "Let's leave these two alone."

Cali and Talen disappeared down the steps. Kase and Lenia made their way to their feet. Kase held the trident in one hand, and wiped away a tear from Lenia's face with another.

"Kase, how ..." she paused. She looked down at the ground.

Before she could say anything else, Kase lifted the trident, held it in both hands, and closed his eyes. A white glow came from its head. He opened his eyes, and noticed that Lenia was shielding hers. The light faded into nothing.

"That's impossible," whispered Lenia. She looked shocked.

"I can't explain how it works." He gripped the trident tight and held it close to his body. "But I know that you understand the same thing that I do. You're the only one that understands. You know the power of it. You know how it feels."

"What happened?" asked Lenia with concern.

Kase handed the trident to her and walked to the edge of the island. The dragon was just a speck on the ground below, but it didn't appear to be moving. "I'll tell you on the way down." He sighed. "Let's go."

Their descent of the Skyland Grind passed quickly for Kase. He was still a little confused, but it all seemed to make sense to Lenia.

"That's amazing." Lenia held her trident tight. "You really are a super warrior. You're a wizard warrior! A wizzarior!"

Kase laughed. "No, I'm not," he replied. "I know we joke about it, but I'm a warrior. I was born a warrior. I have the strength and skills of a warrior. I'm nothing more."

"But what you described to me are the same kinds of things that I've learned by being a wizard," Lenia said. "You just experienced things that wizards take years to study, practice, and perfect. You even teleported! That's not exactly something warriors can do!"

Kase smiled at her excitement. "The power isn't from me," he said simply. "It's from the trident. It's by far the most powerful weapon I've ever used." He remembered how easy it was to summon the light, strong enough to hurt even a dragon. "But I fear that if anyone finds out what actually happened, and how I was able to use it, they would take it away from you. If it fell into the wrong hands," Kase paused. He thought of Mardious Hood, and the destruction he had caused with nothing but his own power; of how many people, including his grandparents, it had taken to defeat him. "It would be catastrophic," he added.

Lenia stopped and looked at her trident.

Kase moved to the edge and tried to see how far they were from the ground. They didn't have much farther to go. He could clearly see the dragon and the crowd that had gathered around it. It looked like some people were trying to keep others from getting too close. There were even a few horse-drawn carriages set up around it.

"I will make sure that nobody takes my trident away from me." Lenia held it tighter.

"Me too," Kase said, and smiled.

They descended the rest of the way and made it to ground level. The crowd around the dragon was chaotic. There were students hustling around, trying to get a better look. There were professors talking and taking notes. There were even some High Guardians of the Triple Crown walking around in their armor. They looked serious.

"There he is!" Tarkin said excitedly. He pointed at Kase. "The Dragon Slayer!"

Everyone turned to look at him, and a hush fell over the crowd. One of the High Guardians stepped forward. "You are Kase Garrick?" he asked in a stern, low voice.

"Yes," Kase said hesitantly.

"Come with us," he ordered. The Guardian turned his back and headed to one of the carriages.

Kase looked back at Lenia. She moved the trident behind her back, and took a few steps away to blend into the crowd. He breathed a sigh of relief, and then followed the High Guardian.

"Dragon Slayer!" shouted Tarkin from the edge of the crowd. He and the rest of Ninety-Nine Problems started cheering. Cali and Talen were clapping too, and had proud smiles on their faces. Other students joined in, and then the whole crowd erupted with excitement. Chants of 'Dragon Slayer' came alive.

He nodded in recognition and tried to keep cool as he strutted towards the carriage. He climbed aboard the back, and looked around at all the mayhem around him. Some of the Guardians were moving the crowd away from the dragon, while others were tying it up and getting ready to move it with the other carriages. He wondered why they were trying to transport the dead monster, and just how they were going to accomplish such.

Four other Guardians joined him on the back of the carriage, and they started to ride off. "Where are we going?" he asked.

"The Triple Crown has requested a meeting with you, Kase Garrick," responded the first Guardian. "They want to know how *you* single-handedly killed one of the most dangerous creatures in the realm." His expression implied that he didn't believe much in the possibility.

Kase sunk over when he realized that he didn't know what he was going to say. The Triple Crown was not going to be as excited as the crowd was, so some detail would have to be provided on how he actually slayed the dragon. He would have to think of something quickly so that he could protect the trident, and with it, Lenia.

⁂

"So, let me get this straight," said Sheeze, the High Scholar. "The dragon swallowed your sword and choked to death?"

"Yes, sir," replied Kase confidently. He was standing in the Great Hall, in front of the three Members of the Triple Crown. There were a few other warriors, all Guardians, standing guard at the entrance to the hall, but they weren't involved in the questioning.

The Triple Crown members were each sitting on large thrones atop a pulpit at the head of the room. The high walls around them were decorated with the most beautiful tapestries and statues that Kase had ever seen.

"He's lying," said Zuke, the High Wizard. The moment Kase had entered the Grand Hall for questioning, Zuke's spiteful gaze had not left him. He continuously snickered through Kase's recounting of the day's events. "A dragon cannot be killed by choking on a sword," he retorted.

"We don't really know that, do we?" replied Sheeze. "Just because it has never happened before, does not mean that it cannot be true. What kind of sword was it?" he asked Kase.

"The sword belonged to my grandfather," Kase lied again. "His name was Roman Garrick."

"We know who your grandfather was," said Mac, the High Warrior. "He was a great warrior, and served the realm well. I have no doubt that his sword was worthy of killing a dragon. I can see a lot of similarities between you and him; perhaps his spirit lives on inside you. I believe that you are, in fact, very capable of killing a dragon, Kase Garrick."

"Thank you, sir." Kase nodded towards Mac. He was trying to hide his smile. He was proud to be recognized by the highest of all warriors in the realm, and all the more so to be compared to his grandfather.

"However," continued Mac sternly, "I don't believe that you killed *this* dragon."

"What?" Kase said in confusion.

"I don't think you killed this dragon," repeated Mac. "I believe that you stumbled upon a dragon that was already dead, and claimed to have killed it, in order to make yourself seem like a righteous warrior. It appears that you were in the right place at the right time, and tried to capitalize on the death of a famed monster."

He paused purposefully, meeting Kase's eyes. "The Triple Crown appreciates your true confession: that you had no part in the killing of this dragon, or any other. We expect your full cooperation here today, in order to bring clarity, and with it, justice, to the events that just transpired."

"But," Kase said, "I did kill the dragon. I am a righteous warrior." A lot of things raced through his mind. On the one hand, he was already lying to the Triple Crown about what happened. On the other, it now seemed like they wanted him to tell a different set of lies in order to discredit himself.

"Simply preposterous," muttered Zuke, seemingly disgusted with Mac's account.

"Look, Kase," said Sheeze in a soft tone. "Dragons are an endangered species, and the law protects them from being hunted in their Skyland sanctuary. We don't believe you killed this dragon maliciously, so we're trying to help you avoid punishment."

Sheeze paused. "We're also trying to avoid word spreading of this improbable situation, because it might cause a bit of a stir. It will give false hope to poachers. It will bring unneeded fear to the innocent. Great debates will start, and politics and policies will be addressed for no good reason at all. In short, it will cause more harm than good."

"You are a great young warrior, Kase Garrick, and we look forward to you continuing your training at The Academy," Mac added. "Thank you for sharing your story, but I'm afraid that we are going to have to … massage the details a little in order to protect those of the realm. Let me ask you something. Are there people in your life that you care about? Family? Friends? Your teammates?"

"Yes." Kase thought about Lenia and her trident.

"Now take the handful of people that you care about, and replace them with everyone in the realm." Sheeze smiled warmly. "If you treated the people you care about with the same respect and love that you treat everyone, then you know what we must do. As the Triple Crown, we love the entire realm. Do you understand why we must do this?"

"This is outrageous!" exclaimed Zuke. "The realm deserves to know the truth, one way or another. You cannot protect the realm from the truth. Tell me Kase"—Zuke clenched his teeth as he said Kase's last name—"Garrick. Tell me how you really defeated the dragon."

Kase looked down for a moment, and then up at Sheeze. "I didn't kill the dragon," he said in a sombre tone. "I made the whole thing up."

Zuke sneered, and glanced at the other two members of the Triple Crown with the eyes of a madman. They refused to meet his gaze. Slowly, he stood from his chair, and stalked out of the Great Hall.

"You are an outstanding individual, Kase." Sheeze nodded towards him.

"Your grandfather would be very proud of you." Mac also nodded in respect. "When you are finished at The Academy, I will personally make sure that, should you wish it, you have a position of honour among the High Guardians," he vowed.

It was a great privilege that Mac had just bestowed upon Kase, but he didn't even care at that point. He knew that his lies had gotten him into a dishonourable position, and although more lies would protect the ones he cared about, it would ruin his own reputation. He knew that Mac and Sheeze were right, but he had also hoped that there would be some better solution available.

"Thank you." Kase nodded to the two members of the Triple Crown. "You are too kind."

Sheeze stood. "I shouldn't have to tell you this, Kase, but please keep this conversation between us. We wouldn't want anyone else causing a stir, or getting into danger, because of these proceedings."

He waited for Kase to nod in agreement. "These warriors will escort you back to The Academy and make sure you arrive safe." Sheeze motioned for them to take Kase away.

Kase's stomach felt uneasy. Everything seemed so complicated, now. He exited the Great Hall and headed back to The Academy.

CHAPTER 15

Graveyards

"Hey, Dragon's Liar!" said a student mockingly as he passed by Kase.

"Get out of here!" yelled Cali, and she stared him down.

Cali, Talen, and Kase were all waiting in the common area for Lenia so that they could read Event Five together.

"Don't worry about him, Kase; he's a jerk!" she yelled loud enough for the student to hear.

"The name doesn't even make sense, grammatically." Talen glared right along with Cali.

Kase just stared at the ground. It had been a long week for him. Word had spread of his encounter with the dragon. Instead of being heralded as a hero, he was made fun of for being a coward. Instead of calling him the Dragon Slayer, they had started calling him Dragon's Liar.

Even his friends within the warrior school had made their disappointment in him known, and excluded him from some of the team projects. The few times he had seen them, Tarkin and the rest of Ninety-Nine Problems looked at him in confusion. They, at least, weren't calling him a liar.

Although he knew the truth, and kept reminding himself that he was showing his nobility to the Triple Crown, it was still hard for him to be at The Academy.

"Hey, sorry I'm late," Lenia said as she approached. She stood beside him, but he didn't look up at her. He didn't want to see any sympathy, or pity, in her eyes.

"Where's your trident?" asked Cali.

"I decided to leave it behind for this event." She grabbed Kase's hand.

He calmly let go, moved his arm away, and kept staring at the ground. He felt his heart cave in a little bit.

Cali saw him move his arm away from Lenia, and called him out on it. "Hey!" she yelled.

He still looked at the ground.

"Look, Kase," she continued. "I don't know exactly what happened between you and the dragon, and I don't know what happened with you and the Triple Crown, but we all know what happened to all of us up there. We saw my brother, our teammate, not hesitate to fight an enormous monster. Talen, what is the probability of a person defeating a dragon?"

"Defeating a dragon with a dagger, or with a trident?" Talen asked. "Because the probabilities vary based on reach, piercing power—"

Cali gave Talen a confused look, and huffed. "It's practically impossible!" she interrupted. "We witnessed the impossible happen, and despite what everyone else says, we know that you are a true, honest, and brave warrior. We know that you put others' safety above your own, and have the integrity to stand tall against all odds. You are a wonderful teammate, an unbelievable friend, and above all, the best brother a girl could ever ask for."

Her voice quivered. "Don't let these fools affect you. Don't let them change you. Don't let them cause you to become closed off to us!"

Kase looked up and into Cali's watery eyes. He turned towards Talen, who was stone cold, as always. He grabbed Lenia's hand and met her hopeful gaze and beautiful smile. All the doubt and confusion that encircled his mind eased. He didn't instantly feel better, but it was a good start.

"Give me the sage mirror," he said.

"He's back!" exclaimed Cali, and she handed it over.

"Dragon Slayer!" exclaimed Talen.

Kase shot her a look.

"Too soon?" she asked.

"Please don't call me that," Kase said with a laugh. "We'll have to think of a better nickname."

"Well, super warrior, maybe we'll discover a good one when we complete Event Five?" Lenia squeezed his hand tight.

"Maybe, super wizard." He smiled at her. "Mirror, mirror, show us the details of Quest Series Event Five." The mirror swirled, and he read the revealed text out loud.

"Stone by day, alive by night. This defines the life of the gargoyle. It is said that gargoyles listen to the prayers of the living when they are stone, and then speak to the souls of the dead at night. Although their intentions and way of life are generally unknown, many are studying their current behaviours in order to better understand their true nature."

"'True nature'?" Lenia asked. "Aren't they stone?"

"The creatures gargoyles, not the architectural decorations," Cali put in.

"Yeah—aren't they stone?"

Cali sighed.

Kase shook his head and continued. "Some professors of the scholar castle have been studying the migrating patterns of gargoyles. An experiment was conducted whereby prayers were written on tiny scrolls and attached to the legs of the creatures, rather than being spoken aloud. The gargoyles were then released to freely roam the realm.

"Teams are to venture out and recover the tiny scrolls. Once found, use your sage mirror to capture your image and note where you are, in order to help the professors document migrating locations. Return all scrolls back to your sponsoring professor to verify the legitimacy of the passage on the scroll, and submit it to the Quest Series officials. The team that retrieves the most scrolls will obtain the most points."

Lenia nodded confidently. "Collecting paper—we can do that."

There was one final line of advice. "Sometimes in order to talk to angels, you must first sound like angels." Kase let out a deep sigh as he gathered himself.

"Hey, it's the Dragon's Liar!" screamed one of the students from across the yard. Kase looked down at the ground again.

"Wow," said Cali, ignoring the hater. "They really left this one open."

"What do you mean?" asked Lenia inquisitively, also trying to ignore the bully.

"The gargoyles could really be anywhere," replied Cali. "And we won't even be able to try and find them until nightfall. This event is really a game-changer."

"How should we start, then?" asked Lenia. They all looked at Kase, as if waiting for him to take the lead, but he just shook his head and stared at the ground.

Cali walked over to him and wrapped her arms around his waist, giving him the biggest hug she could. Lenia, who was still holding his hand, wrapped her arms around them both to form a group hug. Seconds later, he felt Talen's tiny arms wrap halfway around his waist on the outside edge of their giant hug ball.

"To the library," said Kase, who could barely speak he was being squeezed so hard.

The three girls cheered in unison, and they all disengaged. The Liberati headed to the scholar castle. Lenia and Kase were still holding hands, and walking at a slower pace than Talen and Cali.

When they were out of earshot, she spoke softly to him. "Kase, I'm sorry." She sighed. "This week, you—"

"Can we just not talk for a while?" he asked. "I've had a rough week, and I just want to be alone with my thoughts for now."

Lenia looked down, released his hand from her grasp, and slumped forward a little.

He looked over and clutched her hand quickly. "Don't let go," he said softly. He was going through a lot, and he needed the strongest person he knew by his side.

"Never." She tightened her grip. They continued on in silence, following Cali and Talen to the library.

⁂

"Is this really what gargoyles look like?" Lenia flipped through a book of magical creatures. She showed the open page to Cali for verification.

"Yes," confirmed Cali. "They kind of look like miniature goblins, but with wings."

"I think they kind of look like hairless monkeys," replied Talen. "But with wings," she added.

"I think that one looks like Niveous," said Kase with a smirk. "But with wings."

"I mean"—Lenia darted her eyes to the left with a smile—"how are we going to tell them apart? If I see him, I'm going to have to check out his leg for a tiny scroll."

They all laughed. It felt good to laugh again.

"So, how are we going to tell them apart," asked Kase. "Like, actually? Some of these places will have stone gargoyles, and some of them will have real ones."

"We won't really know," admitted Cali as she continued working on her map. "That's the limiting factor in this challenge. We might find wild gargoyles that don't have a scroll. We might find statues that look

205

like them, but aren't gargoyles at all. We'll just have to try and guess which areas are going to be the best for finding them, and keep our eyes open for anything that moves."

"What areas are we going to try and look in?" asked Lenia.

"Talen," said Cali as she stood up. "Can you explain the plan to these two? I'm going to go grab another book."

"Absolutely." Talen put down her map. "During the day, gargoyles want to sleep peacefully, so they choose areas where they can blend in to rest. This means that their natural habitat is usually close to mountains or caves: places that are made of stone. Once they wake up at night, they have the ability to travel to different areas and hunt for food.

"Because of the strong beliefs of many people, monuments have been erected in cities to act as prayer centres for the faithful. Stone monuments help gargoyles blend into their surroundings, and so they will frequent the area to deliver prayers to the dead when they awake for the night. Therefore, our target will be areas that have monuments for gargoyles: specifically, graveyards."

Kase frowned. "Graveyards?"

"Graveyards have a high concentration of different statues, many of which look like gargoyles," Talen explained. "The key to our success will be to try and identify which statues are gargoyles, and which ones are just statues. Once darkness falls, we will only have a short time to try and capture the scrolls; otherwise, the gargoyles will just disappear into the night, stopping in a different location for the next day."

"That sounds like a great plan," said Lenia, who still looked concerned. "But how are we going to identify which are statues and which are gargoyles?"

"We just have to look for statues that have a scroll on their leg," responded Talen confidently.

"Can't we just remove the scrolls when they're statues then?" asked Kase, not really understanding what the plan was.

"When a gargoyle turns to stone, everything it touches also turns to stone," Talen responded. "That means that the scroll will likely be stone, just like the rest of the gargoyle during the day, and will turn back to normal at night."

"So how are we going to get the scrolls then?" asked Kase.

"The clue comes from the last line in the instructions," said Talen. "'In order to talk to angels, you must sound like angels.' It's referring to song. Gargoyles respond well to singing, so that is how we're going to get the scrolls."

"Who's singing?" said Lenia as she looked at Kase with hopeful eyes.

"Not me," said Talen sheepishly. "I don't sing."

"It's okay," said Kase confidently. "I got it. Check it," he said as he brought his hands up to his lips. He started to make rhythmic drum sounds, while he bobbed his head.

He stopped his beat, opened his mouth, and started with his favourite song. "I ..." he said, but then quickly stopped. His voice had cracked as if he'd just hit puberty.

Lenia and Talen burst out laughing. Lenia was trying to fight the tears as she grabbed her stomach. Talen was laughing so hard she literally fell out of her chair.

Kase cleared his throat. "Sorry, let me start over." He tried to get his confidence back.

"That was too good." Lenia wiped away the tears from her eyes.

Talen picked herself off the floor. "Please do that again!"

"You know what," Kase said with a sarcastic smile. "I think I'll save the next show for the gargoyles. I clearly don't need any more practice, so you'll just have to wait for the main event."

"I can't wait!" Lenia said. "My turn though." She sat up straight and cleared her throat. "Check it!" she said mockingly. She started making a beat like he had, but it sounded weird, because she couldn't hide her giggling. She stopped the beat, sat up straight, and looked Kase in the eye. "I …" She made her voice crack.

Lenia and Talen burst into laughter again, but Kase rolled his eyes. He knew he set himself up for that one, but shook his head and pretended to be really upset.

"I'm sorry," Lenia said as she laughed. "I just couldn't help myself."

"You're a jerk," Kase said playfully. He wrapped his arms around her in a quick embrace.

"What did I miss?" Cali returned to the table, holding four cups of steaming hot chocolate.

Lenia turned her head to look at Cali. "Who are those for?"

"Sometimes when my brother was feeling down, our aunt would make us hot chocolate." Cali set the first mug in front of Kase. "She made her own special blend of cocoa powder and mixed it with hot water. It was, and is, the best hot chocolate I've ever had. She ended up sending me some in the care package that you brought for me, Kase. I was saving it for a special occasion, and today seemed like the day."

She smiled at her brother, and handed a cup to each other person in the group. Sipping the cocoa together, each one of them felt a little warmer and happier inside.

For the rest of the night, they all sipped on their hot chocolate, teased Kase's singing ability, and made their plans for hunting gargoyles the next day.

⁂

In the morning, the Liberati met at their usual early time. Their plan was to check a few graveyards in the same area, to increase their chances of finding a scroll. Since Talen was from the capital city of Kimroad, and knew the area well, they decided to start there. She knew of three different graveyards in the same vicinity, so it was the perfect starting point for their quest.

They packed a sac like they had for every other event. Kase had a new dagger strapped to his belt, while Lenia showed up with something new as well.

"Where's your trident?" asked Cali.

"I didn't think we needed it for this event." Lenia shrugged her shoulders.

"We're going to a graveyard, at night, and don't need a magical fire-starter to help us on our quest?" Cali asked sarcastically.

Lenia laughed. "It's just a little bulky to carry." She looked at Kase. He knew that she left it because of its power, and since they were going to the capital, potentially with lots of witnesses, he was glad that she didn't bring it along.

"But I did think of something that can help us." She reached into her pocket and pulled out four fire-starters. She picked up the first one; it had something carved into its handle. "Here, Talen; this one is for you."

Talen was shocked at the gesture. "I don't think I've ever had a friend give me a gift before," she mumbled. She saw the carving. "It's got a shark on it! I love it!" she said in a high-pitched squeal. She held it close to her face and closed her eyes.

When she opened them, there were awkward stares from the rest of the Liberati directed at her. "Thank you so much." She cleared her throat and looked down.

"You're very welcome, Talen." Lenia reached for another fire starter. This one had multiple clouds etched into it. "Here, Cali; this one is yours."

Cali accepted it graciously. "You didn't have to do this." She smiled. "I might not be as excited as Talen, but I really appreciate it. Thank you," she said sincerely. Everyone chuckled.

Lenia grabbed another fire starter and gave it to Kase. "This one is for you." She looked up into his brown eyes. It had a trident carved into its handle.

"This is the coolest thing anyone has ever given me," he said with a smile.

"It matches mine." Lenia held hers up, too. "Now, we're ready to go!" She turned back to Talen and Cali. Both of them were playing with their fire starters. Turning them on. Turning them off. Turning them on again.

"Can you believe these two?" she said to Kase. She looked back at him. He, too, was playing with his fire starter. He looked up at her, and then glanced at Talen and Cali.

"Unbelievable," he said. He shook his head and put his fire starter in his pocket. They both giggled. He put his arm around her, and they started off towards the portal gate.

Talen and Cali both followed, not really paying attention to anything but the fire in their hands.

Because of the large population, Kimroad had a lot of different portal gates within its boundaries. It was not uncommon for cities to have an array of portals compared to the country, where the young travellers had been accustomed to travelling over the last few weeks. People in the big city needed fast transportation for their livelihoods, at least in comparison to travellers in the rest of the realm. The portal door that the Liberati chose to enter was on the upper-east side of the city.

As soon as they set foot in the capital, Kase's eyes fell on the distant castle located in the middle of the city. He felt crushed. He held Lenia closer, and stared at the place that had changed his life just a few days before.

"Should we turn back?" she asked cautiously. "Maybe we should go to another city?"

Cali and Talen also looked at Kase when they realized the affect that the castle had on him, and awaited his answer.

"No, let's stick to the plan." He sighed and faked a smile. The Liberati all appreciated his strength, and they moved forward.

It didn't take them long to find the first graveyard. They entered the gate, and saw rows upon rows of tombstones. Each of them had different engravings; some had flowers around them, and others had statues. There were bare trees spread throughout the area, which gave the graveyard a spooky look, even though the sun was shining bright.

"Do we have to check out every statue?" Kase asked. He was surprised at how many of them were scattered throughout the park.

"Yes," confirmed Cali. "But if we all split up, we can get through it much faster!" she added enthusiastically.

The Liberati took their time looking through the first graveyard. They carefully studied each statue, and gingerly stepped around the tombstones. Although they were meticulous, they were unable to find a single statue with a small scroll on its leg.

They were not discouraged, however, and they made their way to the second graveyard. There were fewer statues at this one, and although they took extra care, their luck did not change.

They entered the third graveyard with less hope, but were still determined.

"I think I found one!" yelled Kase, having studied the leg of one of the statues. He touched the protrusion, but realized that it was just a small branch that had fallen perfectly. He brushed it off in disappointment as the others had raced over.

"You found one!" Lenia said excitedly as she approached. She was the first to get to him, since Talen and Cali were further in.

"No, it's just another statue," he said dishearteningly.

"They all look the same, don't they?" Lenia put her arm on his shoulder.

"They really do!" he replied. "Except for this one." He pointed next to her. "This one looks like a baby gargoyle. It's perhaps the ugliest baby I've ever seen."

"No, wait!" Lenia said as she peered closer. "There's something on its leg!" she said excitedly.

Lenia and Kase both stared at the baby gargoyle, and, sure enough, it appeared to have a tiny scroll attached to its miniature limb. As Cali and Talen approached, they all took a good look at it together.

"Yes!" exclaimed Cali. "That's definitely a scroll! Well done, Kase!"

"Well, I ..." He looked down at Lenia.

"This deserves a break!" Cali interrupted. "Let's all set up here and have a snack."

"What do we do after that?" Kase dropped the sac to the ground.

"We wait until nightfall." Cali pulled out some food and water they had packed earlier. The Liberati laid a blanket down near the tombstone, so as to not disturb any of the graves around it, and rested until nightfall. They had some snacks and drinks, told stories, played the cloud game, and enjoyed the sunshine.

Before night was upon them completely, the Liberati packed up their sac and set it next to the tombstone that the baby gargoyle was on. They surrounded it on all sides and waited for it to reveal itself.

"So, as soon as it appears, I just start singing?" asked Lenia.

"That's right," assured Cali. "Then, we try and take the scroll while you serenade it with your song."

As soon as Cali finished, the baby gargoyle's eyes started to glow. The white light illuminated the Liberati's faces, and then the eye colour changed to a rosy red. The grey stone of the statue melted away, revealing the black, leather-like skin of the gargoyle.

The baby gargoyle shook its head and looked at the Liberati. Its eyes grew soft. Its face seemed to pout.

"It's so cute!" said Lenia, lost by its adorableness.

"I just want to hold it!" said Cali, who also made a pouty face.

"I don't like this." Kase kept a watchful eye on it, making sure to not miss any of its movements.

"Come here, little guy." Lenia reached her hand out to pet the baby.

As soon as her hand was close enough to its face, it opened its mouth and bit her. She screamed.

The baby gargoyle let go of her hand and seemed to laugh. It spread its wings and fluttered them in order to fly away, but Kase grabbed it. "Quickly, let's get the scroll!" he said as he wrestled it to the ground. For a tiny baby, it was incredibly strong.

The gargoyle started to scream wildly. When he had it pinned, Cali knelt down and tried to grab the tiny scroll from its leg. Lenia was shaking her hand, trying to get the pain to subside.

"Can you get it?" asked Kase.

"I think so," said Cali. "Just keep holding it!"

"Uh oh," said Talen softly. She was staring at the trees. "We're not alone."

The baby screamed again.

"Do you have it yet?" said Kase angrily.

"We need to get out of here!" said Talen loudly.

"Oh no." Lenia had followed Talen's gaze.

"Got it!" Cali held the scroll up in victory.

Before Kase had a chance to let the baby go, a claw scraped the top of his head. He quickly looked up and saw the back end of a gargoyle fly into the night sky. He moved his hand and reached back. There didn't seem to be any blood, but his head was still hurting. The baby got up on its feet, growled at Kase, and then flew up into the trees.

Kase turned back to the rest of the Liberati. Cali and Lenia looked horrified, staring up at the tree. Talen was nowhere to be found. He slowly turned and saw that the branches were filled with dozens of red, glowing eyes.

Before the Liberati could react, the gargoyles started swooping down at them. Lenia and Cali screamed while the flying goblins scratched their skin with their sharp claws, messed their hair with their stubby fingers, and knocked them around with their stout bodies.

"This is a nightmare!" yelled Lenia. One of the gargoyles knocked her to the ground. She helplessly curled into a fetal position.

"Well, what do we do?" shouted Kase. He had taken out his dagger and was swinging wildly. He couldn't see where the gargoyles were coming from, or where they were going, so he didn't hit anything with his uncontrolled swipes.

Cali had her face covered, and was flicking her fire starter in a hopeless attempt to scare the gargoyles away. She started singing. She didn't have a great voice, but she was belting it out confidently. She even started to dance, but the gargoyles kept swooping and swiping.

"That's making it worse!" shouted Kase.

"My ears are bleeding!" screamed Lenia from where she was lying.

Cali's poor choice of song was quickly drowned out by the most beautiful voice that the three Liberati had ever heard. The voice was not singing any words; it simply moved from note to note in a heartwarming kind of way. The wonderful voice made time stand still, as everyone and everything stopped what they were doing to listen.

Talen calmly sang in the moonlight. She was standing on top of one of the tombstones, reaching notes that Kase didn't even think were possible to hit. Her angelic tone was mesmerizing.

The gargoyles swooped softly down from the tree and gathered around her. They sat down in front of the tombstone like children listening to a bedtime story. One of the gargoyles landed at Kase's feet. It reached up, grabbed his hand, and led him to where the others were seated so they all could listen to Talen sing.

Cali and Lenia were also welcomed and guided by the gargoyles to enjoy the melodic entertainment. As Lenia sat down, she looked over at Kase and smiled. He was holding the baby gargoyle that he had been wrestling with moments before.

Everyone got comfortable, and Talen moved from the top of the tombstone down to the ground. She broke into a lyrical song. The gargoyles started swaying peacefully.

As she was singing, Talen went through the crowd of gargoyles and looked for more scrolls. They were all docile because of her serenade. She found four more prayer-carrying gargoyles, and easily removed their scrolls.

When she was done her song, all the gargoyles rejoiced. They smiled at the Liberati and bobbed their heads up and down in excitement. They seemed satisfied with Talen's performance. They flew away while Kase, Lenia, and Cali were still sitting on the ground, awestruck.

"I thought you didn't sing?" said Lenia slyly.

Talen blushed. "My parents made me take singing lessons when I was younger. I loved it, but I don't like to perform. It's just a little embarrassing, that's all," she replied with a smile.

"You have the most beautiful voice I've ever heard!" exclaimed Cali. Talen's smile brightened.

The Liberati had obtained five scrolls, and all rejoiced at their accomplishment. They counted their scratches and bruises from their miniature battle, and then laughed at themselves, since none of them were seriously hurt.

Lenia spent some time healing the small wounds, and then the battle-tested Liberati gathered their things and headed back to The Academy.

For the rest of the week, they continued to search different graveyards at dusk. With Talen's beautiful voice serenading the gargoyles, it was easy for them to remove the scrolls. On the last night before the event was over, they took all twenty-three scrolls they found to Professor Bright to verify.

"We're going to win this event for sure!" exclaimed Cali. "And it's all thanks to Talen!"

Talen blushed as the rest of the Liberati cheered. They were all sitting in Professor Bright's classroom at one of the tables, while the professor was checking the scrolls against her own marking list supplied by the Quest Series officials.

When she was finished, she slowly approached the Liberati. "Some of these don't match," she said with a questioning tone.

The Liberati all looked shocked.

"I only count seventeen as being legitimate prayers. Are you sure you got all of these from gargoyles?" she asked politely.

Before any of the Liberati could answer, Kase broke in. "What are you saying, professor?" he said in disgust. "That we're all liars?" All the teasing from the last two weeks came crashing down on him, like a weight pressing down on his shoulders.

"I was just asking a general question, Kase," she replied softly. "I'm sorry about the rumors going around The Academy about you."

"You're sorry?" said Kase. "You're sorry?" he repeated again, louder. "I know what you're thinking, and you don't have to dance around the obvious. You're sorry. Lenia's sorry. Everyone here is sorry. You know what? I'm sorry. I'm sorry that you feel bad. I'm sorry that you have to worry about what you say around me. I'm sorry that you have to be around such a pathetic, cowardly warrior like the Dragon's Liar!" Kase got up from his chair and stormed towards the door.

"Kase, wait!" said Professor Bright. "You don't have to lie to us. You can tell us the truth."

"Kase!" yelled Cali, but he kept moving through the room, trying to escape everyone around him.

"Kase, stop!" Lenia said sternly.

He stopped just as he reached the doorway. He put his hand on the frame and tilted his head back to listen, but didn't look back.

"You told me not to let you go," she said. "So I'm not going to let you let *us* go, either."

Kase dropped his hand from the door and slumped forward.

"The world is a cruel place sometimes," Lenia continued. "But not everyone is cruel. There are people that you can count on, and trust with the truth. There are people that care about you, and truly know you. There are people who have your back, no matter what."

Kase looked down the empty hallway. He knew where it led. It was a lonely path, one that he didn't want to take. He turned, locked eyes with Lenia, and slowly relaxed. He had to let go of the doubt that clutched at his soul.

He walked back delicately to the table. "I'm just afraid to tell you all what happened. I was warned not to, and I don't want to burden you with everything. I also don't want to put you in any kind of danger."

"You won't burden us." Cali smiled softly.

"We understand you, Kase," said Talen, who smiled too.

"Danger is my maiden name," chimed in Professor Bright.

"We're in this together." Lenia grabbed his hand.

Kase sat back down and took a deep breath. He felt safe. He told the Liberati everything.

CHAPTER 16

The Winners Hierarchy of Outstanding Performance

K ase was relieved after he finished telling his story. It felt good to tell those he trusted about his experience. He felt secure. "You teleported?" asked Cali with a raised eyebrow.

"Yes," replied Kase.

"And you were able to use the power of Lenia's trident?" asked an excited Talen. "Can I try it?"

"Where is it?" Kase stared at Lenia.

"I hid it," she replied honestly. "Don't worry; it's in a safe place."

"Can you show us?" Cali asked in a serious tone.

Every member of the Liberati looked at Professor Bright for approval. She was sitting down, not looking at anyone, trying to assess the situation. She had been awfully quiet through Kase's narrative.

"Professor Bright?" Lenia said in a concerned tone, trying to get her attention.

The professor looked up. She shook her head as she brought herself back to reality. "Yes, let's see the power of the trident," she said with a nod. "Can you go get it for us?"

Lenia confidently got up and walked across the room. "I realized that if someone found out about its power, they would come to me to look for it. I didn't want to keep it out in the open, or on my person, so I decided to hide it in a safe place."

She walked to the end of one of the classroom's bookcases. She grabbed the edge of it and leaned back, so that it gently moved away from the wall. After she was satisfied, she reached behind and grabbed her trident. She held it in front of her for a second, admiring its beauty. She turned to the Liberati and Professor Bright, and the head of the trident caught ablaze.

"Cool!" Talen brought her hands up to her face in excitement.

"Lenia!" exclaimed Professor Bright. "That's amazing!"

"You should see it underwater." Lenia grinned. Professor Bright's mouth opened wider. The fire stopped as Lenia walked over and handed it to Kase. "Your turn."

Kase stood up and gripped the trident firmly.

Talen, Cali, and Professor Bright all leaned on the edge of their seats.

He closed his eyes to better feel the power of the trident flow through him, and a brilliant white light started to shine from its head. Everyone in the room shielded themselves from the brightness. Kase opened his eyes, and slowly the light faded into nothingness.

"Cooler!" said Talen under her breath as she stared at the magic warrior.

"Kase, that's ..." said Cali as she shook her head in awe. "Who are you? What are you?" It made Kase feel proud, but a little confused.

"Can I see it?" said Professor Bright as she reached out her hand.

Kase looked at Lenia, and then handed the trident over.

The professor gripped it with both hands and studied it with a quizzical eye. She held it out in front of her, and closed her eyes. The Liberati stared at the trident and the powerful professor, but nothing happened.

Professor Bright opened her eyes. "I don't feel anything." She studied Lenia and Kase, but looked confused.

"Can I try?" asked Talen. Professor Bright handed the trident to the scholar, but kept staring at Lenia and Kase.

Talen cradled the trident and closed her eyes. After a few silent moments, she peeked her eyes open and pointed it at Kase. "Rooooaaaarrr," she said as she jabbed it in his direction.

All of the Liberati burst into laughter, including the professor.

"I think it's broken." Talen sighed. "Boosh, boosh." She waved it from side to side, but still nothing happened.

"You're going to hurt somebody." Cali grabbed the trident from Talen. The Liberati all laughed again. Cali held it in her own hands, but instead of trying to use it, she gave it back to Lenia. "This power is obviously meant for the two of you. I don't know how it works, and I don't know why it works, but I know that it belongs with you."

"Thank you, Cali," said Lenia. "Professor?" she said with hopeful eyes. "What do you think?"

"Truthfully," replied Professor Bright, "I have no idea how this works, what it means, or what we should do now. What you've told me, what you've shown me, is remarkable. I am amazed at what you have discovered from your adventures. But as amazing as it is, I'm not surprised."

Professor Bright stood up and smiled at the Liberati as she continued. "The idea of the Quest Series—the essence of it all—is to bring out the best in students, to showcase their talents. I like to be involved in the Quest Series to help students reach their potential, but I knew from the beginning that this team was beyond anything that I had seen before.

"Cali, your leadership in keeping this team together, even though you all come from different backgrounds, is admirable. You have a logical understanding of the realm, but the things you don't understand aren't disregarded easily: you try to find a way to define them, and accept them. By keeping a scholar, wizard, and warrior on the same path, you have demonstrated the ability to be a truly great leader.

"Talen, your thirst and retention for knowledge is unparalleled. You are already wise beyond your years, and you have demonstrated the ability to continually learn and apply your knowledge. Your intelligence will only lead you down a path of great discovery and innovation. I believe you will help take this realm into new and wonderful places.

"Lenia, your power is even stronger than what you have demonstrated in my classroom. Most wizards are limited by their own doubts and lack of vision, but it seems to me that you're breaking through boundaries. This trident is a demonstration of how you're able to connect to the realm, connect to other magical creatures, and connect with other people. I am proud to call you a pupil, but I cannot wait for the day when I can call you a colleague and a friend, because I know that you will become one of the most powerful wizards the realm has ever seen.

"Kase, you are a strong, courageous, and caring individual. You have said that all you want to do is try to be a great warrior, but let me be the first to tell you that you don't have to try anymore. You already are one. You have stood tall against all sorts of unimaginable circumstances. I feel honoured to be in the presence of someone who demonstrates such poise and power.

"Each of you is strong and powerful in your own right, and I have no doubt that you will succeed in this competition, provided you stay true to yourselves, work together, and keep trusting each other."

Professor Bright brought her hand up to her own heart. She walked back to her table at the front of the room.

The Liberati all looked at each other, and couldn't help but feel proud at Professor Bright's kind words.

"Thank you, Professor Bright," said Cali. "But what do we do now?"

Professor Bright quickly gathered the scrolls that the students had brought her, as well as her own journal. She turned and walked back towards them. "We've already seen the effects that this competition has had beyond The Academy. I think it was right for you to keep the trident a secret from them, even though we now know it only works for you and Lenia."

She looked pointedly at Kase. "And you would do well to continue to keep that particular fact to yourself. The last person to demonstrate two sets of abilities at the same time was Mardious Hood. Even though he claimed he had the abilities of a scholar and a wizard, and not a warrior and wizard, we all know what happened."

The Liberati all nodded. They were all aware of the evil that had followed the Brotherhood.

"I am going to try and see if I can find out some more information from one of my trusted sources," the professor said as she came back to the group.

She reached out and put her hand on Kase's shoulder. She looked him in the eye with a calm confidence. She spoke directly to him instead of the group. "There is one thing I am certain of as we go forward. You are going to be faced with a choice, Kase. You are going to have to choose whether you want to do the things that you want to do, or do things that other people tell you to do. Each option will have its own set of hardships and consequences, and it will take a lot of courage no matter what happens, but I know that whatever you choose, it will be right."

Professor Bright walked up to the door of the classroom.

Kase looked down as he searched for words. "Should we come with you?" was all he could muster.

Professor Bright put a hand on her chin as she thought about it. "Actually, can you come with me, Lenia?" she asked.

Lenia shrugged and accepted the invitation without questioning it. "Absolutely," she replied.

"Who are you going to see?" asked Cali.

Professor Bright smiled at the Liberati. "I'm going to see a friend of ours."

Lenia looked at her in confusion, but Professor Bright pulled down the collar of her garment. On her upper back and shoulder was a design of a whirlpool.

"Anastasia," Lenia replied with a smile.

"Mermaids," said Talen excitedly.

"Can I come?" asked Kase as he watched Lenia gather her things. "I really want a mermaid design on my neck," he said jokingly.

"I don't think it's going to be that kind of trip," she said with a smile. "Plus, I still haven't come up with a design worthy of being on your neck yet."

"You're right, Lenia," agreed Professor Bright. "It's already nightfall, so we will have to hurry. We need to submit your last score, talk to Anastasia, and then be back in time for you to get some rest. Tomorrow is going to be a big day."

"How so?" asked Kase.

"Tomorrow is the announcement of who made the WHOOP." Cali rolled her eyes.

"What's the WHOOP?" Kase asked.

"WHOOP stands for the Winners Hierarchy of Outstanding Performance," Talen said. "It's the tournament that the top eight teams from the Quest Series face off in to determine the winner of the Q. Hopefully, we make the final cut." She looked at Professor Bright.

"You'll not only make it," replied the professor confidently. "You'll win it."

⁂

The Liberati gathered in the common area after their last class of the week. There was no next event to read out on their sage mirror; the only thing left to do was find out if they were one of the top eight teams. The final standings were posted in the great hall, so the team headed there to accept their fate.

"Did Anastasia have any information for you?" Cali asked Lenia as they entered the main castle.

"Unfortunately, no," responded Lenia. "She said she's never heard of or seen anything like it. She even tried using the power of the trident, but couldn't make it work. It seems like Kase and I are the only ones that can use it."

"That's too bad," said Kase sadly. "Looks like we've hit a dead end."

"Not exactly," Lenia replied slyly. She grabbed his hand. He was confused, but let her continue. "Anastasia wants to meet you. She has a couple tests for you. She wants to see you use the trident, and then make your own, to see if it has any magical power. She also wants to see if you can handle getting your neck inked."

Kase's mouth dropped open. "That's amazing!" he said excitedly. "What kind of design are we going to do?"

Cali stopped and rolled her eyes. "This is serious, Kase!" she said sternly. "You two have an unbelievable, never-before-seen power. Maybe you should focus on that before you get a ridiculous design on your neck."

"It's not ridiculous," he said.

"No, Cali's right," said Lenia as she interrupted him. "We need to focus on what's important right now. Anastasia said that as soon as we're done with the Q, we should go back and see her. We'll make sure to figure out our power before we worry about ink designs."

"Hey, Dragon's Liar!" shouted a warrior from the steps of the great hall. Kase glanced over, but couldn't see who yelled at him. He felt his anger rise.

"Let's do this." He walked a little faster.

Lenia, Cali, and Talen all looked at each other.

"Let's do this," Talen said in a low voice, mimicking Kase. She clenched her fists and followed him. Cali and Lenia smiled as they followed suit.

As they joined the crowd in the great hall, they noticed the mix of emotions of all the students. Some were sad, others were angry, and some were overjoyed. Suddenly, every member of the Liberati got nervous. Their eyes fell on the giant sage mirror at the front.

All the team names were ranked from the top. "Number three, the Liberati!" exclaimed Cali.

Kase and Lenia looked at each other and smiled. "Three!" exclaimed Talen. She gave them both a hug. "We did it!" she said proudly.

"It must be destiny!" exclaimed Lenia as she laughed.

"Next time, tell your friend destiny to bump us up a few spots," Cali said with a wink.

"It won't make a difference," said Niveous from behind them. "Are you sure you even belong here, Dragon's Liar?" Kase clenched his fists and turned towards the devious scholar.

"Are you sure *you* belong here?" Lenia stepped in front of Kase. She slammed the base of the trident on the ground, and its head burst into flames.

Niveous and the Headsmen looked at it with nervous fear and backed off.

"Get out of here!" Lenia glared at them. They all turned and walked away.

Kase smiled, but Lenia's face became blank as she looked around the room. All the students seemed shocked as they stared at the power of the trident in front of them. Her shoulders slumped forward, and the flame went out.

"Thanks for having my back," said Kase. He touched her hand.

"Let's get out of here," said Cali. She looked around the room. It was eerily quiet after the recent spectacle. The Liberati quickly hurried outside to avoid more attention.

"What are we going to do now?" asked Lenia as they left the great hall.

"To the library!" said Kase excitedly.

Cali looked at her cute little brother and tried not to laugh. "We can't prepare for the WHOOP like the other events, because the structure of the final tournament is different than the rest of the Q."

"What do you mean?" asked Kase.

"Talen?" said Cali.

"Thank you, Cali," replied Talen. "The WHOOP is a tournament format. The top eight teams all compete against each other as pairs in a head-to-head matchup. Only the winners of each round will move on, so we have to make sure that we beat the team we end up against in order to continue up the hierarchy. It's sudden death; if we lose, we get eliminated. No other matches matter. No other teams matter. The only thing that matters is beating one team at a time."

"That's intense," admitted Kase.

"It's supposed to be intense," replied Talen with a stone-cold look. "It's war."

Cali laughed. "I love the passion, Talen," she said, "but it's just the WHOOP. Like Professor Bright told us, all we have to do is stick together, and do what we do. We'll be fine. We learn of the events just before they start, so all we can do right now is get some rest, clear our minds, and make sure that we're ready for tomorrow. The first matchup starts in the morning, and if we win, we'll continue throughout the day. It's going to be challenging, and it's going to be tough, but it's going to be so much fun!"

"I think I'm both excited and nervous," admitted Lenia. She grabbed Kase's hand.

"I think I'm anxious," he replied. He gripped her hand tight.

"I think those are both the same thing." Talen giggled. The Liberati all laughed, and agreed to get some rest so they were ready for the WHOOP in the morning.

<hr />

"Ladies and gentlemen, I give you the first two competitors!" exclaimed the Grand Master. All the seats in the balcony around the auditorium were filled with students, professors, and fans alike, and they cheered emphatically. There were even some journalists documenting the event to share with the rest of the realm. Kase realized that the WHOOP was something that the whole realm paid attention to, and was definitely different from the previous events of the Quest Series.

The Liberati were standing on stage with a team of four warriors, along with the Grand Master, who was explaining the rules of the first event.

Kase stared ahead at the obstacle in front of the stage. It was a giant, sandstone wall, with two doors at its base. It was too tall to see over, and the mystery of it was making him anxious.

"Here lies The Labyrinth," announced Grand Master Carter. "Much like the Sandcastles of the Eidola in the second event of the Quest Series, The Labyrinth is an obstacle course that challenges the skills and ingenuity of all competitors. However, it is not a stand-alone castle that favours scholars, wizards, or warriors; it is a maze that challenges all three.

"Each team will enter their own Labyrinth, and race through identical trials to the end. The team that successfully makes it to the end of their course first, wins. This event will not necessarily challenge your strengths, but will certainly expose your weaknesses. Know who you are, but don't be discouraged by who you are not. Good luck!"

The Grand Master lifted his hand to quiet the crowd.

"Hey, Dragon's Liar," one of the warriors sneered. "You're not going to be able to fake your way through this event."

Kase couldn't help but turn. The warrior had a stupid grin, which only made him more determined to dominate in the first event.

"You won't be laughing after we beat you." Talen took a step towards the warrior team and puffed up her chest.

The warrior laughed harder. "Do you normally have the smallest girls stand up for you, Dragon's Liar?" he joked.

"Team Tayhas, are you ready?" yelled the Grand Master. The crowd cheered again.

"Dragoon!" they yelled in response. The warrior sneered at Kase and ran his finger across his neck.

"Team Liberati, are you ready?" yelled the Grand Master. The crowd went quiet, and a mix of cheers and boos echoed through the stadium. Kase felt guilty at his team's poor reception.

"Don't worry about them." Lenia moved her head underneath his.

"C'mon team, focus." Cali put her arms around Kase and Lenia. Talen joined in the centre of their huddle. "Let's not worry about Team Tayhas, or the crowd. It's us against the world right now, but that's okay. We can handle it. Let's just do what we do."

"Whoop!" yelled the Grand Master.

"Whoop!" the crowd cheered in return, and the doors to the Labyrinths opened. The warriors ran to the steps of the stage, and sprinted to the door on the left. They started their maze before the Liberati had even taken a step.

"Let's do it!" Kase bounced in place. The Liberati cheered for themselves, and then hurried down the steps. They may have been behind, but there was more to the obstacle than just speed.

When they entered, Cali took the lead. They wound their way through a hallway until they came to the first junction. To the left was another sandstone passage, and to the right was one that looked exactly the same.

"Which way should we go?" Cali asked the group.

Kase turned to Lenia, who was staring up above the walls. The roof of the Labyrinth was open, and the crowd was staring at them. Some were cheering, others were yelling, and flashes of light reflected from sage mirrors. Kase put his hand on her shoulder. "Focus," he said reassuringly. It might have been more for himself than for her.

"What's that on the wall?" Lenia pointed. There was a marking high on the top edge, which looked like an eye with ancient writing underneath. He had no idea what it meant.

"It looks like the language of the Eidola," Cali exclaimed. "Good eye, Lenia!"

"Well," Lenia said as she smiled at Kase. "Some people call me Hawk-eye."

"Unbelievable." Kase laughed.

"Talen, what does it say?" Cali asked, oblivious to the inside joke.

"It says 'to the left'," Talen replied. "It must be a clue!"

The Liberati followed the advice of the ancient Eidola, and continued through the maze. They kept their eyes peeled for other markings, and found eight more. Even though there were endless turns and multiple hallways that all looked the same, they were confident that they were on the right track.

Kase thought the Labyrinth was a pretty easy event, until they discovered that they weren't alone in the maze.

As the team rounded a corner, they were met by the mean glare of a giant, crimson-skinned Minotaur. It was twice as tall as Kase, with arms the size of tree trunks. Its white snout snorted angrily as it stared down the Liberati.

"Get back!" Kase jumped in front of the group and shielded them. The Minotaur lifted its head into the air and let out deep bellow. The crowd cheered. It tried to take a step forward, but it was chained to the side of the wall. It let out another bellow.

"It can't move." Cali gently nudged Kase's arm down. "But it's blocking the way. What do we do now?"

Kase breathed a sigh of relief. "Did we make a wrong turn?" he asked.

"We followed the signs exactly," confirmed Talen. "I don't see any more, though."

Lenia just stared at the beast. "It's not real," she said.

"What?" asked Cali, Kase, and Talen at the same time.

"It's an illusion." Lenia started walking towards the Minotaur.

"Are you sure?" Kase reached out and touched her arm.

She stopped and turned. Her eyes were twinkling. "Trust me," she said with a smile.

As she kept walking, the Minotaur seemed to get more disgruntled. It started kicking up dust, snorting crazily, and screaming loudly. It looked like it was getting ready to demolish her. She kept moving closer.

She stopped inches in front of the beast and reached out. It snorted one last time, but it didn't have any effect on her. As soon as she touched its snout, it disappeared. The pathway was clear. She turned around and gestured for the Liberati to join her.

They jogged down the hallway, which led them to an open area. There was a wall that looked like the side of a mountain, with a few stairs off to the side. It was at least thirty feet high. At the top was a stage that marked the end of the Labyrinth, where the Grand Master was standing proudly. The crowd cheered.

"This is it!" said Cali as the Liberati rushed to the wall.

As soon as they got there, another step slowly slid out on the side. "The stairway is slowly revealing itself, but the climb up the wall must be faster. Let's go for it!" She grabbed hold of the rock and held tight.

Kase smiled at Lenia and then put his hands on the wall. "Wanna race?" he asked.

"You have an unfair advantage, super warrior," she said as her eyes moved to the left. "You don't have to carry a trident."

Kase laughed. "I'll—" he was interrupted by Cali, who fell to the ground and landed on her back with a thump. He knelt down to help his sister. "Are you okay?" he asked.

"It's a lot harder than it looks," Cali replied as he helped her up. He looked back up at the wall. It looked relatively easy to him.

"How about you take Lenia's trident, and jump on my back," he said. "Then I'll come back down for Talen," he instructed.

"Done," Lenia said. She tossed him her trident and started climbing up the wall. He couldn't help but laugh.

"You think you can carry me the whole way?" Cali asked as she stared up the wall.

"Absolutely," Kase said confidently. His body felt good, and the excitement of the competition was making his heart pound faster. He knew it would be a hard climb, but it didn't look that high to him. If Lenia was willing to climb it herself, then he only had to climb it twice.

Cali held the trident in one hand, and then wrapped her other around his neck and shoulder. She locked her legs around his waist, and he started their ascent. He grabbed hold of a rock, steadied his foot on another, and began his climb.

When he got to the halfway point, his arms felt like they were on fire. He persevered. He didn't even look back to see how far ahead he was of Lenia; he was just focused on getting to the top.

He pulled himself over the edge of the stage and helped Cali stand. "Well done, Liberati!" The Grand Master exclaimed. The crowd cheered and booed. "You'd better hurry though," he added, and he pointed to the other Labyrinth. Team Tayhas was standing in front of their Minotaur illusion, trying to figure it out.

"Hurry, Kase." Cali nudged him. He shook his arms out, and then quickly scaled back down the wall, passing Lenia on his way. "Lenia, pick up the pace. Team Tayhas is almost through!" he yelled.

Kase helped Talen secure herself on his back. He was relieved that she was a little lighter than Cali. He started his ascent again, but this time, he kept an eye on Lenia. She was three quarters of the way up the wall, and was dangerously high. She was trying to move faster, but he could tell she was being careful about which rock to grab.

When he was halfway back up the wall, he noticed her hand fall from its hold. Her foot slipped, and then her body slammed against the rock. She was dangling by one hand. Her grip was slowly giving way.

"Lenia!" screamed Cali.

Her fingers slipped. She drifted away from the wall. Her arms and legs flailed aimlessly in her perilous drop.

Kase let go of his hold and launched himself towards her. With one hand, he grabbed her waving arm. With the other, he clutched the rock. Talen tried to help steady them all as they swung back and forth, dangling from the wall. The crowd cheered. Kase's eyes locked with Lenia's.

"Don't worry, Hawk-eye, we've got you!" Talen looked down and over her shoulder. They all giggled.

"Nice catch," Lenia replied. She looked down, then back up at him. "You know I was just testing you though, right, super warrior?"

Kase was about to reply, but Cali yelled at him from the stage. "Team Tayhas made it to the wall!"

Both Lenia and Kase got serious. He pulled her up to the wall and steadied her. "Keep going," he commanded. "You can do this," he said reassuringly. They weren't about to lose to Team Tayhas.

Kase and Lenia moved up the wall side by side. He helped her decide which holds to grab, and it helped her move faster. Cali kept cheering them on. The crowd got louder. Talen shouted a warning. At least one member of Team Tayhas had made it to the top.

Kase's heart was pounding. His arms were sore. They felt like they were seizing up, but he tried to focus on his goal instead. They were almost there.

When they were close to the top, Kase picked up his pace and launched himself to the edge of the stage. He swung himself up, set Talen down gently, and then reached down on his belly to grab Lenia's arms and lift her the last little way. Cali helped him stand. He checked on Team Tayhas. Two members were still climbing.

"We have a winner!" yelled the Grand Master.

The Liberati all celebrated together at the win of their first event. Even the crowd seemed to change their tune; only cheers echoed through the auditorium. The Liberati didn't care. They were happy for themselves. They were proud of each other. Kase was glad to beat the fast-talking warrior, and the rest of Team Tayhas, and relished the victory.

After Cali handed Lenia back her trident, they made their way across the finishing platform. Only the first three members of Team Tayhas were there, since the loudmouth was still struggling on the last challenge.

In honour of the Quest Series, and in respect to the Grand Master, Team Tayhas wished the Liberati good luck in the rest of the tournament.

The crowd grew quiet as they talked amongst themselves and stretched their legs during the break in action. The Grand Master started to lead the two teams away to the exit of the platform. Cali and Talen were already reminiscing about their strategy from the obstacle course, and Lenia and Kase were hand-in-hand.

Team Tayhas stayed behind for their last member, who stepped onto the platform. He had finally finished the race.

"Hey, Dragon's Liar," he yelled, but none of the Liberati turned around. "I have a prize for you," he said slyly.

Kase turned his head slightly to look at the sore loser. The warrior was hunched over, cracking his knuckles and clenching his fists. He was ready for a fight.

Kase stepped in front of Lenia to protect her.

She didn't need protection. She slammed the base of the trident on the ground. "No," she said in a strong voice.

Before the warrior could even attempt to throw a punch, Lenia's trident caught fire and sent a pulse through the air. Everything stopped. Lenia and Kase were encompassed in a sphere of fire.

The warrior dropped his hands. The rest of Team Tayhas stopped; their jaws dropped to the floor. The Grand Master smiled. The whole crowd froze and looked on in wonder.

Lenia and Kase were standing in her protective cage of fire. Kase wasn't surprised by her action, but he was concerned about her reaction to it. She looked afraid. The crowd muttered among themselves, and reflected lights from sage mirrors glittered as the crowd captured images of the spectacle. He clenched her hand tight. Because of her, they were safe.

CHAPTER 17

Water Shadow

L enia let go of Kase's hand. The flame went out.

Grand Master Carter rushed over and stood between the Liberati and Team Tayhas. He called over a couple of other administrators, and they quickly led Team Tayhas away. He turned towards Lenia, and smiled as he studied the trident.

"That is some wonderful magic," he said. The crowd was still bustling with excitement, but it didn't drown out their conversation. "Where did you learn how to do that?" He squinted and tilted his head to get a better angle. His hand slowly reached out in curiosity.

Lenia didn't say anything, just gently tilted the trident back out of reach.

"Lenia is an exceptional student with her fire control." Professor Bright stepped up onto the platform. "Her power is really growing here at The Academy." She walked up behind Lenia and put her arm around her.

"But it came out of nowhere," the Grand Master said softly. He only had eyes for the magical trident.

"You are incorrect." Professor Bright nervously laughed. "A true wizard is always prepared; isn't that right, Lenia?" She winked.

Lenia looked up at Professor Bright, then over towards Grand Master Carter. She slowly nodded.

"I can see that you're quite talented, Lenia," the Grand Master said with a wry smile. "I'm looking forward to your next event.

Professor, please lead your team back to their competitor's room. We need to keep going on with the WHOOP."

Professor Bright guided the Liberati off stage and down the narrow corridor to their competitor's room. Each team was segregated during the final competition, so they couldn't share any clues about the events, or gain an unfair advantage by conversing with other teams. It also gave them a chance to rest, and grab some of the food and water provided.

As they passed the room full of students and journalists, they were bombarded with questions. They rushed down the hall as fast as they could.

"I shouldn't have done that." Lenia looked at the ground.

"You mean, save my life?" Kase said from behind her. He was trying to make her feel better. He reached out and grabbed her hand. She stopped walking and turned to him. He saw her start to smile. "I mean, you did owe me one," he said sarcastically.

Lenia's expression grew brighter as she laughed. Professor Bright and the rest of the Liberati stopped walking down the corridor and looked back at the heroes. "What do you mean?"

"I saved you from your fall off the wall, so I guess we're even," he said playfully.

"Okay, I guess you did; but saving people's lives isn't really a game." She looked to the left and smiled. "If we're keeping track though, I guess I saved you from the banshees, so that means I'm winning two to one," she conceded.

"Oh yeah?" Kase laughed. "I guess you did, but do you remember when I saved you from that pigeon?" She nodded and laughed. "Two, two," he said jokingly.

"Twos?" she said with a wink. "I guess we're tied then. I just hope that you don't put yourself into any more situations where I have to save you in the WHOOP, because that means I'll win this game. I always win. I won't even give you a chance. I'll have your back, Kase Garrick, whether you like it or not," she said with a smile.

Seeing her happy again made him happy.

"Alright, you two." Cali rolled her eyes in disgust. "Let's keep our focus on the task at hand."

"You're right, Cali," responded Professor Bright. She smiled at Lenia. "But as much as you think you're going to win, Kase, my Aileron is on Lenia." The Liberati laughed.

☆

"Ladies and gentlemen," said the Grand Master. "I give you the next two competitors of Round Two!"

The crowd grew louder as they responded to the announcement.

"Competitors, I give you your second challenge." He waved his arm towards the grounds of the auditorium. The Liberati examined what they were up against. There were two giant, glass tanks filled with water. One of the tanks was directly in front of where they were standing, and the other was in front of the wizard team dressed in bright yellow, ironically named Team Pink.

"In front of you lies the Curse of Treasure Cove," explained Grand Master Carter in a loud, eerie voice. "Long ago, there was an evil mermaid known as The Water Shadow, who was obsessed with gold and jewels. She would scour the ocean floor for treasure that was lost by sailors on their journeys from one corner of the sea to the other. Over the years she had collected a legendary bounty. It was a treasure so magnificent, it would have made anyone the richest in the realm."

For the number of people in the auditorium, it was oddly quiet.

"As the Water Shadow collected more treasure, the legend grew. Soon sailors and hunters alike started searching for the place she hid her precious items, and became as obsessed as she was. She, in turn,

237

grew more cautious, paranoid, and destructive, which made the other mermaids worried.

"Since she was causing harm to other creatures in the realm, the Mermaid Queen decided to confront the Water Shadow and save her from her own obsession. The Queen tracked the Water Shadow to a secret cove in the heart of the sea. Instead of explaining herself, or surrendering her bounty, the Water Shadow cast a spell on the treasure, which ended up costing her the most valuable thing of all: her life.

"She spread her soul throughout her collection of treasure, and bound it to the cove. The sacrifice she made caused anyone or anything that removed an item from the cove to be cursed. The other mermaids made sure that any evidence of the cove was forgotten, and have sworn to protect anyone, or anything, from finding it and facing certain doom."

The Grand Master smiled and gestured to the tanks. "Like Treasure Cove, the tanks of water in front of each team are cursed. Teams are to search for pieces of treasure in each tank, remove them, and hang them from the golden chain on top of the stage. There is only one piece of treasure in the tank at a time, and once it is removed, the next one will appear.

"However, with each additional piece of treasure that gets removed from the tank, a different obstruction will be added because of the curse. There is a thirty-minute time limit for this event. The team that hangs all five items first, or has the most pieces when time runs out, wins the competition. In the event of a tie, the team that finds the last piece in the shortest amount of time is the winner.

"Sometimes the hardest part about finding something beyond your reach, is finding yourself first."

The Grand Master lifted his hand, and the crowd went silent. Before he could continue, someone yelled, "Show us the fire shield!" The crowd roared in support. The Liberati were surprised at the overwhelming support, but Lenia looked down in embarrassment.

She took a deep breath, closed her eyes, and then glanced at the balcony. Kase scanned the crowd and realized that her power was appreciated instead of feared, and he couldn't help but feel proud of her. He even noticed her friend Aura sitting on the edge of the balcony, waving and cheering supportively.

He turned to Lenia; she looked relaxed. The trident came ablaze. The crowd roared louder with excitement.

The Grand Master swung his arm down. "Whoop!" he yelled.

"Whoop!" the crowd replied, and it echoed through the auditorium.

Cali gestured for the Liberati to come together, so they could talk in the deafening auditorium. They gathered in a circle, and put their arms around each other to form a huddle.

"All right," said Cali in a stern voice. "Let's focus. What's our strategy?"

"We find the treasure," Kase answered simply.

"Of course." Cali rolled her eyes. "But how do we find it. Do we all take a different portion of the tank? Do we each dive down individually, or do we focus on a certain area and all make our way down together?"

"Don't worry," said Lenia cockily. "We have the trident. When Anastasia led me through the sea, all I had to do was keep a hand on her, or my, trident, and I was able to breathe underwater. I think so long as all of us can touch the trident, we'll have an advantage, because we won't have to keep coming up for air. That way, we can all look around the tank together, as a team." Lenia spoke with poise and confidence.

"Okay." Cali smiled and shrugged. "Let's jump in, then!"

The Liberati all turned calmly towards the tank, except for Kase. He sprinted towards the edge. He jumped off the stage, tucked his legs into his chest, wrapped his arms around his ankles, and braced for impact. The rest of the Liberati all turned to avoid the giant splash that he made.

His youthful spirit inspired Cali and Lenia, and they both trotted towards the stage edge and jumped in after him. Instead of causing a big splash, they both elegantly dipped themselves in the water.

As Lenia came up from under the surface, he playfully splashed her. Unfortunately for him, she was holding her trident, and jabbed him in the ribs in return as she gently wiped the water from her eyes.

Talen slowly walked over to the edge of the stage and looked at the rest of the Liberati nervously. "I can't swim," she admitted sheepishly.

"That's okay," said Cali brightly as she treaded water. "I'll teach you! Just jump in; I'll catch you."

Talen smiled, but still looked nervous. She dipped her toe in the water, and then stepped back from the edge. Cali was about to give her some more encouraging words, but then Talen jumped in.

All three Liberati members grabbed hold of her quickly and helped her get her head above the water. She started moving her arms and legs in a dogpaddle.

"I'm doing it!" Talen said. She spit water everywhere. Cali brushed Talen's wet hair out of her face and giggled at her enthusiasm.

"All right," said Lenia as she led the team. "Grab hold of the trident." She held the trident upright in the middle of the group, and everyone put their hand on its stem.

"Amazing," said Cali as she felt her body with her free hand. "I feel so warm."

"You're kind of amazing," Kase said to Lenia. She blushed a little bit.

"Just wait until we head underwater," Lenia replied with a wink.

"Let's do it!" He pulled the trident and dove down.

"No wait!" said Talen as she was pulled underwater. "I'm not ready!" But her head was already beneath the surface. Kase stopped pulling his team down and looked back. Cali and Talen were bewildered, while Lenia was relishing their wonder.

"Pretty cool, right?" she said, and she started to laugh. "Just make sure you keep touching the trident."

"How is this possible?" Cali touched her face with her free hand.

"This is awesome!" Talen wrapped both arms around the trident. "Don't let me go," she said nervously.

"Don't worry, Tal." Kase looked over at Lenia. "We've got you." He turned away and started kicking his legs. His powerful strokes pulled the other three members along with him. They all moved to the bottom of the tank to search for their treasure.

Cali and Lenia joined in on the swimming, so that Kase wasn't just blindly pulling them down. They kept their eyes peeled towards the bottom of the tank. "What are we even looking for?" asked Lenia.

"I don't really know," admitted Cali. "I'm guessing that we'll know it when we see it."

"Look at that." Kase pointed in front of him. "It looks beautiful; like Lenia's ankle."

From above, it looked like the bottom of the tank was a rainbow, but when they got closer, the details of the coral revealed themselves. There were even some small plants and fish scurrying around. It was like the ocean floor.

"I think my ankle looks a little more beautiful than that," Lenia said with a smirk.

"I don't think so. There are too many wonderful things to look at!" Talen said excitedly. Her eyes were moving back and forth with lightning speed as she identified all the creatures she saw. "Look at the seahorses! The angelfish! The baby sea turtles! The puffers! The rainbow coloured fantails! The starfish! Is that a mantis shrimp? I hope there are sharks here!"

Kase stopped swimming and turned to Talen with a worried look. "You think there might be sharks?" he asked.

"Are you afraid of sharks, Dragon Slayer?" Lenia giggled.

"First of all," Kase said defensively, "I'm not afraid of anything. Second, I actually think you should be worried about sharks, because you don't want to put me in a position to save you from any danger. It might cause me to add another point in the life-saving game."

"Oh really," Lenia said with a wide smile. "Well, I hope—"

"Can we keep moving, please?" Cali looked annoyed. "We're kind of in the middle of the WHOOP. We can talk about sharks later; right now, we have to find that missing treasure!" Her voice reached an angry tone.

Kase and Lenia lowered their heads in shame, because they knew that Cali was right. "I still don't even know what we're looking for," Kase said under his breath.

Cali rolled her eyes and threw her hands up in disgust. Her face quickly grew worried. She moved her hand up to her throat. She grabbed hold of the trident and coughed as the magic aided her breathing again. A few tears formed in her eyes. She kept coughing. "This is so weird," she admitted.

"Not as weird as that coral-shaped treasure chest." Talen pointed ahead. Kase, Lenia, and Cali all looked around, but couldn't see what she was referring to. Everything seemed to blend together into one lump.

"What are you looking at?" Kase started swimming forward again.

"Yeah, Talen," said Lenia. "I can't see anything that looks like a chest."

"It's just a little farther," Talen replied. She guided the other swimmers. "Just a little farther," she said as they got closer. "Farther. Okay stop! It's right there!"

The three Liberati members looked again at where Talen was pointing; this time, they all saw the square-looking chest. "How did you see that?" Cali asked in bewilderment.

"I guess you're the new Hawk-eye!" Lenia added. Talen smiled proudly.

Kase reached forward and grabbed the lid of the treasure chest. A bright, green beam of light emerged from the chest as he flung open the lid, and the Liberati all covered their eyes. When they looked back, they saw a large, circular, golden medallion with the letter 'W' on its face.

"That's it!" exclaimed Cali.

"It's heavy!" Kase lifted the medallion with one hand. Its diameter was as wide as his forearm. He grabbed the thick edge with one hand, and held on to it as he started kicking the other way.

Cali and Lenia followed suit, and even Talen started to kick as well. Together, they all made their way to the surface and back to the stage.

As the Liberati lifted themselves and the medallion onto the stage, the crowd roared with excitement. Kase carried it over to the chain while the rest of the team followed.

He turned to Talen. "You found it; would you like to do the honours?" he asked.

"I would!" Talen sang. She happily took the medallion from Kase. The Liberati laughed. She held it with both hands, and was barely strong enough to lift it up. With a valiant effort, she lifted the circle just high enough so that she could hook it on the chain. The crowd roared again.

Before the Liberati could all celebrate, they noticed the water in the tank bubble. It turned from a clear blue to a dark, murky green.

"There's something in there," Lenia said with concern.

"Yeah, our next piece of the treasure." Kase ran over to the edge of the stage and jumped back into the tank. "C'mon, super wizard!"

"Look out!" Lenia yelled. She ran to the edge of the stage, dove into the water, and stuck her body in front of him. She started treading water, and looked around frantically. He saw something slither up to her as she stuck her trident out.

The tiniest eel swam around her. It was the width of his finger, and circled the young couple. It flashed a couple times with the electricity that surrounded its body, but it dove into the water and swam away. Kase laughed hysterically.

"My hero." He pretended to wipe tears from his eyes. "You saved my life! I am forever grateful. Looks like you're in the lead, three to two now."

Lenia giggled. "Okay, we won't count that one," she admitted. He was about to say something else, but she splashed him.

Cali and Talen jumped back into the tank. "Let's get going! It looks like the other team got their first medallion!" Cali exclaimed.

The Liberati all looked at the tank next to them, and saw Team Pink emerge onto the stage with their first piece of the treasure. They were all now in pink; the water had turned their clothes a different colour. The crowd cheered.

"Crafty wizards," Cali muttered under her breath.

The Liberati submerged themselves again. The water may have been murky, and the floor of the tank may have been muddy, but the Liberati persevered again. It didn't take them long to find the second piece of treasure: a square medallion with the letter 'H' on it.

The crowd roared as the Liberati hung the second piece from the gold chain on the stage. The water bubbled again. Its colour changed from murky green to bright yellow. The bottom of the tank appeared to be littered with gold.

"It smells." Talen pinched her nose.

The Liberati reluctantly jumped back into the tank and submerged themselves again. As they made their way to the bottom of the tank, they were overwhelmed by all the gold pieces that were strewn across the floor. All of them were flat, with no inscriptions or letters on them.

"One of them should have an 'O' marking on it, and look similar to the first two medallions," said Cali.

"Why an 'O'?" asked Kase.

"I'm thinking that all the medallions together will spell WHOOP," replied Cali. "It will look pretty cool when we hang all of the letters on the gold chain."

"That is pretty cool," Kase admitted. "I kind of wish that I had a gold chain with WHOOP on it."

"Challenge accepted!" said Lenia with a wink.

"What do you mean?" Kase said.

"Don't worry about it, dimples," she replied with a smile. "Just keep looking for the medallion."

The Liberati continued with their search. They took their time, because they knew that studying each piece was better than having to double back and search again. It may have been slow and tedious, but they eventually found what they were looking for: a triangular piece with the letter 'O' on it.

The crowd roared as the Liberati hung the third medallion from the gold chain on the stage. The water bubbled again. It turned blue, but the surface froze over in solid, white ice. Lenia glanced over to the other tank to see what the other team was up to; their tank was still bright yellow. There were only two medallions hanging from their chain.

"What do we do now?" asked Kase. He walked to the edge of the stage. He stepped onto the surface, and then jumped up and down to test how solid it was. "This ice is pretty thick."

"It's not ice," said Lenia as she joined him on the water's surface. "It's crystal."

He reached down and touched it. "I don't know; it feels pretty cold." He brushed his hand across it.

"Trust me," Lenia replied with a smile.

"Always," he replied. He put his hand on his chest.

"So, what do we do now?" asked Cali as she and Talen joined them. Talen moved her feet quickly, and then stopped as she slid across the crystal surface.

"We have to look around for an entrance of some sort," advised Lenia. "This crystal is magically created. Look for any part that doesn't look like the rest. It'll be a magical spot. That should be the entrance to the water below."

The Liberati split up and started walking slowly across the crystal. Cali and Kase moved cautiously, not letting their eyes rest. Lenia walked at a faster pace, since she had a better idea of what she was looking for. Talen kept walking and sliding, walking and sliding.

"I think I found it!" Kase yelled. He was staring at the crystal below his feet. The spot was barely distinguishable from the rest visually, but it felt right.

Lenia raced over. "This is definitely it, super warrior," she said proudly.

Cali and Talen made their way over, but didn't seem to know what was going on. "This looks like everything else here." Cali looked down in confusion. "What do we do now?" She sounded irritated.

"Watch this," Lenia said as she took a step back. She closed her eyes, smiled, and fell forward. Kase, Cali, and Talen watched as Lenia fell through the hard crystal and into the water below.

Lenia looked back up to the surface.

"Awesome," said Kase. He closed his eyes and fell forward, just like her. Instead of passing through the crystal, he fell flat on his face.

He leaned up and rubbed his forehead. Lenia was laughing underneath the surface. The crowd was laughing too.

"What just happened?" He shook his head.

Lenia looked down and dove deeper.

"What do we do now?" asked Cali.

Kase stood up and felt his head again. At least he wasn't bleeding. Before they could come up with a plan, Lenia pushed the medallion up from beneath, and popped up after. "Hey dimples." She smiled up at Kase. She put her hands out and tried to climb out of the water and onto the crystal surface. He grabbed her arms and lifted her from the water into a hug.

"How did you find it so fast?" Cali said excitedly.

"It was right below the entrance," Lenia said as she disengaged. "Sorry, I would have come back for you all, but I saw it right away."

"Perfect," replied Cali. "We only have one more medallion to go!" She skipped towards the stage. Talen followed, and skipped and slid on the crystal as she went. The crowd cheered with excitement.

"How did you make it through the crystal?" Kase asked as they casually walked back to the stage.

"The trick is believing that the door is there, even though your eyes and your mind are telling you it's not," she replied calmly. "It's about letting go of everything around you, and trusting that feeling you have inside of you. Believing everything inside of you."

She looked down as she gathered herself. "Maybe you wouldn't understand, because you're a warrior."

"Well, other warriors might not understand, but I'm a super warrior. I understand completely."

"You're such a nerd." Lenia giggled and grabbed his hand. They stepped back on stage as Cali put the fourth medallion on the chain. The crowd cheered loudly. The Liberati all turned to the tank again, but this time they didn't see a change.

"That's weird," said Lenia as she studied the surface.

"Looks like I get another chance to try the crystal door!" Kase ran across the stage and onto the surface of the tank. Lenia raced after him.

He slid to a stop at the edge of the doorway that he'd found before. He knelt down and touched the crystal. "It's not here," he said.

Lenia stopped running and looked down. She was about twenty feet behind him. "No," she shouted, "it's right here." She smiled, and then fell forward and through the crystal.

He raced back to where she'd been standing, and couldn't contain his excitement. He peered through the crystal and saw her trident come ablaze in the dark water below. His smile disappeared. It looked like a giant serpent was circling her.

"Lenia!" he shouted.

"What's going on?" Cali and Talen finally rushed over.

"There's something in there." Kase kept his eyes on the tank. The trident flickered, and then went out.

"Oh no." Cali put her hand over her mouth.

Kase didn't have time to think anymore. He closed his eyes. He focused on Lenia. "There is a door," he whispered to himself. He let go. He fell forward.

His head hit the surface of the water, and the cool liquid surrounded him. He swam down and started searching for her frantically. The water was too dark. He couldn't see anything. He felt something brush against his leg. He turned in the water towards it, but nothing was there. He felt something brush his shoulder, and he turned again. This time, he was staring at a pair of dark, red eyes. He stopped moving.

The eyes moved closer, and Kase could see the outline of the serpent's head. He was so hypnotized, that he didn't notice its tail curl itself around his body. When the tail was around his torso, it wrapped itself tighter and squeezed.

He panicked, and tried to wiggle free. He couldn't move his arms. He closed his eyes. He was running out of air. The serpent moved Kase around the tank, tossing him through the water. He felt helpless, until he felt something touch his shoulder. He was warm. He coughed. He took a deep breath, and the serpent let go of him completely.

"You made it!" Lenia said with a smile.

Kase grabbed her trident. "The serpent!" he said as he tried to catch his breath. "We have to get out of here!" He tried to swim, but Lenia started laughing.

"Did the little snake scare you? He was just playing." She laughed again. "He's so gentle!" The snake had moved his head beside Lenia. It was the size of her torso. She placed her hand delicately on his scales before he slithered off. Kase realized that he wasn't in any danger.

"Little?" Kase said defensively. "I thought I was going to drown!"

"I guess it's a good thing I was here to save you," Lenia said. "Three to two," she added with a wink.

Kase shook his head and smiled. "You win," he admitted. "What about the final medallion. Did you get that already, too?" he added sarcastically.

"Obviously," Lenia said. She was confident. She was amazing. She waved her hand, and the snake's tail returned. It was holding the medallion.

They swam up to the surface and placed the medallion on the crystal. Cali and Talen ran it back to the gold chain together, and hung it up. Lenia and Kase joined them. Their event was complete. "We have a winner!" shouted the Grand Master.

The crowd cheered, and then they started chanting Lenia's name. Lenia looked down at the floor. Kase started chanting her name along with the crowd. She looked over at him and laughed. She turned her attention to the balcony, and the crowd cheered. She waved and smiled, and then lit her trident up again. The crowd cheered louder.

The Liberati gathered together and embraced in excitement. They shook hands with Team Pink as a sign of good gamesmanship. They waved at the crowd one last time before they were led back off stage. Just before they entered the passage, the Grand Master stopped Lenia. "That trident really is remarkable," he said.

"Thank you, sir," she replied uncomfortably. She clutched her trident a little tighter. She joined her team as they walked down the hall and into the competitor's room.

249

CHAPTER 18

Eternal Flame

"Ladies and gentlemen," said the Grand Master, "welcome to the finale of this year's Quest Series!"

The crowd exploded with excitement.

"The final two teams are: The Headsmen and The Liberati," He turned towards the two teams to acknowledge them.

The crowd cheered, overwhelmingly in favour of the Liberati. People were calling for the trident again, and Lenia seemed like she was enjoying being the fan favourite.

Kase glanced over at the Headsmen, but instead of seeing the glares he expected from them, they were worried and nervous. It made him smile.

"In front of you lies the final challenge," Grand Master Carter explained. The teams were standing on the stage, and looked down at the ground level of the great hall. There were hundreds of small, concrete stands scattered about the floor, but only one of them held something valuable on it. The golden WHOOP trophy stood alone on top of one of the stands, shining in all its glory.

"The event is simple. The first team to grab the trophy wins, and is crowned champions of the WHOOP!" The crowd cheered again.

"However." The Grand Master waved his arm, and the room was instantly filled with hundreds of trophies that all looked alike. Each of them occupied the space on one of the small concrete stands. "The winning team must obtain the correct trophy. If the wrong one is touched, the trophies will all get rearranged, and the correct one will

250

be moved to a different spot. It will be difficult to keep your eye on the right target; even more so with other obstacles in your way."

Grand Master Carter waved his hand again, and a door opened at the right side of the great hall. Slowly but playfully, ten baby bears came out of the entrance, each a different colour. They tumbled over each other as they ran out to the auditorium floor. The crowd and the Liberati all sighed as they looked at the adorable creatures.

The bears not only crashed into each other, but they started running into the trophies as well. As soon as one of the bears touched a trophy, the stands opened and the trophies disappeared into them. Seconds later, the stands opened back up and the trophies returned.

"I would like to introduce a rare species of bear that the professors of the wizards' school have been working with and studying. They are known as Kaber bears, since they only reside on Kaber Island. Although these bears are cute and beg to be touched, their fur contains a chemical that acts as a defense mechanism. Any living creature that comes in contact with the Kaber bears becomes paralyzed for around sixty seconds. In the wild, this gives the Kaber bears time to elude any predators. In this event, it delays anyone's chance of reaching the WHOOP trophy.

"This final event will challenge a team's patience, speed, and strategy. Not only do you have to compete against each other to become champions, but you have to be aware of your surroundings as well. The team that is able to come together and obtain the WHOOP trophy will be crowned champions. Good luck to all."

The crowd started cheering again as the Grand Master held his arm up to signal the start of the final event. "Whoop," he yelled as he swung his arm down.

"Whoop," The crowd echoed.

Cali gestured for the Liberati to come together one final time. They gathered in a circle, and put their arms around each other, but they all kept an eye on the spectacle in front of them.

"All right, team," Cali tried to keep the smile from creeping onto her face. "I know we're going to win this challenge; I can feel it!" she exclaimed.

"Look how cute those Kaber bears are!" Lenia stuck out her lower lip. "I want one!"

"You realize you can't touch them, right?" responded Cali seriously.

"That baby-blue one is taking a nap!" said Talen in a high-pitched voice. "It's adorable!"

"Was anyone listening to the Grand Master?" Cali's tone clearly showed her lack of patience with the rest of her team's silliness.

"That pink one has a tiny little bow in her hair." Kase covered his mouth. He started dancing on his toes in excitement as he watched the loveable creatures. "I'm going to name that one B-Town!"

Lenia and Talen couldn't stop giggling. They started pointing at the other Kaber bears and tried to name the rest of the slew.

"I'm going to name that yellow one Noodle!" exclaimed Lenia.

"Obviously," Kase said in support.

"And that purple one should be called—" started Talen.

"Enough!" Cali screamed at her team. They all stopped and looked at their leader.

"Sorry, Cali," said Kase. "What would you like us to do?"

Lenia and Talen also turned their attention away from the cute Kaber bears and awaited orders.

"We need to hit this challenge as a team, with everyone doing a different part for the greater good." Cali explained her thoughts on the event. "There are three major areas of concern. First, we need to identify which trophy is the real one. Second, we need to keep an eye on the Headsmen and make sure that they don't reach it before us. Finally, we have to distract those Kaber bears so that they don't interfere. Talen, do you know anything about the trophies, Kaber bears, or this event?"

Talen looked back at the auditorium floor. Her face was expressionless. "The trophies reset whenever something touches the wrong one," she said in a serious tone. "The Grand Master implied that they get randomly rearranged, but there must be a pattern of some kind, or some other kind of trick. All we have to do is figure out the pattern, and we can predict where the trophy will end up.

"The Kaber bears are doing a good job of resetting the sequence on their own, but when we figure out where the trophy is going to be, we need to contain the bears so we can get to it before it switches places. If the bears keep touching the trophies, it may be difficult to get to the right one, even if we're a couple steps ahead.

"As for the Headsmen, it looks like they're taking a different approach. They are all splitting up, trying to find the right trophy on their own." Talen pointed to the floor. Each member of the other team was walking towards a different stand. They were moving with precision, but looked lost.

"Great work, Talen," Cali said casually, but Kase was blown away by Talen's description. "Do you think you can figure out the pattern?"

"Yes," Talen said confidently. "As long as I can stay up on stage, I should be able to recognize something if I concentrate hard enough."

"Perfect!" said Cali. "Kase, since you're our fastest team member, you should stay with Talen. When she figures out the pattern, she will tell you which trophy to get."

"Dragoon!" Kase said in response to his captain's orders.

"Lenia," Cali continued. "Since the Headsmen are afraid of you, I need you to occupy their attention. Do whatever you have to in order to throw them off their game. Do you think you can do that for us?"

"Dragoon!" Lenia said in response, and elbowed Kase in the ribs. He smiled proudly.

"Since I'm the only one that isn't obsessed with the Kaber bears' cuteness, I will contain them. Once I see Kase start to run, I'll do my best to get them to stop moving. All right, let's do this!"

"Let's do this!" the rest of the Liberati cheered themselves on.

Talen and Kase moved to the edge of the stage and sat down. Talen didn't take her eyes off of the trophies, which were already rapidly changing. Kase didn't take his eyes off Lenia.

Lenia and Cali moved off the stage and down to the ground level. Cali started to move closer to the Kaber bears, studying their every move. It seemed like they were busy playing with each other, and didn't even recognize anyone or anything else on the floor. They were in their own magical world.

Lenia moved towards the leader of the Headsmen. Before she was even close to Niveous, he was staring at her. A look of fear fell over his face, and he started running away. He had recognized her wicked game.

"Come back here, Niveous," she yelled. "I just want to talk to you." She sparked fire from the head of her trident. The crowd cheered with excitement.

"Do you notice anything yet?" Kase said to Talen. He still kept his eyes on Lenia. She was faster than Niveous, and was catching up to him.

"The Headsmen seem to be looking at the base of each trophy," Talen said as she stared straight ahead. "There must be something different about the base of the championship trophy."

"How do they know what to look for?" he asked, not really expecting an answer.

"They're cheaters," Talen said simply. "Cheaters are going to cheat."

Lenia had caught up to Niveous, who still looked scared. She was saying something to him, but another member of the Headsmen was sneaking up behind her. He threw something on her.

Kase stood up and was about to jump off, but Talen grabbed his leg. "You're supposed to stay here," she said.

Lenia was pulling some sort of goo off her skin. The Headsmen laughed. They ran away in victory.

"Don't worry," he said. "I'll be right back." He leapt off stage and sprinted towards her. He didn't care if he hit the trophies. They disappeared like an illusion, and then reappeared moments later.

His attention turned towards the Kaber bears. They, too, were headed towards Lenia, but they were growling. He ran faster.

All the bears were barking. Lenia screamed, and tried to wipe away the gooey substance from her face, but she couldn't see. The crowd gasped. The Headsmen laughed. The bears were getting closer.

Kase grabbed Lenia's arm, and she screamed again. He turned his head away from her shrieking voice. "Don't worry; I got your back," he said.

He ran away from the terrifying, adorable bears, pulling her along behind him as he had in the steam pits. She followed, trusting him even though she couldn't see. He zigged and zagged, touching trophies as he went. The bears followed erratically as they hunted them down, like they were sharks attracted to blood.

Kase made his way back to the stage and threw Lenia on top of it. He jumped, grabbed the edge, and pulled himself up. He looked back down and saw the bears pacing below the stage, unable to climb up.

"We're safe," he said to Lenia. He knelt over her. He used his shirt to wipe away the goo from her face. "Is this honey?" he asked, and smelled it.

"Yes," Lenia replied. "I don't know why the Headsmen had it, but the Kaber bears are certainly attracted to it. What do we do now?" she asked. Kase glanced at the Headsmen across the room. They didn't have the obstacle of the bears anymore, and were able to focus on winning the competition instead.

On the opposite side of the floor was Cali, repeatedly touching the same trophy so that they would reset. It was helping Talen solve the puzzle, and throwing the Headsmen off at the same time. Kase admired Cali's determination and spontaneous thinking, but their team was still in a worse position than the Headsmen.

Kase took a deep breath. "I have an idea to level the playing field a little bit," he said as he looked down at the Kaber bears. He reached over to Lenia and wiped some more honey off of her garments.

He held his honey-soaked hand over the edge of the stage. "Here B-Town," he said in a calming voice. He let the honey drip down onto the face of the pink bear, and watched her insatiable lips devour the golden treat. The other Kaber bears started fighting her for the dripping honey, each of them getting a mere taste of the wonderful nectar. "Stay here," he said to Lenia. He winked.

He leapt off the stage, landing away from the Kaber bears. They turned towards him, their noses alive with the sweet smell. They took off after him in a mad scramble to devour more of the tasty treat.

He didn't even look back at the hungry beasts, but held the honey hand in front of him and headed directly for the Headsmen.

The Headsmen saw him and the sloth of wild Kaber bears running towards them, and tried to scurry away. Unfortunately for them, he easily tracked them down, and buttered each of them with honey. Instead of chasing one person around for the delicious honey, the Kaber bears were now going crazy, running after everyone in the arena. Chaos ensued.

Niveous froze as a couple of Kaber bears playfully ravaged him from behind. They licked him until the next moving target caught their attention. Sharaine was victimized by Lenia's favourite Kaber bear, Noodle. Even Kase was eventually caught. He froze for sixty seconds. Lenia had jumped off the stage and scurried about, joining him in his madness. She was frozen by the sleepy blue Kaber bear.

The crowd went wild as the students and bears ran around in pandemonium. It was highly entertaining for them to see everyone and everything flying about randomly on the battlefield.

At times, it seemed like the crowd was cheering for the bears instead of the teams. It also seemed like the bears were playing with the students, chasing anything that moved instead of being obsessed with honey. Just as the craziness was hitting its peak, the trophies in the room disappeared from view.

"We have a winner!" the Grand Master yelled. Below the stage, on the right side of the auditorium floor, Talen was holding a WHOOP trophy high above her head in victory. The crowd roared in support.

"Talen, you did it!" exclaimed Cali, just before she was frozen again by a Kaber bear. The doors to the right of the stadium opened, and a bell sounded. The Kaber bears stopped what they were doing and dutifully ran towards it. After a few more seconds, the rest of the Liberati all unfroze. They gathered with Talen and the WHOOP trophy. The crowd roared. The Liberati had won.

⁂

The fire was so inviting. It drew everyone in. It was warm. It was magical. Lenia was happy to show off the power of her trident, and the crowd cheered. She wasn't trying to hide it anymore. The power was hers. In the moment, it represented their bond and the way they felt. They were champions.

It was the final ceremony for the Quest Series. The Liberati were being officially crowned the number one team.

The Grand Master placed the final gold medal around Lenia's neck, and the crowd cheered again. She pulled it away from her body and turned it so she could examine it. It had all the symbols of The Academy on it: the three-headed dragon, the midnight owl, the unicorn, and the peach tree. The phrase 'Strength in Unity' was etched underneath.

"That concludes this year's Quest Series," the Grand Master yelled. He put his arms up and gestured for the crowd to quiet down. The balcony was filled, and all the other teams were gathered on the auditorium floor. "Let us commemorate it by dancing the night away. Please enjoy yourselves responsibly, and unite in celebration."

Music started to play in the background, and the celebration quickly got underway. The giant sage mirror on the stage started reflecting different colours. Students began to dance on the auditorium floor, and people from the balcony were moving to join them.

Lenia turned back to Kase and grabbed his hand. "Would you like to dance with me?" she asked.

"Let's all dance together." Cali put her arms on their shoulders.

"I have some moves I have to show off," said Talen. She ran ahead of them. They all looked at each other and laughed.

They made their way across the auditorium floor, and gathered in a circle. Other scholars, wizards, and warriors joined them, but they all made sure that Talen still had enough room for her 'moves'. The music was upbeat. Drums were beating loudly and steadily. Trumpets were being played grandly.

Kase and Lenia were beside each other. He nudged her playfully. "I guess you won the lifesaving contest," he said.

"No," she replied as she smirked. "You saved me from B-Town when she tried to freeze me in the last event. That tied it up again. Three, three."

"Threes?" He laughed. "A tie seems fair, but I thought you were going to win?"

Lenia smiled bright. Her green eyes glowed. "I did win," she said as she grabbed his hand. "I have you in my life."

Kase felt warm. She was the greatest person he had ever met. They did great things together. She owned the most powerful weapon he had ever seen. He had fought a dragon, and won. They had defeated Niveous and the Headsmen. The Triple Crown had recognized him. They had beaten the odds, and conquered adversity.

Even though the celebration was grand, the music was lively, and their medals were golden, the Quest Series was rewarding because they discovered the greatest thing in the world. They had each other.

CPSIA information can be obtained
at www.ICGtesting.com
Printed in the USA
BVHW091402120921
616597BV00007B/86

9 780995 900202